THE GHOSTING TIME

Jeremy Esekow

ISBN: 979-8-218-46754-8

To Shelley, Ali, Barak and Rafael. I would never have finished this book without your support.

Prologue

Human time travel became a reality in June 2090 when a laboratory in Montana, under the guidance of Professor David Leventhal, sent a volunteer scientist, Lucy Findlay, back to the date May 29, 2020, for one hour in the prototype time travel vessel the Adventurer. She returned with a vial of atmosphere and a video of the BLM protests in Minneapolis. Lucy participated in numerous follow-up missions and experiments. After a few reentries, though, her genetic structure had become so unstable that she died. Her death set testing back several years.

Because of the obvious potential and the incredible danger should the technology be available to all, everything related to the scientific achievement was immediately classified. A global conference was held with representation from governments worldwide to decide how the technology should be used and, more importantly, controlled. They banned any time travel until a set of protocols could be developed and enforced that would regulate the entire domain and ensure that nobody would be harmed. For twenty years, various laboratories worked on the safety, stability, and efficiency of the technology.

Simultaneously, the philosophy and practicality behind time travel were exhaustively debated. A governing body, the Time Traveling Authority, or TTA, was set up to control, manage, and enforce all time travel endeavors around the world. Eventually, policies were created that governed time travel and restricted any nonapproved use or activity. Every expedition was to be comprehensively supervised, acceptably secure, nonintrusive, and undetectable to locals from the past. The TTA also decreed that time travel into the future was forbidden.

Initially, and for the first twenty years, all time traveling expeditions were scientific in nature. Authorized samples of the atmosphere, oceans, and earth's crust from many different periods in history were collected. With each expedition, the technology improved. Security and safety became dependable, and none of the trips impacted the past or future. Almost every nonscientific group in the world was also itching to attempt special-purpose time travel missions. The pressure on the TTA from all walks of life became immense. And the loudest voices of all came from tourism. There was an extensive lobby demanding that ordinary people and not just scientists be allowed to experience the past. Several operators began to design their own vessels and technology to accommodate tourists and short tours, all under the watchful eye of the TTA. In 2120, the first tourism operators were licensed.

Three fundamental protocols were introduced by the TTA and had to be obeyed for the full duration of every trip, by every operator and tourist:

1. *NO TALKING*

    No unsupervised interactions are permitted with any locals. Voice suppression solutions must be administered to all tourists.

2. *NO CARRYING*

    Tourists may not bring any personal items on ground trips. They may pick up and touch items during ground trips but may not collect and return with mementos.

3. *NO VISITING YOURSELF*

    Nobody is permitted to journey to the future, nor are they allowed to journey to the same place twice. Time travelers are also not permitted to contact their parents in the past.

Wormholes remain open for a maximum of ninety-six hours. Time tours must be completed well within the limits. Tourists must be connected (tethered) to their TourPod and must remain tethered throughout the tour. Tourists who stray from their group and become disconnected from the TourPod may become lost in time.

The regulators also recognized the danger of being able to travel to specific dates and events. All efforts to sharpen and perfect the time-mapping and navigation systems were strictly regulated. Navigation was designed to be imprecise. The tours would generally land within two weeks of any specified time destination. The tours were designed for visitors to experience a place, period, or movement but not to witness specific events. As time tourism gained popularity, the TTA faced a constant battle to ensure the operators followed the guidelines.

CHAPTER 1

RACHEL--1893

Edvard Munch mashed the clumped bristles at the end of his paintbrush into his tired palette and soaked up another helping of oranges and reds. He looked up at the sunset for the hundredth time and then back down at his depiction of it on his canvas. The shades he had created were dazzling, with mad, bending, swirling strokes, yet his painting was lacking. There was no message. No meaning. He'd produced yet another lifeless landscape. His hand lingered on the canvas as he patiently studied the path that ran around Ekeberg Hill, overlooking Oslo. And then, a frenzied girl suddenly appeared. She sprinted toward him, her hands at her cheeks framing her desperate expression. Munch lowered his brush as he watched her approach. She was a curious mix of innocence and panic. Their eyes met, and she slowed in an instant. Coming to a stop several feet away on a slight incline, she hugged her arms around her as she searched the hill.

Munch called out to her. "Excuse me, miss?"

She turned to look at him.

"I know this may be a strange request, but would you mind doing that again?"

The girl squinted at him, puzzled.

"The way you ran toward me....with your hands..." He raised his hands to frame his face, bobbed his head from side to side, and opened his mouth, mimicking a scream.

Cocking her head slightly to the side, she pondered his request. Strange indeed. And then her stare stiffened to one of recognition. Rolling her eyes, she vigorously shook her head and turned her back toward him while continuing to search the surrounds.

"Nobody is here. Just you and me," Munch hollered above the wind.

He stared at the girl, switching his attention between her and the disappearing sunset. Shrugging, he plunged his brush against the palette and got back to work as the girl desperately paced backward and forward, purposefully ignoring him as she kicked up dust. Circling crows swept towards the bare branches of looming trees as the sunlight faded. The girl's slowly lengthening shadow increasingly played with the splashes of color on Munch's canvas each time she passed him, and he finally packed his art away, politely wishing her well as he departed.

Rachel was bruised, battered, frightened, alone, and now canonized in Edvard Munch's most famous artwork as his Screamer. Five thousand miles and 230 years from home, she had no way to get back. Violently separated from her school tour three hours earlier, she was desperately hoping they would find her on the hill. They had all been on the way to it when she was grabbed and assaulted. A low buzzing deep within seemed to flatten the vividness of all sounds and colors around her. She should be shivering, hatless and scarfless in her flimsy jacket. It worried her that she didn't feel cold. Just a dull sense of disconnection. And a deep gnawing pit of worry in her gut. She knew what would happen if she got separated from the group... what happens to anyone left behind.

Most of the locals were indoors now and smoke rose like wiggling white fingers from all the chimney stacks in the valley below. A wagon approached, the horses snorting as they trudged along. The driver, a cloaked and bearded man with deeply creased skin and a long, curled pipe, squinted at Rachel in disbelief as he tugged back on the reins.

"Ride to town, young lady? You will die of cold out here," he hollered above the wind.

Recoiling at his stained teeth, Rachel shook her head. She couldn't speak, so she moved to the side of the path and gestured that he be on his way. There was nowhere he could even take her. Nobody in the world could help. She felt the bile starting to rise from her stomach and stopped herself from throwing up by gulping down a gust of icy air. Would she never see her friends again? Or her father and Daniel?

How could I be so stupid?

She reeled back to the center of town, passing a small group of vagrants huddled around a fire on the outskirts. The dancing reflection of the fires and streetlamps against the snow lent a serenity that contrasted with the rising levels of panic creeping through her body. The crackle of the fire scratched at her ears, while the hazy smoke stung her eyes.

Relax. I can figure this out.

Rachel stumbled in a daze through the dark, windy streets. Shadows flickered on the faces of staring strangers, distorting their features, as she searched in vain for a familiar face. Tripping aimlessly over cracked and uneven pavement tiles, she felt like a failing jester in a circus arena.

So tired.

She found a barn next to a mansion with a single awkward light shining in the upstairs window. Ancient trees surrounded her, heaving under their thick, soaked canopy of dark leaves, seemed to encroach, closer and closer. Rachel approached the barn door and tried to open it, but her hand struggled to grip the latch. She panicked. Had she already started dematerializing?

Her head was throbbing as panic seemed to creep over her eyes, blinding her from seeing anything clearly. It felt like everything in her guts had made its way up into her brain, leaving her with an empty pit in her body, and a packed, throbbing skull.

I've got to think.

Need to get inside. NOW.

Rachel slumped against the rough wooden door. The matted hair that wasn't already tangled stuck to her forehead and eyes drawing the tears and raindrops away from her face. She kicked the heavy wooden barn door with a soggy, mud caked boot, barely registering a dim thump. Powerless. There was nobody to help her and not a soul in sight. Gusting wind and the gentle, incessant dripping of drizzle drowned out all other sounds. The gloomy grounds with the looming house were deathly still.

Rachel had never felt so alone. Well- actually, every single day since her mom had died…

Yes, Daniel was usually hovering about, consumed by some new toy or Eyecam clip. And while she didn't see him much, dad was always in his study down the passage if she really needed something. Assuming he remembered she was even there. But this right here was a whole new level of isolation.

I need to figure this out.

Rachel concentrated and calmed herself. Then she grasped the latch again and tugged the slippery iron bolt firmly until the barn door shuddered open. Entering, the stale waft of damp hay was a welcome change from the ceaseless drizzle outside. She collapsed in a tight ball on the nearest stack of hay and squeezed her stinging eyes closed.

JOE--2130

Joe and Daniel entered the arrivals hall with ten minutes to spare. All metal and glass, the room was littered with floating magnetic HoverStools, most of which had already been clustered together to seat waiting groups of friends and relatives. Joe caught the faint scent of disinfectant masked by a strong waft of pine and lavender. Tourists no doubt returned with all manner of deadly, historical viruses that had to be killed. He craned his neck to see the TourPod arrival schedule scrolling across a giant window that separated them from the landing bays. "Welcome" holograms and children sitting on parents' shoulders made the tour names difficult to read. Daniel spotted some unoccupied

HoverStools and ran to claim them.

"Dad. Over here," he beckoned as he pulled two of them behind him.

Joe headed over, occasionally lifting his eyes to study the strangers he passed as he cautiously weaved his way through. His thoughts were mainly on Rachel. He could already picture her gushing nonstop about the trip. All the artists she had seen, the food she ate, the sketches she drew. She'd left three days ago with her art teacher, Ms. Sender, and some classmates. Her school had planned to go on the Impressionist tour for years and booked it the previous January. Rachel had developed a passion for oil painting, a rare art form these days. She was talented.

He had almost refused to let her go, only consenting after realizing that her mom, Liz, the fun adult in the family, would have approved the tour without a second thought. Joe, adopted as a baby by a single mother and never having known a father, improvised as a family man, sometimes awkwardly. He'd never really been taught what fathers were supposed to do and used AutoParenting apps that made his behavior predictable and overly cautious. Keeping children fed and educated seemed to be the most important thing. More comfortable admiring from the sidelines, he was rarely in the thick of the action. Liz had been the passionate, energetic, and hands-on parent, delegating none of the child-rearing. She knitted the children's blankets, mashed homemade baby food, and refused an android NightMinder. When the kids were older, she spent hours researching new destinations to explore with rented submarines or rocket packs and always found new stores that sold raw materials, crafts, and supplies. They even did yoga together.

Liz got sick when Rachel was ten years old. Almost every illness was curable, but not the gradual genetic deterioration that afflicted her. Joe withdrew from his family. He spent all his free time researching and analyzing her illness. He slowed her deterioration by removing everything risky--strenuous activity, sensory stimulation, and complex foods--but ultimately lost an impossible battle. After she died, he tried to assume both parenting roles, minus the adventures. Their lives became routine and empty, but stable. Sending Rachel on the tour that would inspire her was his way of showing how much he cared about her passion for painting, even though he hardly ever expressed it. Or looked at her artwork, admittedly. The trip cost Joe a full year's salary, but he was sure it would be worth it.

He smiled as he remembered his last words to her at the departures hall next door when he waved her off a few days ago.

"You'll love it. You'll come back inspired and paint beautiful things. Mom would be so proud of you."

It was funny that he couldn't really recall what Rachel had said to him.

Joe reached Daniel, who was grinning as he spun around on a HoverStool. He was circling in a small trajectory, the stool automatically detecting and correcting its path to avoid bumping into passersby.

"That one's for you."

As Joe readied himself to sit, a tall, distinguished man grabbed the second stool for his bag and coat.

"Hey!" Daniel yelled.

"Oh, sorry." He turned to Joe. "Do you mind?"

"Go ahead." Joe yielded.

Daniel seemed disappointed but quickly forgot as another TourPod entered a landing bay behind the tall glass screen facing them. The ship steadily lowered as a measured, eloquent voice filled the room.

"Castles through the Middle Ages arriving now."

"Does that lady sound like Mom?"

Joe smiled at Daniel. "Rachel's tour is soon."

There was hollering and waving as friends and family hugged and greeted. Groups left the hall as new ones entered.

The voice again: "Ancient Greece arriving now."

And again a few minutes later: "The Wild West arriving now."

Daniel tired of his spinning HoverStool. Joe rested against a pillar as his legs were aching. Where was Rachel's tour? They zigzagged through the crowd to the front window to get a better look at the landing Pods.

Maybe he hadn't heard them announce Rachel's tour. He spotted some official-looking ground crew at the far end of the landing bay who seemed to notice him too. He gazed through the clear panes at the newly arrived tourists and guides bidding each other farewell.

"Nineteenth-Century Impressionist Artists arriving now."

"Dad. That's Rachel's group!" Daniel had his hands pressed against the glass.

A third TourPod descended through the open ceiling and gently landed. The name 'Bradbury' was embossed on its sleek silver surface. Joe turned away and glanced at the ground crew. The frantic manner in which they were pointing and gesturing, made him certain that they were talking about him. As the Bradbury hatch slid open and the landing ramp lowered, the officials hurried over, diverting the tour guide from the Arrivals door. Joe and Daniel craned their heads to spot Rachel. Her teacher, Sara, was the first out after the tour guide. Head bowed and shoulders sunk, she headed over to an official clutching a ClipScreen. Rachel's classmates sluggishly followed. Still no Rachel. A firm voice behind Joe called out.

"Joe Hasselback?"

Joe and Daniel turned to face a Time International Experiences representative. Her stern, sorry eyes and tightly pursed lips were a stark foil to the smiles and laughter otherwise filling the room.

"Yes?"

"Please come with me."

They took Daniel to a play area as Joe followed, trancelike. The unthinkable was happening. As he sat speechless behind the single, square desk in a dimly lit office, faceless staff members presented him with vagaries, regrets, and waiver forms.

"We're so sorry that she ran off."

"You'll need to sign another waiver, or we won't be able to send a team to look for her."

"She never let anybody know."

"All tourists are instructed not to wander away from the group."

"Trying to find her yourself will never work, and we can't help you do that."

"The paperwork seems in order now. We'll be sending drones to try to locate her."

Empty and sick, over the next few hours, he'd been back and forth to Time International Experiences headquarters and met with their managers and lawyers and officials from the TTA. They reminded him of the risks, showed him all the forms that he had signed, and explained sympathetically that neither the TTA nor the tourism company bore any responsibility for her safety. They told him they would do everything they could to get her back, but also that they couldn't really do much and had never actually recovered anybody before. He'd been patient and hopeful at first as they bustled him out of the offices with concerned frowns and reassuring nods. Daniel had been inconsolable at first and refused to fall asleep alone. He woke up throughout the night and several nights afterwards demanding answers to Rachel's whereabouts. Joe started every morning with a call to the TTA but gradually realized that he would get nothing from them.

"Yes, Mr. Hasselback. Unfortunately, the drones haven't turned anything up. We'll call you as soon as we detect her presence. No problem. No. Thank you. Goodbye… yes… good bye sir… goodbye."

A dull fire started to build inside. He'd been polite and cooperative for long enough. He wanted answers, and he'd get them himself. First, from Sara, Rachel's teacher, who had supervised her tour.

CHAPTER 2

RACHEL--1893

Rachel woke up and shot to her feet, startled and confused. After scanning the room, she remembered flopping on a bale of hay in the musty-smelling barn. Straw clung to her clothing and hair. An uninterested cow was the only other inhabitant emitting a slightly sour, earthy odor as it gently munched on a bale of straw. Early sunlight glinted through the gaps and cracks in the walls and the door that she had left ajar. Milk pails were neatly stacked against the stark, wooden planks lining the building. She glanced up at the crisscrossed puzzle of beams suspended from the ceiling. Confusing. She looked back down at her fidgeting hands. Unsure what to do next, she sank back down, holding her legs and rocking gently. She'd never been completely alone. Rhythmically swaying while trying to keep calm, she thought of her mom. If she were alive, Rachel was sure she would have chaperoned the tour, and this would never have happened. She couldn't panic. Mom never panicked. Her mom used to do yoga, calming her mind and helping her tackle problems serenely.

Dad was also calm. Robotically calm. He always thought things through and came to the right answers, even if it took weeks to come to a decision. Rachel knew she didn't have weeks. Days at best. Rachel rocked as she pondered what to do. She assumed that all expeditions that came to Oslo in 1893 would center around the life of the artist Edvard Munch, painter of The Scream, one of the most recognizable paintings of the Impressionist and perhaps all periods. Her group was supposed to visit the bridge on Ekeberg Hill where he painted it. Munch also presented many of his works at the National Museum, so she decided to stay close by.

Outside, Rachel heard chatter approaching. The cow mooed. Footsteps intensified. Somebody was coming to milk it. She needed to get out of there.

Jumping up, she squeezed through the barn door and sprinted away, gusting past a startled farmer and his teenage son. Her elbow started to throb. The bolt on the door had caught her. Gritting her teeth, she headed towards the town center, blindly following a dusty path. It was a chilly morning, with a post-rain freshness, and enough light to guide Rachel to the center of town. She soon found a quiet alley with a view of the gallery. Rachel stopped. Thoughts buzzed through her head.

Her familiar, safe home.

Her mom painting.

Daniel looking up at her.

Glorious brushstrokes on an evolving canvas.

Sara pointing and explaining.

The tall man with the cruel eyes

Whack!

The last memory was so jarring that Rachel reached for a crate pressed against the narrow walls to steady herself while she watched the museum entrance. She breathed deeply, inhaling slowly like her mother used to do. This slowed her heart rate and restored the sensation in her face. She sucked in a breath through her nose and pushed out her stomach as she squeezed her eyes tightly closed. She tried to clear her mind and focus only on the roughness of the walls. Reassuringly, she began to feel the icy wind against her cheeks as it gusted through the streets and alleyways. She tried to keep the oxygen in as long as she could. It stopped her from freaking out.

JOE -- 2130

"And then what happened?"

Joe had arranged to meet Sara at a coffee shop on the River Walk in San Antonio. They sat at the end of a long table that lined a largely robotic kitchen. Sara was Rachel's graphic design teacher and a technically capable, if somewhat unimaginative, artist who struggled to sell her work. She had connected with Rachel when teaching Impressionism, and the tour was to be the highlight of their year.

Her puffy, red-rimmed eyes were a welcome change from the indifferent expressions of the TTA bureaucrats. At least she answered his question.

"Rachel was having a ball. We'd been pretty lucky. Rachel had caught Monet's eye by his studio in Vétheuil, and he'd doodled a sketch on her sleeve."

Joe raised his eyebrows and faintly smiled. It was just like Rachel to get herself noticed.

Sara continued, "We'd done the Impressionists in France, and we'd gone across to England in 1889 to see Whistler painting a landscape. We had a few hours before we needed to return, so they took us to Oslo to see Munch. We were making our way toward Ekeberg Hill when Rachel grabbed me and gestured behind us."

"What did she want?"

"She couldn't tell me. We'd all been silenced for the ground excursion. I looked behind, but I didn't know what I was looking for. She seemed excited and urgent. Like she wanted me to see something, but at the same time, she didn't want me to keep staring."

"What was it?" Joe pressed.

"She was trying to tell me with her hands. It could have been that some hoodlums were following us. Or that somebody had tailed us all the way from London, which was impossible. Right? I looked again. I saw a few people. There was one man who stood out. His outfit seemed too modern. All black, fewer fastenings. Formfitting. Rachel kept looking. I decided to try telling our guide, Toby, so I moved forward. We turned a corner, and when I looked back, she was gone."

"What do you think happened? Do you think you were being followed?"

"I don't know. Why? And by whom?" Sara pleaded, clearly torturing herself with the same questions.

The table began to glow and pulsate, giving Sara a chance to compose herself as the DrinkMaster requested their orders. Everything on the menu was prepared instantly in the industrial-size gleaming silver hulk of graphene that could accurately synthesize almost every beverage from almost every part of the world. Joe mindlessly ordered two black coffees as Sara continued.

"I got Toby's attention. We all turned back, but we couldn't find her. Everyone was frantic, searching everywhere we could think. We went back to the ship and tried to locate her, but she wasn't giving off any signal. When we got back to Alaska, I gave them a full report. I told them everything I could remember."

Joe felt himself trying to grasp the unfathomable. Of course, Rachel would never have been irresponsible enough to wander off on her own. She hadn't gotten lost--she had been kidnapped!

He composed himself, head bowed. Sara, staring blankly at a space above his head, stirred her coffee mechanically. She hadn't sipped from it. Eventually, Joe looked up.

"And the guy who might have been following you?"

"Strange-looking man. Very tall and pale. Very pale."

***

Five days later, the thought of someone kidnapping his daughter still burned in Joe's gut like a vial of acid, but he was running out of leads.

He had already interrogated Rachel's teacher and then her tour guide.

He had spent hours upon hours at the TTA, working his way through the managers, guides, controllers, and trainers, the special operations team, as well as their so-called resource and surveillance departments. He'd been to Time International and questioned the tour company's safety commission.

Then he hit the books, grilling professors and scientists who specialized in the theory of time travel. He taught himself about wormholes, space-time foam, and negative energy. He studied the nanomaterial tracking technology that was supposed to keep time tourists safe. And with the same grim fortitude he had once used to study his wife's medical scans, Joe forced himself to learn about the ghosting effect--the inevitable dematerialization and disappearance of every stranded time traveler, lost to history.

Rachel's ship, the Bradbury, had returned without her on the afternoon of September 22, 1893. The journals suggested that she would turn into a ghost by September 25th.

Three days… if she was lucky. An insignificant window of time in which to find her, and he would only have one shot.

Joe threw himself back into the search, digging through online forums where time tourists described their most harrowing experiences. He contacted a lady who had been captured by Incas and been only narrowly rescued from certain slavery or death by her pilot's quick thinking and a StunGun. Another man had been attacked by a drunken Viking and was lucky to escape with eight of his fingers. In desperation, Joe even read the accounts of blacklisted tourists--those who misbehaved on their tours and were permanently banned from time travel.

As he continued to dig, back to the earliest days of time travel tourism, the film and the stories got more obscure and outlandish. Finally, something sparked in Joe's conscious: Things went wrong more often when time tourism was new. The guides seemed less prepared and the tours a little more improvised.

That was what Rachel needed: an improviser. No modern luxury TourPod operator these days knew how to do anything but push buttons and run through checklists. She needed an Amelia Earhart, a Marco Polo, or a Lucy Findlay--an explorer, a survivor, someone bold and quick-witted and confident...

...someone utterly unlike him in every meaningful way.

Joe had no clue how to start. Overwhelmed and helpless, his head stuffed full of facts, his thoughts darting in every direction and his guts twisting, Joe suddenly hungered for stories of tours that fell apart. He had to get more practical, to learn from real-life stories. Joe hunted for footage on the pioneering, smaller-tour operators. The TTA had regulated all activity since the very beginning, so Joe did not expect to uncover any scandalous secrets. And then he stumbled on a strange little marketing video from the very bottom of the internet.

The advert started with a group of tourists dressed in loincloths nervously approaching bewildered, frightened-looking Stone Age men. It cut away the moment one of the cave dwellers reached for a sharp-looking rock. Then a different group raced away from a marauding gang of Bolsheviks, in the thick of a revolution. The visitors seemed genuinely terrified. Suddenly, a clunky-looking TourPod was speeding across an African plain, buzzing herds of wildebeest. Then there was a cut to more tourists slowly advancing on a group of alarmed lions. A boisterous voice-over rose over the barely contained chaos.

"Nobody will bring you closer to the greatest, most humanity-defining periods in history. At Morton Tours, you will experience beauty, excitement, wonder, adrenaline pumping adventure, and the triumph of the human spirit. See ten thousand years in two days. Join us for the time of your life."

Joe smiled, appreciating the independent, gritty quality. The final scene showed the narrator, thumbs up, confidently smiling and inviting the viewer to swipe right to request a quotation.

"I'm Milo Morton, and I'd love to make some memories with you."

Joe held up his SmartGlove and nervously cleared his throat. "Call Morton Tours."

The SmartGlove chirped. No record exists.

Joe frowned. Ran another search. Apparently, Morton Tours had ceased trading five years ago under a cloud of legal trouble. Joe searched further, eventually finding an archived copy of one of the last Morton brochures. He could only hope the contact information was still valid-- and that there was still someone on the other side of the line.

He called into his SmartGlove, "Hello, Milo. Can I meet you? It's about time tourism. It's really important. Joe." Send.

Hours passed with no response. There was no time for patience. He tried again. "Hello, Mr. Morton. I need some information urgently. My daughter is missing. Please reply as soon as you can."

Nothing.

By the time Joe gave up waiting for a response, it was almost midnight. Daniel was asleep in the other room. Joe hadn't closed his eyes in almost two days. He was gritty-eyed and unshaven, his head pounding and his back stiff from hours spent at the screen. As he paced the living room, one glance at Rachel's empty bedroom rooted him to the spot. The canvasses littering her floor looked grey, the livelihood that had always filled her room seemed to melt away like the unfinished spaces on one of her works in progress.

"Please," he found himself pleading into his SmartGlove. "I am trying to find out what happened to my daughter. She went on a time tour and never returned. Nobody can tell me anything. Please, please, answer me, Milo." Joe's voice cracked. He hit send and threw his SmartGlove onto the sofa. Turning away, he stood motionless in the darkened room, listening to the empty hum of a dozen useless devices in power-saving mode, imagining what he was going to tell Daniel in the morning.

After a couple of minutes, his SmartGlove vibrated. He ventured over apprehensively and stuck his hand in.

1 Beachcrest Drive, Burlington, Vermont. Tomorrow morning. Come alone.

CHAPTER 3

BARRETT--2130

Superintendent Dan Barrett stared intently at the sleek graphene contours of the DrinkMaster as coworkers in his compliance department bustled about. His concentration was broken as Yulia rushed up behind him, clutching an electronic file.

"I can never decide," Barrett said, sensing her presence. Despising any sense of indecision, he quickly ordered what had become his regular.

"Double tall espresso, Peruvian beans, umm…fully roasted. OK. One sugar. But I want Demerara sugar." An afterthought: "And a little goat's milk on the side."

Barrett's coffee and a tiny tub of milk slid out moments later. He cradled the cup to his chest as he walked back to his office, with Yulia keeping up beside him.

"The commissioner wants to see you on Wednesday about increasing the tour slots. Should I confirm for two o'clock?"

Barrett grunted.

Yulia continued, "The Compliance and Oversight Committee are meeting on Friday to decide on the new licenses. You will need to submit your report by Thursday evening. OK?"

In her three years working for Barrett in Regulations and Compliance, Yulia had brought order to his chaotic schedule of demands and deadlines. He had hired her straight out of school and increasingly relied on her efficiency, discipline, and energy. After she'd asked about the program, he'd enrolled Yulia in the upcoming TTA agents' course and worried about how he would replace her.

Barrett didn't answer her. He set his coffee at his desk and swiped at his holographic display, activating it.

"Pull up the footage from the lost girl's ship."

A series of screens appeared, each marked by date and venue.

"London first."

Footage of the group inside the ship appeared. By flicking his wrists, Barrett played the footage forward and backward, speeding it up and slowing it down. Occasionally, he paused an image and spun it around, viewing the ship from different directions.

Yulia watched him silently, absorbing his every action. He scrolled through videos, flicking several into the archive. Ultimately, Barrett lined up three paused images and stacked them together above the side of his desk.

"Show me outside."

A new series of holograms appeared. He pointed at the first, bringing it to the front of the batch. The image displayed the horizon surrounding the TourPod. With his index finger, Barrett could switch the perspective from the sides of the ship to the sky above and the terrain below. Barrett paused and stared at the second video. He opened and closed his right hand, causing the image to expand. Straining his eyes, he expanded the horizon, revealing an ominous new blot.

"There it is," he affirmed. "It's the Dark History ship. Right there with the Time International group. In London. From 1889."

"Right, sir," Yulia agreed.

"And look," Barrett continued.

He pulled one of the footage files that he had saved to the side. It was a view through a porthole from the ship. He expanded it gradually, drawing her focus onto a ship hovering in the distance.

"There is another Dark History ship. Or maybe the same one."

Yulia nodded, waiting for instructions.

"This footage is from Oslo. From 1893."

The TTA had blocked all development of improved navigation systems to ensure that groups of tourists would not arrive at the same historical events at the exact same time and draw attention to themselves. Regulations stated that ships were permitted to target destination dates within two weeks, but no closer.

Barrett was baffled. "What are the chances that two ships jumped to the exact date and hour of the same day? Twice. Unless one of them was tracking and following the other. Highly unlikely. Almost impossible. Was the Dark History ship following the Time International TourPod? The other way around?"

"Almost impossibly?" Yulia offered.

"Get me Jethro Wenger from Dark History Tours."

"Now? You have to report to the Executive Committee in thirty minutes."

"Try him. He's a cagey character. Never stays on the line for more than three minutes, anyway."

Barrett studied the vessels until Jethro appeared in his holographic feed. He was a slight, cunning man with sharp features. Jethro took in the entire room with his stare, never blinking.

"Superintendent Barrett? I'm a little busy. Can I help you with something?"

"Mr. Wenger. Thank you for taking the call. I'll get to the point. I'm sure you heard that another tourist went missing this week."

"I heard about it. Doesn't really have anything to do with me, though."

"What did you hear?" Barrett pushed.

"Nothing interesting. A girl on one of the Time International tours never returned to the ship. That's all."

"Her name is Rachel Hasselback. She is sixteen years old. She's the tenth person to disappear this year. And the first ever on one of their tours."

Jethro replied with callous indifference. "Very sad. Again. What does that have to do with Dark History?"

Barrett's jaw tightened. "As your tour operator's license is in review, all your trips must be prearranged, supervised, and logged with us. And I'm looking at footage from a Time International TourPod of one of your ships that launched two weeks ago without a TTA agent onboard, in 1889. What were they doing?"

Jethro was unfazed.

"They were on a quality assurance check. Perfectly legitimate. They were back within the hour, as required by the TTA. Are you suggesting that we know more about the tourist's disappearance than we do?"

Barrett paused and stared at Jethro for what seemed like minutes.

"Let's see what comes out."

Jethro terminated the call.

JOE--2130

Joe headed to the local SlingShot station on autopilot. He'd traversed the same route to work every morning for years and took comfort in the routine. Entirely underground and providing sound barrier breaking, seamless, intercity transport throughout North America, SlingShot had become the reliable mode of transportation that Joe used exclusively to navigate his way around. He hadn't changed his routine even once for years and could find his Bullet, order a sandwich from a passing drone and read a research report, without even glancing upwards.

Today was different, of course. The butterflies in his gut reminded him that he wasn't going to work. Arriving at the station exactly at the time he'd planned, he headed down the conveyor to the departure area. His SmartGlove told him to head for Tunnel D and to catch the 7:08 a.m.

Burlington Bullet D1050. He paced up and down the platform, squinting to read the carriage numbers as they slowed, stopped to board and release passengers, and darted off. He wavered too long and missed the first two bullets to Burlington.

A third soon emerged from the tunnel on his left, and he hurriedly stepped forward. The glistening jet-black carriage door opened to welcome him--just as they always did. He stepped inside the glass-and-carbon-fiber capsule and took one of the familiar, elegant leather seats, dropping his travel bag by his feet, and sinking backward into the safety of the commute. But he didn't feel comfortable. He kept his gaze fixed on the trip-progress screen at the front of the car to avoid unwanted eye contact with the other passengers--just as everyone always did.

For the first time in a thousand commutes, Joe felt uneasy. He shifted in his seat. The bag at his feet kept getting in his way, and the cabin seemed smaller. He glanced left and right, searching for a control panel. There wasn't one. He wondered, for the first time, what would happen if the Bullet broke down.

On the front screen, an advertisement was promoting holidays on Mars. Parents could spend their afternoons sightseeing and hiking craters, while the kids raced around on space-skis. Those were things that Liz used to do with the kids, leaving Joe to his computers and his virtual lab. He went on the occasional long weekend away, particularly after Liz got substantially weaker, but nobody seemed to have as much fun. Their Moon Fountains trip had been a disaster, and he still wasn't sure why. Rachel had been so upset, screaming at him about who knows what, that they all came home a day early.

Joe felt as fragile and vulnerable as the glass window beside him. Daniel was at home with no mother or sister, and here he was, putting himself in a dangerous situation. What if the bullet crashed? Milo might be a crazy lunatic! What if he disappeared, just like Rachel?

The old man next to Joe turned to him. "I still remember when the flight from Texas to Vermont took three hours. You could at least order a drink and watch a movie."

Three hours! It had been ten minutes, and Joe was already well beyond his comfort zone. He could not rise quickly enough as the Bullet eased into the Burlington SlingShot station. The air outside was thick with frozen clouds, and he hurriedly summoned a self-driving Bubble from his SmartGlove. Almost nobody owned or drove a car. The odd collector still played around, but that was mostly recreational and on Sundays.

Arriving at Beachcrest Drive, Joe climbed out of the Bubble and stepped out onto a dusty suburban street. The surrounding structures were all farmhouses with covered wooden porches, thatch roofs, and small vegetable patches. The neighborhood struck him as strange, rustic, and backward. Joe made sure not to lose his footing or to step on a discarded shovel, broom, or snake.

He carefully wandered down the street, observing the property numbers--13, 11, 9, 7, 5…and then …the end of the road….. a boundary fence(?)

Strange. Joe checked Milo's original message again: 1 Beachcrest Drive. He double-checked for house number 3, crossing to the other side of the street again. There definitely wasn't a property number 3, 2, or 1. Had Milo meant to write 11 Beachcrest Drive?

Joe circled back, but 11 Beachcrest Drive had a swing set in the front yard and recently used colorful children's toys. The perennial Christmas lights framing the porch did not seem the style of a man who had made his living selling low-budget time travel tours.

Joe walked over to the fence dividing 5 Beachcrest Drive from the protected forest beyond. He ran his finger along the cool metal wire while stretching out his neck to peer beyond the first layer of majestic, green birch trees. As he noticed a glint of metal behind a thicket, his hand brushed across a small knob concealed within a rusting post. He pressed it. After a few seconds, a voice answered.

"Joe?"

"Yes?" Joe replied.

"Just climb over. I'm right behind the big sugar maple." Click.

Joe looked behind him to make sure nobody was watching and pulled himself over the tall fence. Does he live in a forest? How does he live in a forest? What if I hadn't found the buzzer for his illegal home? Who is this guy?

Joe grabbed at the top bar and grunted as he sprang, briskly stuffing his right foot through a hole in the fence. He pulled himself over to the other side of the fence, wiped his pants, and headed toward the smoking chimney. He found a quaint little stone cottage soon enough, with an antique hoverboard parked outside. The strange dwelling had a fishpond, a vegetable garden, and a small pen with goats and chickens. Joe steadied himself and knocked on the heavy, gnarled door—officially surrendering his last chance to abandon this mad errand and go safely home to his son.

Milo opened the door. A tall, solidly built fellow with a thick mop of greying hair, he squinted suspiciously into the sunlight.

"Are you alone?"

"H-hi. Yes?" Joe stuttered.

But Milo had already retreated indoors.

Was Joe supposed to follow him? "Thank you for seeing me, Mr. Morton," he said.

"Did you bring money?" Milo called over his shoulder.

"You…didn't ask me to bring money."

Milo's only answer was a grunt as he ambled down a dark hallway.

But it was rude enough that Joe himself left etiquette behind at the door and followed the strange man, past the photographs, ornaments, and objects that seemed to occupy every inch of wall and shelf space. As he shuffled after Milo, he turned to stare at a conspicuous titanium door poorly concealed behind a tall, thirsty-looking potted plant.

At the end of the hallway, they came to a study bursting with books, maps, a PocketHolo, VisonPlayers, antique guns, and various unidentifiable contraptions. Milo walked around to his chair, gesturing for Joe to take a seat, overlooking the fact that there was no uncluttered place to sit.

Joe anxiously decluttered a chair as if he were working out a strategy in a game of Pick-Up Sticks.

Milo did invite me, he reassured himself.

He glanced at the titles as he shifted a pile of books and papers towards the desk. Darkest Secrets of Time Travel, by Milo Morton. Adventures in the Fabric of Time and Space, by Milo Morton. Final demand notice, from Powersoft Lumber. Notice of eviction, from Leddy Park Management Committee.

"You mention that your daughter disappeared during a time tour?" Milo made no eye contact as he scrolled through messages on his PocketHolo.

"Yes. In Oslo, around 1890. Her tour set off two weeks ago. I want to get her back," Joe said, speaking in measured, short sentences, resisting every urge to snatch the device out of Milo's hands to command his full attention. "But nobody who was involved knows anything. I don't think anybody who has gotten lost has ever come back before."

Milo was busy typing something, muttering to himself.

"Yes, yes, you'll get your money… What were we saying? Oh. Well, they're all bureaucrats. Nobody has a clue what to do. I wouldn't get my hopes up. So…what do you want from me?"

It took everything Joe had not to shout the first thing that sprang to mind: Nothing. Just forget it. Clearly, I'm wasting your time. And mine.

But that would be of no help to Rachel.

And it wasn't what Liz, her mother, would say.

Groping for patience and inspiration, Joe glanced around the cluttered room. He thought of how excited Daniel would be to see the treasures Milo had accumulated through his years of adventuring. He thought of how indignant Liz would be that this pioneer of time travel had been sidelined and thrown away by the same industry that had profited so tremendously from his trailblazing. And he thought of the younger Milo from the commercials, who so enthusiastically volunteered to launch himself and anyone brave enough to come along for the ride into every kind of situation imaginable.

That was who Joe needed. Was that Milo still in there somewhere?

Joe leaned forward, uncharacteristically steepling his arms against his knees at the very edge of the seat. "I need you to help me do what nobody else has ever done before. I need to bring Rachel back." And then, in a moment of irrational confidence: "I'll give you whatever you want."

Milo looked up with a cunning gleam in his eyes and a smile that melted years away.

"Mr.... Hasselback, did you say? A pleasure to make your acquaintance." The handshake he offered then was as firm and vital as a rescuer's first grasp of a drowning man's wrist.

"I can't promise that you will come back, but we just might find your daughter."

CHAPTER 4

JOE--2130

Joe shifted in his chair, his eyes lingering on a large blaster mounted in the corner of the cluttered study. Milo was jabbing impatiently again at a keyboard.

"You'll get paid," he muttered at the screen as he sent a message.

"Thanks again, Mr. Morton…"

"It's Milo."

Joe tried again. "My daughter went missing two weeks ago. From what I can gather, somebody separated her from her class tour."

Milo paused and studied Joe. "Did she run off? Maybe she was eaten or sacrificed?"

"Her teacher said my daughter seemed to recognize somebody before she vanished. Nobody knows anything else. I need guidance."

"Oh," Milo groaned, "you heard about that group I lost in the Crusades."

"Nope." Joe folded his arms tightly to his chest.

Milo waved his hands, signifying that nothing had happened. Joe's uncertainty intensified. Maybe he was making a mistake talking to this shady character.

Milo admitted, "You're right. The TTA wouldn't have a clue what to do. Around four hundred people have disappeared since the trips began. And they've never brought back a lost tourist. Ever."

"Why not?" Joe asked.

"Other than that they are total bastards? Nobody ever figured out how. The TTA are hopeless bureaucrats with no reconnaissance skills. And the TTA would never take a chance on one of the operators figuring it out."

"Why is it so hard to get somebody back?"

"A lot of reasons," Milo began. "First, you need to know how the system works." Milo reached behind his chair and pulled out two fishing rods. "Take this." He passed Joe one of them. "You don't know anything. We'll need lunch."

Obviously in no mood to fish or even to eat, still, Joe followed along out to the back of Milo's property. A faint shimmer glowed off the walls and roof of the cottage, making them blend in with the surrounding trees. Milo was clearly hiding the property from the park rangers and visitors. He was squatting in their forest. They strolled to Milo's surprisingly large pond and cast their lines into the water. The pristine water was filled with perch and trout, clear water lapping up against the deeply green grass.

As Milo unpacked his fishing tackle he continued.

"When they started offering time tours, the TTA wanted the tours to run in the same way as if a person went on a guided vacation overseas. Every aspect had to be controlled and had to operate within the limits of law and nature. People would get a visa. A guide would accompany all tourists. The tours would run for only a limited number of days. Actually, three, maximum. And tourists would age normally. There is no cheating time."

Milo gently prodded a fishing hook with his thumb. Joe leaned back against a tree as he grappled with the facts.

"Why three days?" Joe asked.

"Time travel began when scientists worked out how to open wormholes through the space-time continuum, to the past. But stepping through was much more complicated. Your body--your matter--is attuned to the time that you live in. You are a part of the present. When you are plunged into a previous time, the energy…the matter of that previous time rejects you. The same way that the body of a transplant patient may initially reject the new organ that gets introduced."

Milo handed Joe a fishing rod, and then expertly cast his own line into the center of the lake, before continuing.

"So, when you travel back in time, the technology on the TourPods hides you from the past. At the same time, the ship keeps a strong connection through the wormhole to the present. It's like an embassy in a foreign country. The TourPod and the people are still attached to the present time. We use all kinds of tricks and technologies to 'convince' the past that we're not imposters for as long as the wormhole can be kept open. The longer the wormholes are kept open, the more likely the cloaking procedures will fail. So, the TTA mandated that TourPods are to return, and the wormholes are to be closed within three full days of the ship leaving. You can only fool nature for so long."

As joe fumbled with his rod, Milo rhythmically swung his line backwards and forwards. Joe paused, watching Milo as he expertly lured fish to the water's surface. Then Joe pushed ahead.

"They talked about becoming ghosts at the TTA. What does that mean?"

"Like I said, matter can only survive in its own timeline. When an object that doesn't belong is introduced, the surrounding matter feels 'disrupted.' Everything starts to close in on the unwanted intruder, trying to restore things to what they were before the disruption. Like antibodies fighting a virus. The foreigner gets bombarded until they lose their physicality and become shadows of who they were, retaining only a thin, intangible shimmer of their previous appearance. That's what happens to time tourists who get left behind for too long."

"So, people start to look like ghosts?" Joe exclaimed.

"Not just to resemble ghosts! That's what ghosts are. They're tourists who got lost in the past. Their spirits left to roam in a time that won't allow them to exist."

Joe gulped. "And that is what will happen to Rachel?"

"Could be," Milo responded.

"How long does it take to become a ghost?"

"You need a bit more background."

Milo paused. He pulled his line back in, adjusted the bait, and then recast it into the pond.

"For the last eight years, tourists have been allowed to leave their TourPods and walk around, visiting people and places. How did we know that was safe?"

Joe shrugged.

"Tourists get 'tethered' to the ship. Before they disembark, we apply an electromagnetism to each tourist that replicates the cloaking that protects the ship. But it's connected to the ship. If the TourPod leaves, the effects of the veiling wear off. So, it's crucial that tourists stick with their tour groups and don't wander too far from the TourPod. And if somebody gets lost, we try to find them before coming back."

"So, how long does Rachel have?"

"Hours. A few days maybe."

It felt like another punch in Joe's stomach. "But then she is already a ghost."

"It's more complicated than that," Milo added ominously.

"What do you mean?"

Milo was silent for what seemed like hours to Joe. The wind picked up. Milo gathered his thoughts and then told a story.

"I was one of the first tour operators. I built my ship in the early years when the TTA was still finalizing the regulations that would govern how time tourism would work. It was a crazy time. The tours could run for two days, and the tourists were only allowed three-hour ground excursions. I took a group to witness the American Civil War. We arrived in Gettysburg just before the actual battle was to break out. We'd been watching a few skirmishes and disembarked to try to get closer to the action and the soldiers."

"What!" Joe exclaimed and dropped his line. "Isn't that dangerous?"

"That's what my customers enjoyed." Milo offered a peculiar smile. "A little bit of action. Right?"

Joe tried to nod, but couldn't.

Milo continued, "One of my customers was a young girl, Millie Johnson. She could trace her family back to a slave plantation in South Carolina. Anyway, we set down near the Harrisburg Road and soon realized that we were caught in a particularly dangerous position, surrounded by troops from the Union and Confederate armies. Foolish girl panicked, refusing to hide with us until the TourPod could land. She upped and ran, straight into a company of soldiers who were marching captured freemen back into slavery. They took her."

"You couldn't stop her?" Joe blurted out and immediately regretted it.

"Obviously not! They almost killed us in the crossfire. Anyway, we found the company of soldiers who had taken Millie. But she was away from us for too long and was dematerializing. We stunned the soldiers. Millie tried to get on the TourPod, but she was already turning into a ghost. She wasn't solid. Just couldn't stand inside the ship. Kept falling straight through the floor. She had such fear in her eyes. We had to leave her there in Gettysburg. We had only fifteen minutes to get back before the wormhole closed."

"That's horrific."

"Pretty bad. Yeah." Milo's face had tightened.

They were quiet for a while. Thrashing in the water broke the silence. A large perch was tugging sharply at the end of Joe's line. Milo helped Joe reel it in, and they retired to the cottage to cook it with vegetables from his garden.

"You know," Milo said eventually, "I found her again a few years later."

"You mean they let you run your time travel operation after that?" Joe exclaimed, half-jokingly.

"They tried to stop me. There was an inquiry. I presented my side to their committee. I told them I did everything to stop her from running off and put myself at significant risk to rescue her. They understood that. The TTA had more courage back then." he responded firmly.

"OK." Joe wasn't convinced.

"I went back to Gettysburg a couple of years later," Milo continued. "I took a tour to witness the Confederate withdrawal and Abraham Lincoln's Gettysburg Address, if we got lucky. That night, I went to look for her. She was still on that same road where we left her. The soldiers captured her a few weeks before the Lincoln speech. But that time had taken its toll."

Milo paused in thought as he threw the fish down on the kitchen counter. He poured himself a glass of water. Joe felt a little thirsty but was not offered. Milo turned on the gas and began to gut the fish as he continued.

"She'd lost her spark. Millie was like a faintly colored shadow drifting around. She still wore the slave trader's chains on her arms. I approached her. I told her that I hadn't forgotten about her. When she looked at me with her haunted eyes, I felt a bit rough."

"It was good of you to go back." Joe offered.

Milo shook his head.

"The air grew colder as she stood there, staring at me. But then her black eyes burned like a cut into hell. And her sadness turned to rage. She ran at me, shrieking soundlessly, reaching me in seconds. But she passed straight through me. I was never so terrified. I couldn't do anything for her, so I hightailed it back onto my TourPod."

Joe was almost speechless. He twisted in his chair as he contemplated Rachel's fate.

"You told me that girl was on the ground for a few hours before she started to disintegrate. How long does Rachel have!?"

"The technology is better than it was. Rachel should be fully intact for at least twelve hours. Maybe twenty-four. She'll ghost after that. After that

– two days maybe?"

"So, how do I find her? How do I get her back in time?"

Milo placed the fish on a pan and set the timer. He led Joe back to the study. Joe realized that he wasn't going to be offered any dinner either. Passing the imposing titanium door again, Joe paused, but Milo just shook his head, unambiguously telling Joe not to ask.

They reached Milo's study. When they were seated again, Milo explained some of the challenges behind recovering a lost tourist.

"The key problem is finding them before it's too late. The navigation systems are getting more precise, but the TTA will never allow the technology to develop enough that we can jump to specific dates. They don't want to risk tourists going back and compromising famous events in history. It wouldn't look good if a group of excited, time-traveling strangers crowded the signing of the Declaration of Independence out."

"I guess the passengers could also change history. Wouldn't that be a bigger problem?" Joe suggested.

"You would think so. They used to call that the butterfly effect. If somebody goes back in time and kills a butterfly, shouldn't that create ripples in time that change the course of history? Turns out that we have no evidence of that happening."

Joe squinted at Milo in disbelief.

"In one of my first tours, I took a group to see the Deccan Wars in seventeenth-century India. We got lucky, and then we weren't. We arrived during the Mughal attack on Fort Panhala and set down to watch from a nearby hillside. A scared soldier ran into our clearing just as we were landing the Vonnegut, and we crushed him like a bug."

Milo smashed a fist onto his desk, emphasizing the point.

Joe jumped in his chair. "Not great…"

Milo pressed on, undeterred.

"The battle was spectacular, but we were all a bit worried about going back, thinking that we might have changed the future. Maybe that coward was the great-great-grandfather of an important scientist who would never be born? Maybe the whole world would be different? When we got back, everything seemed the same. I reported the incident to the TTA. Other than further irritating the Compliance and Oversight Committee, I don't think anybody gave my accident much further thought."

"Seems a bit irresponsible." Joe folded his arms tightly.

"There are two theories as to why nobody thinks the butterfly effect holds water. One is best told with the old joke of the time traveler who steps back out of the time capsule announcing, 'I killed Hitler,' and his colleague in the lab says, 'Who is Hitler?' Nobody but the time traveler would be any the wiser that the past or present changed.

"The other theory is that everything that is supposed to happen will happen. Though we don't see it, we are all just living out a plan that was set in stone at the beginning of time."

"My accident was one of many cases where tour groups messed with the past. Everything here still seems normal, right?"

Listening to Milo's crazy stories, Joe was unsure of the answer.

"We still don't tempt fate. The TTA is very cautious to limit the chances of changing the past, so they regulate all ground activity with their restrictions and rules. Guides and pilots--"

Joe was getting annoyed and pushed himself away from the desk. Milo had been talking too much without telling him what to do.

He interrupted: "So, the main challenge is finding Rachel within twenty-four hours of her being on the ground?"

"Assuming she hasn't gotten herself arrested, imprisoned, committed, or killed, there are still major questions. If she's already started to dematerialize, you will have no way of knowing if her body will restore itself on the ship or back in the present."

"I don't know how I am going to do this..." Joe muttered.

"The odds are totally against you," Milo added. Milo stared at Joe. He looked around at the clunky artifacts and strange inventions he had used over the years. Everything seemed useless to Joe. "I might be able to help, but--"

"But what?" Joe answered abruptly. He felt like he was back at square one. Milo seemed flaky and unreliable, and Joe questioned whether they could even do anything to save Rachel.

"You'd have to do something for me in return."

Joe sat back uneasily. "What do you mean?"

"I mean that I have a plan and some technology that will help you find Rachel. I can't guarantee anything, but the way I see it, you don't have a lot of options."

"I don't have a lot of options. But I don't know what you want. And I don't have a lot of money."

Milo stepped over to a shelf cluttered with books and artifacts. Picking up a small, translucent, green figurine and with his back to Joe, he answered. "Maybe I'll ask you for money later. Or maybe you'll bring something back for me. I don't know. Don't worry about it now." He put the figurine down, turned to face Joe, and grinned.

"Well, I don't know. What will you do? What do you want?" Joe hesitated. He reached for his bag and stood up, threatening to leave.

Milo came around and put his hand on Joe's shoulder, reassuring him.

"Relax. I'll help you. Let's see if we can get your daughter back. Come back on Monday. Bring credits. And Rachel's toothbrush."

CHAPTER 5

Jethro sat motionless in his windowless, sparsely decorated office. The exotic objects on his desk were the only indicator that the room was in use. Barrett's call had bothered him. Realizing that his fists were tightly clenched, he breathed in gruffly and turned to the door of his office.

"Gater."

An unusually tall and sinewy man appeared in the doorway. Wide mouth grinning, his entirely black ensemble mirrored his stringy long hair and dull, passionless gaze. Standing still like a muddy pool at midnight, his eyes, framed by a snow-white face, darted from side to side, taking in the empty room.

"Are there any loose ends?"

Gater hid a snarl. He hated to be questioned.

"Take a seat, please," Jethro offered, his sharp smile not reaching his eyes.

Gater squeezed into a chair across from Jethro, his legs with their bony knees pointing to the ceiling like the sails on a yacht as he studied the antique weapons and ornaments on Jethro's desk. No HoverClips depicting children's birthday parties or family holograms. Just immaculately polished finger traps, daggers, batons, and spiked ratchets.

"Tell me about the girl again," Jethro said.

"She knew me from London," Gater said. "I don't know why she noticed me or what she saw me do. But, in Oslo afterward, she recognized me. She's just a nosy little girl. I grabbed her and asked her what she saw."

Jethro was deadpan. Gater squirmed in his seat, finding Jethro's examination unsettling.

"And she didn't tell you?"

Gater answered, "She fought back. Then an old man showed up with a gun."

"An old man?" Jethro exclaimed, surprised.

"Look. She was just scared. That's all. She knows nothing."

Gater seemed a little flustered. "Anyway, she is stuck in Oslo now. She'll disappear soon."

Jethro considered his response in silence while Gater nervously shifted in his small chair, searching for a sign of approval.

Finally, Jethro said, "After Superintendent Barrett called me, I contacted somebody in the TTA. They told me that Barrett didn't know anything. But he won't stop investigating the girl's disappearance until he is convinced that nothing funny happened. He needs to think that she just got lost."

Gater interjected, "Nobody saw anything different."

Jethro picked up a seventeenth-century wooden baton. He cut Gater off by jabbing the air dangerously close to Gater's head.

"I've been told that the father's been asking questions and might try something." He stood up and started to pace.

"So, do we let him investigate? Just leave him alone?"

"Maybe he will get lucky. It seems to me like you left some loose ends."

"Do we stop him dead in his tracks now?" Gater asked nervously as he followed Jethro around the room with his eyes.

Jethro loomed behind him, his imposing presence pressing in like a ton of lead.

"I can handle it. I'll do whatever you think, sir."

Jethro leaned in behind Gater, close enough that he could smell Gater's sour scent.

"Gater. If this blows up and anything blocks the granting of my license, you will have cost our company a delay that neither you nor anybody in your family will ever be able to repay. You need to sort it out. No loose ends."

RACHEL--1893

For a never-ending two hours, Rachel desperately watched the museum entrance. Everybody who approached seemed familiar at first. She'd seen her dad's shuffling walk a hundred times already. She wanted to run out each time but cowered backward as soon as the memory of the strong, wiry man with the twisted grin roared into her head. He had been right here where she was standing now. What if he still was, and he saw her? How had he not killed her yesterday? She touched her head where he'd pulled out her hair as he struck her face, and she shuddered. Calming herself, she studied the street again. Anyway, maybe she was being presumptuous, expecting somebody to come for her. Dad probably wouldn't notice that she was missing. She smirked as she remembered the last time she tried to show him one of her new watercolors, and he told her it was great before she had even turned the pained side around to face him. Pinching her arm, she brought her mind back to Oslo.

Another tour group was bound to pass by, and she just needed to spot them. A handful of bewildered-looking misfits following a confident, boisterous leader would be her clue. She would hide until she was sure. No false alarms. A small group approached, and she strained to see them. A round man who seemed way too excited, his head span from side to side, drew near. The lady beside him was at least twice his size, and her bright, feathery hat bobbed with a flamboyance that didn't match the gloomy surroundings. Rachel squinted, ready to charge out when they got closer, but then, unexpectedly, a large man in a black uniform stepped in front of her, blocking her vision. She recoiled in surprise. He didn't budge and started to address her as she tried to step around him.

"Good day, madam. May I help you?" he asked. The man had sad eyes and a long, droopy moustache. He also had the telltale badges and hard black hat of a police officer.

Rachel immediately shook her head. She did not want any help or attention from a nineteenth-century Norwegian police officer and gestured that she was fine. She tried to encourage him to go along with his day.

"What are you looking for?"

Rachel repeated her signals but realized that she was not making herself understood. As she motioned more vigorously, the policeman's expression grew from polite to confused to annoyed.

When his eyes widened in fright, Rachel froze. She followed his gaze and noticed her left hand had penetrated the lamppost next to them. Like a hologram, her fingers, mist-like. dissolved into the cold steel, reappearing on the other side. She smiled at him calmly and slowly withdrew her hand and rested it deliberately by her side. He started to shout and blow his whistle. Rachel ran. She dodged past him, lifting her skirt and corset, and hurried down Universitetsgata Street as the policeman hollered behind her. She headed toward the crowded Studenterlunden Park hoping to lose him in the crowd. Glancing behind her, she saw that there were now three clunky men in black police suits, batons raised, huffing, and wheezing in pursuit. The locals circling the area had all stopped their morning activities. All eyes were on her.

As she got closer to the park, Rachel noticed two more constables, frozen mid-duty, in a clearing ahead. Ticket books temporarily lowered; they had turned towards her, searching for the source of the shrill whistle blowing. She ducked into the university grounds to her right and headed for a doorway. It was the science building. She scrambled up the stairs, almost knocking over a small group of students, and jerked the doors open as one of them came around the corner. Rachel ran through the corridor, searching for an unlocked closet or empty room. Finding none, she darted down a set of stairways and found herself in a darkened, abandoned passageway. She slowed, not wanting to trip on anything, and progressed up the passage, trying to open every door. The last room on the left was unlocked, though the thick wooden door was jammed. She pushed, slamming her shoulder against it, and forced it to open. She stepped into the dark room, closed the door behind her quickly, making sure not to jam it again, and stopped to catch her breath. Her mind was racing. How did her hand go through a steel lamppost? Was she dematerializing? She could still feel the door. Mostly whole. Relief.

Rachel calmed herself. She breathed slowly, deeply. She was sure it would be safe to get back outside in a few minutes. Then she sensed someone watching her.

JOE--2130

Joe returned to Milo's illegally built cottage in the woods a few days later, Rachel's toothbrush in hand. Another Impressionist tour was due to depart in the coming week, and Joe hoped to be on it. Milo rushed him inside when he arrived and took him past his mysterious titanium vault to his cozy, cluttered office, where they both sat.

"First, you'll need to book the tour." Milo opened the Time International Expeditions booking page, a grin on his face. He handed Joe a bio-coded time travel passport.

"Your name is John Holtzman."

"I'm sorry. What?" Joe asked, taking the card and turning it over in his hands.

"Well, you can't go as Joe Hasselback. They won't let you on the tour."

Joe had never seen a fake document before. He was honest and straight to a fault. Careful to pay every bill he owed and scrupulous with his taxes, Joe even felt guilty if he didn't floss his teeth before bed. How was he going to carry fake travel documents?

"Right!" Milo began. "You'll need to be prepared."

He presented the possibilities to Joe as he saw them. One of two things had happened to Rachel.

Either, she had been the victim of an ordinary crime. A common criminal or mugger spotted her and attacked her. She might have been knocked unconscious, or worse. If this had happened, Milo asserted that Joe had no chance of finding her.

Milo's stronger suspicion was that Rachel was targeted because she was a tourist. Somebody recognized her or her tour group. Joe tried to guess why anybody would attack her. Rachel was a harmless, sweet girl. People loved her. She had no enemies.

Milo speculated that it was an attack on the Time International group by a competing tour operator. He suggested that Rachel witnessed something that she wasn't supposed to see. In this scenario, Joe had a better chance of recovering her. If her time-traveling attackers had found her once, they might be able to do it again.

"Will this work?" Joe was still fumbling with his fake passport like it was a blood-stained dagger.

"You need to make damn sure the ship goes to Oslo," Milo stated firmly, "Now, if Rachel was attacked by another tour operator, and they think that you're connected, or if they think you know what she knows, you'll need to be prepared. They might come for you too."

Milo unlocked a desk drawer and took a set of keys from it. He walked to a bulky, locked cabinet and inserted one key after the next. Joe sat in silence, wondering what to say, as Milo struggled with the cabinet lock.

"You must take some equipment with you," he continued once he'd forced it open.

Joe came over to him, peering curiously at the contents of the shelves. He was expecting to see easily concealable nano-knives, laser cutters, and blasters. He was not expecting to see a collection of small vials and cloth. Milo noticed his look of confusion.

"You obviously can't take modern knives and guns. The TTA won't let you bring anything onboard except essentials that stay on the ship. They can't have more stuff landing up in Area 51. Whatever you take with needs to look plain and harmless."

Smart, Joe thought.

"At Morton Tours, I developed some stuff. Best to keep it to yourself."

He handed one of Joe two tiny, colored glass vials that looked like single doses of eyedrops.

"This will create a lot of smoke. Empty the contents onto the floor. It will paralyze anybody who walks into the cloud. Make sure the wind is blowing away from you."

"Will they let me on out the TourPod with it?" Joe asked as he held his trembling hands out.

"No. But it's tiny and glass, so their scanners won't spot it."

Milo handed Joe another vial of the same size but a different shade, pressing it into his palm.

"This one will create a blinding flash if you throw it on the ground. If the liquid touches anybody, it will temporarily blind them. Again, don't get it in your eyes."

"Thank you," Joe said and put them in his pocket.

Next, Milo held out a long-sleeved yellowish vest. It looked unwashed. The armpits were stained a curious gray. Joe did not like second-hand clothing. At all. Especially not well-worn undergarments.

"Feel it!" Milo said, beaming with pride.

Joe hid a displeased grimace and took it.

"It's my own design. It's made from reinforced linen. Looks and evaluates exactly like common linen. It will withstand most bullets and even a knife attack."

Joe took it with hesitation. "I sure hope I won't need this."

"You never know. Best to be safe. And don't worry. It's a little stiff and itchy, but quite snug."

Finally, Milo pulled out a device the size and shape of a silver pen with a small, flickering-red bulb at the base.

"Did you bring Rachel's toothbrush?"

Joe pulled it out of his bag, and Milo swiftly grabbed it.

"I hope you didn't wash it," Milo cautioned. He firmly pressed it against the sides of the thin silver object. "This is a BioSensor. I designed it myself. It will pick up misplaced matter a mile away."

Joe stared blankly at Milo.

"Misplaced matter is matter that doesn't belong. What I mean is that if even if a hair fell from Rachel's head and you get within a mile of it, this tracking received will blip."

Milo calibrated the device while Joe gingerly placed all the contraband in his bag. He glanced up at Milo. Maybe he had been wrong to doubt him.

"By the way, none of this stuff has been approved by the TTA. If you get caught with any of it, I will deny ever meeting you."

BARRETT--2130

Superintendent Barrett was frazzled. His office line was ringing incessantly, and he was still working through new investigations and complaints. He'd received another grievance from the business alliance community. Celebrity Time Tours passengers were securing extremely rare autographs from long dead personalities and selling them online.

He had a court hearing later that day to censure Epic Party Tours. According to reports, three separate groups had gotten into drunken brawls at a Roman orgy, a twentieth-century Manchester United game, and a nineteenth-century Hasidic bar mitzvah. He still had to review the outrageous footage.

Milo Morton, an old operator that he hadn't heard from in years, had left him a message. And he still had to deal with Rachel Hasselback, the missing girl from the Time International class tour.

The office line persisted. It was Senator Pearson. He accepted that call.

"Senator Pearson, how can I help you?" Barrett answered, doing his best to cover his frustration at the interruption.

"Barrett. How are you?" Edward Pearson didn't wait to hear how Barrett was. "I'm calling about the committee on Friday. We have some new applications for operator licenses on the agenda."

That reminded Barrett. He still had to go through the recommendations for the new operator licenses. Another deadline to add to his work pile.

"I'm interested to see the recommendations you have on the applicants," Pearson concluded, as though reading Barrett's mind.

Barrett uploaded the list of applicants: Aspire Tourism, Dark History Tours, Freedom and Fun-Time Tourism, High Times Travel, and Wellsprings Roots Tourism.

"Senator Pearson," he said, "the reports aren't ready yet. Is there any specific application you wanted to draw to my attention?"

"I'm interested in your recommendations," Pearson repeated but added, "on the Dark History application."

It would have been inappropriate to ask Pearson why he was concerned with Dark History, though it was a legitimate question. Senator Pearson was one of the most influential and powerful personalities on the TTA Compliance and Oversight Committee. Pearson understood the hierarchy very well—how close he was to absolute power, and who was beneath him and needed to obey. He had a short fuse and did not tolerate delays.

"I'll have a look through the report today. Is there anything specific that you need to know?"

"Just your recommendation. I think they are a very professional operation, and I'd like to get them approved without delays."

"I'll have a look and submit my report accordingly."

"Good. Thank you." Pearson ended the call.

Barrett disliked these kinds of conversations. He had to present a report on each of the applications that were appearing before Pearson's committee. His department focused on the applying operator's regulatory compliance, technical readiness, safety measures, and employee training. The committee would review his recommendations as a part of their decision to approve an application.

An approval meant a license to launch a new tour operation. Licenses were very expensive and hard to come by. The TTA were very strict with their votes and only approved a handful every year. They needed to make sure that only responsible, honest, technologically sophisticated operators were running the tours. Barrett's recommendations were an important part of the review. But he had no vote and no direct say in the outcome. Senator Pearson and fourteen other directors, professors, ministers, and industry leaders bore ultimate authority and responsibility.

Barrett had to be very careful. He would not ignore any findings that his team uncovered. But he had to tread delicately while simultaneously making sure that he did not mislead or hide any facts. He looked up who was preparing the report on Dark History.

Barrett called Yulia.

"Yulia, is Agent Chen around?"

"I believe so."

"Please ask her to send me her report on Dark History ASAP. I don't care if it's incomplete. I need to see it now."

"Oh, and, Yulia," Barrett added, "please get me Milo Morton. He used to run that operating company - Morton Tours. He was that guy who got expelled and jailed for smuggling a couple of years ago."

CHAPTER 6

Joe stared at the glowing blue numbers on his SenseAlarm. Finally, almost five, 4:48 a.m. He'd been awake for hours already. Just twelve more minutes and he could start his day. He knew that if Daniel heard him from down the passage, he would want to help with the packing. Which meant more begging to come along. He couldn't bring Daniel.

Joe had watched the fatherly advice clips warning against leaving without saying goodbye. Still, this seemed easier, and he was already running on empty. He hadn't slept through a night since Rachel disappeared. Ghosts filled his mind as soon as he drifted off, jarring him awake.

The alarm puffed out an invigorating cloud of jasmine and citrus. He sat up immediately to shut it off and quickly got dressed.

The front door glowed a soft green, signaling Pam, Daniel's grandmother's approach. He glanced at Daniel one last time and hurried to let her in.

"Hi, Mom. Let me help you," Joe whispered as he reached for her overnight bag.

"It's light. Daniel still sleeping, love?" Pam stepped inside.

"Yeah."

"Don't you want to wake him to say goodbye? I'm sure he'd appreciate it," she suggested.

Joe turned toward Daniel's bedroom. He paused indecisively.

"No. I should just let him sleep."

While Pam thoughtfully agreed, Joe had already changed his mind yet again and headed to Daniel's bedroom. He quietly poked his head in, still unsure whether to wake him. The wolf occupying half of his bed raised its head and opened its piercing-blue eyes for a moment before pushing the anaconda with its foot and settling back down.

Joe could not understand how Daniel slept with a gray wolf and an anaconda curled up beside him. However it worked, Joe let him continue and sluggishly made his way to the kitchen. He hated this break in his routine. Not going to work after breakfast with his children. Joe found comfort in routine—methodically checking the implications of other people's mistakes, never risking the possibility of making his own. His coming week would be another matter entirely. For years, he'd spent every day at a desk searching through reports for trends and clues. As the quality assurance manager at Zoo Synthetics, he tested the newly manufactured animals, working out why they sometimes malfunctioned and ensured that they were 100 percent harmless to people before they were rented or sold. His relationship with Daniel thrived on the synthetic animals, thrilling his son with a steady supply that he borrowed from work. That was easy enough. Rachel was more complicated. He never figured out exactly what she needed from him. Trying to uncover why Rachel vanished, and where she went, was another matter entirely. The possibilities made his head spin. He put his bowl back in the cupboard unused and continued to sit silently with Pam.

"What time do you need to leave?"

"The tour leaves at ten. I need to be there by eight to check on some things before I leave. I'll take off in a couple of minutes."

Joe opened his bag again and checked that he'd packed all the gear

Milo had given him, making sure to conceal it. He glimpsed his fake passport, his heart sinking even further.

"You will know something soon, love." Pam smiled, though her eyes couldn't disguise the worry. "Didn't I read about that young man they found who went missing in Medieval China?" Pam offered as she poured a cup of coffee.

"The TTA Recoveries department doesn't seem to have any plan. I don't think they've ever really brought back anybody that went missing. If this trip doesn't work, I'm…" Joe ran out of words.

"You'll bring her back. You will." Pam hugged Joe, and they finished their coffee in silence.

"Thanks for looking after Daniel while I'm gone, Mom. I'll be away for, max, three days. Oh. He has a wolf and an anaconda in his room." He grabbed his overnight bag and stepped toward the door quickly, but he didn't escape the effect of his bombshell.

"A snake!"

Joe paused. Most people, Pam included, didn't like snakes. Even synthetic ones.

"That son of yours. Go. I'll be fine."

Joe checked his ticket again on his SmartGlove as he set off for the SlingShot station, destination Time International Experiences departures in Alaska.

Two Bubbles and a Slingshot later, he was standing at the entrance to Departures. That same sterile smell stung him, memories of Rachel's tour returning without her.

"Check-in," he mouthed into his SmartGlove. The holographic directions on his palm guided him through the maze of rooms and corridors, past a collection of tour groups and office workers. There was a buzz of joy and exploration filling the cavernous spaces. As Joe progressed, he heard bites of chatter from clusters of excited holidaymakers.

"…to see real dinosaurs…"

"I've heard the Crusades were unimaginably cruel. I'm a bit nervous."

"…they say more bison were crossing the central plains…"

Adverts flashed across massive screens mounted on the walls, displaying ancient cities, erupting volcanoes, sweeping plains, and brutal battles. It cost the average tourist one year in salary credits to book a trip, but the appeal was undeniable. One could experience firsthand some of the most profound events in history. Tour packages of the Stone Ages, First Crusade, Middle Ages, US Revolution, and Impressionist Europe were departing that morning.

Joe found an open counter and where a tall, athletic woman with shining red lips and wavy blond hair greeted him.

"Good morning, sir. My name is Inga," she said in Swedish. "Where are you off to today?"

Joe instinctively squeezed the Revelate implant in his earlobe to make sure it was translating the counter manager's instructions. Almost everybody had a Revelate implanted. Most parents had them put in soon after their children were born. The advantages were obvious—when activated, the instant translations meant that everybody understood everything, regardless of the language being spoken. Nobody bothered to learn a second language.

"Ahh. Yes. The Impressionists Tour," he answered hesitantly.

"Oh, wonderful. That will be interesting. Passport?"

"Yes, of course."

Joe swiped his bag open and dug for the passport, feeling a bead of sweat form above his upper lip. He felt the first pangs of nausea welling in his throat. Finding it, he awkwardly handed it over like it was a bag of heroin. She glanced at him strangely as she studied the biometric data.

"Everything OK, Mr. Holtzman?" Inga asked. She held the passport over her counter, waiting for clearance. Joe felt the urge to run. He looked over his shoulder, expecting officers to be looming behind him. "Mr. Holtzman?"

He turned back to the counter. Inga cheerfully gave him the passport back.

"Please hold up your confirmation and place your bag on the conveyor belt. You will be reunited with your bag on the ship."

Relieved, Joe handed over his bag and raised his SmartGlove.

Period clothing was synthesized for all ground activities. Passengers were not permitted to carry any of their own possessions off the ship. Other than Milo's contraband, Joe had packed his pajamas, a couple of changes of underwear, a pair of pants, an extra shirt, and his toiletry bag. He knew that the TTA would remove anything they felt was risky. Again, as he shifted from foot to foot, Joe just wanted to run away.

Inga looked up at him for a moment and squinted. Joe shifted on the spot as her blue eyes narrowed before looking down again.

"All clear," she said, beaming. "Please proceed to Bay D2. Your TourPod, the Crichton, leaves at 10:00 a.m. sharp."

Head purposefully bowed, he reached the departures point hastily, avoiding all contact, and followed the ramp up and into a small, sleek, and perfectly round TourPod. The center of the Crichton had six comfortable seats surrounded by six passenger compartments. He was the last on board and nervously acknowledged the group, who had happily turned to meet him. Hating the attention, Joe ducked into the compartment allocated to John Holtzman. His bag was on a comfortable-enough bed situated between a shower and a small desk-and-chair set. Vera, the guide, called him back and introduced herself.

"Hello! Vera Johnson, your guide on this wonderful adventure," she gushed. "Welcome onboard the Crichton. I will be at your service for the next seventy-two hours on this Impressionist expedition. And standing over there is Ashar Demian, our pilot."

Ashar waved. "Call me Ash."

There was a murmur of excitement as the Crichton's hatch slid closed. Joe gazed longingly at the benches circling the departures hall.

"We'll be mostly based in Paris, spanning the late nineteenth century and early twentieth century. Depending on how things go, we hope to meet Manet, Sisley, Monet, Cézanne, Renoir, Caillebotte, van Gogh, Rodin, and Pissarro. We'll have a quick stopover in London to see Whistler and then close the tour out with Edvard Munch, in Oslo, time permitting."

Everybody began to chatter with even some clapping, forcing Vera to raise her voice above them. Joe didn't like Vera's indecisiveness. What did she mean by 'time permitting'? And why did Oslo have to be last on the agenda?

"Please remember the rules. You'll be tethered shortly. This will keep you connected to the ship. Without tethering, your body would quickly disappear. Never stray from the group or you can lose the tethering." Vera continued, "We're also going to muffle your voices before each ground excursion, so you won't be able to talk."

One by one, they stepped forward nervously into the small steel tethering chamber. It was a completely innocuous experience, much like the bio-healing chambers in the hospitals. Strobes of thin blue light ran up and down Joe's body while a soft buzzing reverberated through the space. Then the door slid open, and he exited, making room for the next passenger.

"Remember—observe only. Do not interact with the locals or run off with them. Never pick up or carry anything or take your possessions with you during the activities. And most importantly--enjoy!"

Everybody took their seats and strapped themselves in, awaiting takeoff.

Vera chimed in one last point: "By the way, this ship goes fast. You might pass out for a short while. Good luck!"

Ash took his seat and activated the control panels, triggering a complex array of lights, humming noises, and gentle swaying motions. The interior lighting faded, and the windows surrounding the ship darkened. The Crichton lazily climbed.

Leonard Lambert, a lanky, retired history teacher seated across from Joe, piped up in a British accent.

"It's a pity we don't expect to see Gauguin. He'd probably left for Tahiti already."

He looked around for a response. Anxiously waiting for the time jump, Nellie van Donnel, a young bride from the Netherlands, was clutching her husband Carl's hand tightly.

"Would be nice," Leonard continued. "You know, he left his wife and children behind in Europe and never saw them again. He painted nude island ladies for the rest of his life and probably wooed most of them. If you know what I mean."

"Wooed. That's a sweet word." Nellie remarked.

"Nude island ladies?" Carl asked, looking up.

"Watch it, Carl van Donnel." Nellie playfully pushed him.

Joe craned his neck to see outside. The departures building, followed by the streets and parks surrounding the Time International Experiences campus, grew smaller as the ship steadily rose. For a fleeting moment, he thought of Rachel, and of Daniel, whom he had just left behind. Was he being reckless? And then the vessel blasted forward with a breathtaking force. Joe passed out instantly.

GATER--2130

Gater was the first person at the Dark History embarkation station in Sweet Grass, Montana, the morning following his tense meeting with Jethro. He arrived before dawn and waited for the launch technicians.

"I arranged a Solo Pod with Sally from logistics yesterday. One of the new recon ones. For three days."

The technician checked his Planning Scheduler.

"I have you booked for a two-seater DualPod, just over there."

Gater ground his teeth. He called Sally, growing more and more agitated as the call progressed.

"Whatever the boss wants," he finally retorted and disconnected. He headed for the larger vessel without a word to the technician and climbed inside. The craft was oddly shaped--like a pillbox with no hard edges or distinguishing contours. A cockpit seating two faced a large display that seemed to cover every surface. Behind the pilots, a small common area accommodated the provisions store, work counter, and bathroom. At the rear, a retractable partition separated the common area into two sleeping cubicles.

As Gater was activating the guidance system, Shiner stepped onboard. Without looking backward, Gater grunted a sort of acknowledgment. Shiner was older than Gater by at least twenty years. He'd been a mercenary, contracted to the US foreign reconnaissance services for most of his working life. He did not possess all the technical or robotic skills that his colleagues in the operations and security departments had. They liked to undermine him behind his back for that. But nobody ever challenged Shiner directly. He never quit or surrendered.

In a company physical training session the previous week, the participants divided into groups of four. Three of the participants were required to pin the fourth for thirty seconds. Nobody succeeded with Shiner. Two of his coworkers had to go to the medical center with bite wounds and broken fingers. Gater found Shiner overly cautious and unpredictable. Neither enjoyed working with the other. In fact, Gater didn't like working with anybody. It bothered him that Jethro had not let him deal with this mission alone.

"This operation seems complicated," Shiner started. "I wish we'd had time to plan."

"I'm not concerned," Gater responded. "What's so difficult? We're going to follow a tour group to nineteenth-century France, find out what some father knows. And if he knows something, we make him forget it."

Though Gater had a reputation for ruthless efficiency, Shiner thought this mission sounded way too unstructured. Bloodshed or death on a mission meant that something had spun out of control. He always tried to avoid messy outcomes.

"Do we have any transmitters planted along their planned itinerary?" he asked.

"Yes, in Oslo and London. Somebody put a tracer on the father's TourPod before they set off. We'll find them quickly."

Gater activated the nuclear propulsion and calmly glided the pod upward and out of the hangar.

55

Chapter 7

JOE--1870

Joe stirred and then jumped out of his seat startled, his eyes wide open. Vera, and Ash, were already awake and arranging for the day.

"Rise and shine. You've been asleep for 270 years."

She beamed and then tittered. Joe could tell it was a very scripted joke. She gave him a headache.

"We've arrived in France in 1870. Have a look through one of the portholes."

Joe nodded and carefully made his way to the translucent paneling surrounding the common area of the vessel.

It was late afternoon outside. Five thousand feet below them lay sprawling Paris. Joe had expected that the nineteenth-century world would be greener and lusher. A cloud of smog sat stubbornly below the vessel, obscuring much of his view. The forests around Paris were largely ravaged and silent. Most of the trees had been cleared to satiate the populations' unquenchable appetite for food and energy to power their factories.

The surrounding areas were flat--covered with agricultural fields, and likely tree stumps and large mounds of horse manure, Joe thought. As they descended, Joe saw overloaded carts and wagons of wares or passengers. Throngs of people crowded the muddy streets, lively and pulsating. Smoke poured from the chimney stacks. He experienced a sense of belonging that he couldn't understand. The world below him seemed grimy and hard, yet full of purpose. A sense of compassion stirred deeply inside him. The people, slogging away at everyday tasks seemed busier and less distracted. He felt a pull to move among them, experiencing their challenges. Joe was captivated. Soon enough, though, the creeping sense of dread and loss returned. He was here to find Rachel.

The rest of the small group stirred.

"Goodness. How long have I been out?" Leonard asked.

Nellie sat up a moment later, rubbing her eyes, and began to poke her husband Carl, who was still out cold. "Wake up," she whispered loudly, "no time to waste."

Carl grunted.

The tour was seventy-two hours, and deadlines were tight. TourPods that didn't get back before the wormholes closed would be lost forever.

"Welcome, everybody, to Paris, France, 1870. We left Alaska twenty minutes ago, so you really haven't missed anything...well, except 270 years."

Vera tittered again and then continued.

"Take a few minutes to look outside and have a snack. The views are certain to be different from anything you've ever seen. Afterward, we will all return to our cabins. You will find period costumes. Please dress quickly, so I can start the tour. While you eat, I'll explain where we are, what we plan to do, and most importantly how not to get yourselves killed."

Vera grinned as if joking, though everybody knew that this was a possibility. Joe was paying full attention.

Ash opened one of the holds and took out six prepacked sandwich meals. Nellie, Carl, and Leonard ate while they gasped at sprawling, lively Paris below them. Joe took his sandwich into his cabin and tore open the sealed clothing parcel. It contained a dully colored lounge coat, long trousers, waistcoat, and collar shirt. He dressed quickly and returned to the common area.

After a few minutes, everybody was strutting around in their nineteenth-century regalia. Leonard tipped his hat and straightened his tie, while Nellie flapped her long skirt and played with the ruffles and ribbons. Joe preferred uncomplicated clothing, the less fastening, the better. He loosened his collar.

"Attention," Vera shouted above the chatter "You all look perfect, and you'll fit in fine!"

"As explained to you before the trip, before disembarking, we're all going to get scanned quickly by what we call the Silencer. It creates a tiny magnetic field around your larynx that will prevent any sound from coming out. The TTA mandates this for every tourist on every ground excursion, to ensure that nobody causes any panic in the past or tells the locals things that will get you all locked up in an insane asylum. I'll be the only one speaking." Vera continued, "Ash will also apply a nanodrop on the back of your hand. This will make you immune to any of the germs floating around as well as protect the population from your germs."

The group lined up, and Joe found himself at the front. Ash picked up a small vial with a dropper while smiling gently in Joe's direction.

"Who doesn't have a Revelate implant? Anybody?" Vera asked.

Leonard raised his hand. Carl and Nellie both nodded and automatically reached for their ears.

"Ahh. Good. The Revelates will work perfectly in all the cities and times we will be visiting. Leonard, you'll just need to follow my instructions even more closely."

Looking at Ash, Joe could not pin him down to a single distinguishing feature. His face was neither too round nor too square. He had brown eyes and brown hair. He resembled one of those acquaintances one is happy to bump into but whose name one can never recall. He had a detached, invisible quality and never looked others in the eye, even while speaking to them. Normally Joe appreciated that in a person, but in this case, he found it unsettling.

"A drop on your wrist…aaand you are done."

Carl and Nellie were next.

Vera continued setting out the day's activities. She gave a lengthy introduction to the period and style of Impressionist art. It was obvious that the group was familiar with the subject, but the floor was Vera's, and nobody could argue or object.

"We'll hopefully run into some of the most famous Impressionists. Ash will take us to an empty clearing inside the Bois de Boulogne, Paris's second-largest park, constructed just a few years ago. After making our way to the sixteenth arrondissement, it's a short stroll to the art studio of Charles Gleyre, whose students included Alfred Sisley, Frédéric Bazille, Claude Monet, and Pierre-Auguste Renoir. We'll sneak into the back and hopefully see some of them at work."

Vera waved animatedly, acting out the day's activities as she spoke. Joe's headache got worse just watching her. She would undoubtedly make his pressured trip feel even longer.

"Then it's off to the Avenue de Clichy and the Café Guerbois, a favorite meeting place for many of the artists. We will hopefully get a table and enjoy some of the local beverages. I will order them for you! Finally, we'll wonder around the neighboring Montmarte neighborhood and then head back to Crichton."

By now, everybody had been immunized and silenced. The excitement was palpable, though; Joe was apprehensive, hoping by some miracle to find Rachel in the first hours.

"How about we go around the cabin, and each of you tell the rest of us what you hope to see or experience? Ladies first. Nellie, let's start with you."

Joe would have to pretend to be an art tourist like the others. It shouldn't be so hard, but he knew that he wasn't a very convincing liar. And that was when the stakes weren't high at all. He knew at least one

Impressionist painter. Monet. He'd say that he was a huge fan of Monet. Nellie rose first, face glowing as she delighted in the attention, though her awkward stance betrayed a slight level of self-consciousness and inexperience as a public speaker.

"Well. Carl and I love Monet. Everything about him and everything that he did. It would make the tour for us if we could see him in action. And also--you know--just to see the people, and the fashion--"

"And the food," Carl interjected.

Joe slumped in his chair. He could feel beads of sweat starting to form on his upper lip.

"Lovely," Vera replied. "Leonard? What about you?" She spoke with a hint of apprehension, which seemed justified when Leonard removed a speech from his pocket.

"'The Impressionist Movement: The Birth of Color and Feeling,'" Leonard began and cleared his throat, as he prepared his vocal cords.

Vera gently interjected, urging Leonard to keep it short and to the point. Unfazed, Leonard launched into a detailed analysis of the period, focusing on the artistic representation of shade and color as a contrast to the political movements that were awakening at the time. After ten minutes and the increasing level of groaning and yawning from Leonard's captive audience, Vera interrupted him.

"Leonard, that was lovely and interesting, but time is short, and we need to start the tour."

Clearly dismayed, Leonard huffed as he sat down, placing the stack of unread pages on the mess table. Joe exhaled, relieved. Surely there was no more time for chitchat. Maybe he was off the hook.

"John. Let's have a quick word from you. Why did you decide to join the tour?"

Joe rose to his feet slowly. All eyes were on him. He nonchalantly dabbed at his sweaty face with his sleeve and nodded at the faces in the room. His mouth was bone-dry. Leonard loudly folded his speech and shoved it back in his pocket. The room fell silent again, with just the faint pinging sound from the console and navigation systems.

Keep calm, he thought. *Nobody suspects you.*

"Monet," he simply stated and then paused. He realized that he had nothing else to say that wouldn't make him seem suspicious.

"Yes?" Vera said encouragingly.

"Umm. That's it. I really, really like Monet."

An awkward silence persisted until Nellie clapped her hands together. "Just like us!"

Vera checked her watch. She looked over at Ash to prepare the TourPod for landing and ended the group dialogue.

"Thank you, friends. Remember that everybody is to always stay close to me. If you wonder off, and I lose sight of you, and we can't find you, you're in a world of trouble."

Vera paused for a moment. Her voice became serious, and she reminded the group.

"If you're separated from the ship for too long, you will start to disappear. You will become a ghost. And we don't yet know how to stop that or to reverse it."

Nellie grabbed Carl's hand and squeezed it. Joe was sure that Vera glanced at him specifically. Had she somehow figured out who he really was?

"So, there is no room for misbehaving. Any deviating from the rules, and you will be confined to your cabin for the remainder of the tour."

Ash had activated the cloaking apparatus as they flew into Paris. The Crichton zipped to a wooded area above Bois de Boulogne and then gently descended to a flat clearing among the trees. The ship was camouflaged so that it blended in with its ever-changing surroundings.

He checked the visuals to ensure that nobody was approaching. After landing in a dusty, sheltered clearing, he powered down the engine, brightened the internal lighting, and released all the seat locks. As he opened the ramp, Joe felt a gust of chilly, air from the unexpectedly familiar world outside.

Before disembarking, the group again lined up in front of Ash. He held the Silencer, a thin, silver rod up against the head and neck of each passenger. It made a series of delicate beeping sounds. Joe, who was first, tried to thank him and quickly realized that no sounds came out.

"Your voice will come back on its own in a month."

Nellie looked horrified.

"But we'll restore it when you return later tonight."

"You're safe to exit," he told Vera.

Joe took in a deep breath, enjoying the feeling of cold on his face and body. Clothing in his time was all climate controlled, he couldn't remember the last time he had noticed the temperature. Leonard struggled to his feet, while Nellie and Carl stood and stretched. Nellie was still enchanted with her frilly dress. They all made their way to the exit, and Joe gingerly stepped onto the grass outside the ship. It was sunset, and a glorious pink hue filled the sky. He was struck by the cacophony of chirping birds. Once everybody was gathered in the clearing, the hatch closed, and the Crichton quickly took off and disappeared.

Vera rounded everybody up, and they set off toward the outskirts of the park, heading for the Boulevards des Maréchaux. Nellie beamed at Joe as they all shuffled into a group behind Vera, who walked briskly as she pointed out the history of the park and the expansion of Paris's borders.

They passed a small lake with a fountain burbling out a neat circular spray of cool water. Children were pushing toy boats around the edges while impatient parents were pleading with them to be careful. Joe thought of Rachel. When she'd found out that her parents met at a fountain, she'd turned fountain spotting into a family project. Their family couldn't walk past one without her and Daniel splashing each other. She'd photographed and painted a hundred of them. Joe choked back his angst and wondered if she had passed by here too.

As they entered the street, the din of birds and children gave way to the clopping hooves from scores of horses pulling wagons, carts, and carriages. Bicycles, a recent invention, weaved between the larger wagons, their riders tinkling their bells.

Men with neatly cropped beards and moustaches filed past them wearing frock coats and carrying canes. Even the children wore suits and caps. Most women wore stiff, puffed-out skirts and tops with fancily embroidered hats.

The sensory simplicity struck Joe the most. All of the sights and sounds were real. There were no billboards, no promotional holograms and advertising jingles, and no whirring engines, only powerful horses pulling creaking wagons, chattering pedestrians, and squeaking bicycles. The group briskly made its way down the wide avenues toward the Artists Quarter, Vera explaining all the way.

As they approached Charles Gleyre's studio, the streets got busier. Joe gagged at the powerful stench of horse manure. Vera wanted to get the group to the studio quickly, always wary of losing their low profile. She instructed everybody to stay close and cross the streets carefully. And to watch their step!

Joe covertly slipped his hand into his jacket, feeling for Milo's BioSensor. Finding the activation button, he pushed it, turning the device on. As he followed Vera, he kept glancing at the device, waiting for it to detect Rachel. Nothing. Joe kept it hidden, making sure Vera wouldn't see what he was doing. She kept looking backward at the group, checking that they were keeping up.

They hastily crossed the boulevard and ducked into a side street, cutting through onto the Rue de l'Université. Leonard seemed to be trying his hardest to explore every shop window and office. The EyeCam embedded in his contact lens recorded everything. Carl and Nellie, delighted by the sidewalk cafés and rowdy bars that they passed, were pointing at the loudest tables.

Within the hour, they reached the studio. Joe was glad to stop. He turned aside and fiddled with the device hidden in his pocket. Still nothing. Was it broken? He could hear boats along the Seine behind the buildings, the river sloshing against the boats and jetties. Vera gathered the group.

"In a moment we'll go up to the studio of Charles Gleyre on the second floor. As well as being a great painter, he was--is--the teacher of Renoir, Monet, Sisley, Bazille, and other famous Impressionist painters. Pass these photos." Vera handed copies featuring profiles of several of the Impressionist masters to Leonard, who promptly circulated it.

"They come here several times a week to paint and to learn. The studio is busy, and there are many artists, models, and passersby who like to visit, so they're used to seeing people walking in and out. We'll enter in pairs. Keep close to the back wall. A couple of minutes and back out. If anybody addresses you, just smile."

Vera opened the delicately carved, heavy wooden double doors, and the group filed in. As Joe entered, he imagined how excited Rachel must have been when seeing this place. Sara had confirmed their group visited the studio. She would have come face-to-face with her idols, watching them work.

They walked up the wide staircase, each clutching the banister to steady themselves as a collection of female models came down the other side, faces still painted and hair fashionably styled. Joe couldn't resist looking them over. The boldest of them said something that he didn't hear, and the others laughed.

Vera indicated to Carl and Nellie to go in first. A young artist was entering. Carl and Nellie sneaked inside with her. Joe smiled at Leonard, who was grinning in anticipation.

The clock was ticking for Joe. His chances of running into Rachel were minuscule. Her trip had lasted seventy-two hours and spanned fifty years. It was almost impossible that they would visit the same sites at the same times. When he'd booked, he wondered what he would actually do. Milo's BioSensor might help him figure out where she'd been. Although, if Vera caught him trying to find her, she'd shut it down. He couldn't carve a message on the wall for her. That would be almost pointless. He'd have to be smarter. There was a small chance the Crichton would detect her if they crossed her timeline. The tethering process might allow Rachel to sense their ship, the same way that he could sense it. Then she would come looking for him.

Maybe whoever took Rachel would come for him. He'd get answers but might find himself threatened as well, leaving Daniel an orphan. Maybe it was helpless. No! Rachel was strong when she needed to be. Joe saw how, when he withdrew after Liz died, she stepped up for Daniel, showing a level of responsibility beyond her years. He prayed that she could be strong now. He covered his face with his hands as he waited for his chance to enter the studio.

Carl and Nellie came out a moment later, radiating. Nellie was wide-eyed, bursting to tell the group what she saw. Carl seemed satisfied but a little flushed. Noticing his expression, Joe guessed that there was a naked female model in there with the artists. Vera indicated to Joe and Leonard to go inside. Leonard went first. The room was large and spacious with the anticipated attractive naked model sprawled across a chair in the front center. The group of artists, forming a semicircle around the girl, were diligently studying and painting her. There were around twelve of them, mostly men.

Leonard froze, starstruck. He could barely breathe. He turned to Joe and tried to speak, but no words came out. He tried to point at one of the artists stealthily, but like a child in a candy factory, his attention and his limbs swung about, almost knocking over an unused easel. Joe trying to follow him, noticed Sisley deep in concentration. After barely a moment, Leonard had poked him again, this time gesticulating in the other direction. Joe looked over and now spotted Monet hunched over a canvas filled with swirling strokes and lines.

The artists were engrossed in their work, so nobody else noticed Leonard's flapping and swooning. Joe watched the artists for a moment longer, admiring the different stages of creation taking form.

He indicated to Leonard that they better leave. Leonard seemed appalled but put up no fuss. They shuffled out. Vera was glowing at her success. Two heavyweight Impressionists in one room! They headed down the stairs.

As they approached the street level, Joe felt a strangle prickling sensation. The feeling strengthened as they proceeded. Vera had turned her head back toward the group as she walked, enchanted by her own voice. She had begun to explain the origin of the various municipalities.

The prickling in his neck gave way to a rushing buzz behind his eyes as Vera was about to step out of the building and into the road. He felt like he had been removed from his present surroundings and plugged into another reality. His vision blurred, though his other senses heightened. Leonard, walking toward the door just ahead of him, seemed much smaller and fuzzy. He could hear the French ladies passing by the building as if they were inside his head. His hands felt strange, and his hair felt electric. Like a dandelion, the follicles were standing on end. Dancing with static electricity, his fingertips stung and jolted as he touched his ears.

Something bad was about to happen. He felt a powerful urge to act. He scrambled to the front of the group as a large double-decker horse-drawn carriage thundered toward Vera. She hadn't seemed to notice. He knew he had to do something. He hesitated. He wanted to yank her out of the way without hurting her but only managed to awkwardly brush her on the shoulder. A worker standing by them had also noticed Vera, Joe, and the charging horses and jumped forward, pulling her to safety.

"What are you, crazy!" the driver cursed as he rode past. The horses would have trampled her. She pulled herself up and brushed herself off while glancing quizzically at Joe. She thanked the French worker. Joe was disappointed with himself. His feeble attempt to save Vera accomplished nothing. He always seemed to overthink and ultimately froze when it counted. But how had known she was in danger?

Chapter 8

RACHEL--1893

Rachel held the rough, heavy wooden door shut as she listened for the policemen. The only light in the room from the crack beneath the door, came from the few lit lanterns in the deserted passage outside.

She suspected that she had lost the policemen, but now she had more immediate problems. She felt a growing sense of dread that she was not alone. She steeled herself and wheeled around, sporting the most aggressive look she could muster. Gloomy shadows hid most of the room. A series of empty laboratory tables and benches stood out. The walls were lined with rickety shelves holding jars stuffed with creepy organs and reptiles. A stench of formaldehyde filled the air. Rachel slowly moved toward the center, scrutinizing the sides and corners of the room. The thick layer of dust on the tables suggested that no classes had been held here for years. There were no school bags, papers, or binders lying about. She glanced at the jars and shuddered. There were fetuses, lungs, eyeballs, snakes, and other ghoulish objects she couldn't identify bobbing in clear liquid. As she got closer to the other end of the room, she noticed an outline in the corner. Rachel froze, as did the shadow. She grabbed a laboratory stool and hurled it toward the corner. The stool crashed onto its side, making a loud clattering against a lab bench.

A withered man emerged from the corner, silently screaming. He advanced toward Rachel with his hands waving in the air, fingers curled outward as if to attack, eyes wide open and staring. She picked up another stool and held it aloft, thrusting the legs toward him to fight him off. The man slowed, having moved faster than his legs could sustain.

Rachel swiped at him with the stool. It passed straight through him, throwing her off balance. She fell over a desk but bounced back, fists extended. The man relaxed. His claws became fingers, and he dropped his arms to his side. The two stood there and stared at each other silently. Rachel gradually lowered her clenched fists.

After realizing that the old man could not talk either, she walked over to the chalkboard at the front of the classroom. Rachel picked up a piece of chalk and wrote.

Why are you here?

Rachel offered him the chalk, but he declined, indicating that she should do the writing.

She thought for a moment, wrote the alphabet on the board and started to point at each letter. The man indicated what she should write, letter by letter.

Stranded Hiding
Huh?
Missed ride
I'm Rachel. U?
Harry
Where is home?
England
U can't take a train?
Trapped
How long?
Years

Rachel froze. She looked at Harry. How did she miss it? She played the events over in her head. He seemed to float and couldn't touch her. When she had taken a swing at him with the stool, she hadn't missed. He was a ghost.

U were on a time tour?

Yes

Me 2

Harry's eyes widened with hope. His bottom lip began to quiver with emotion. Rachel was the first tourist like him that he had seen in a very long time. Rachel had a million thoughts of her own. She was terrified at the prospect of being stranded like Harry.

U live in this lab?

Yes

Why?

Safe Quiet

Rachel understood why; the basement floor, and particularly this laboratory, looked like they had not been used for such a long time. A faded, stained calendar lying on the lecturer's desk displayed the date April 1853, forty years obsolete. She guessed the administration had moved all the lectures years ago after the students had insisted the floor was haunted.

When did U come to Oslo?

1829 Battle of the Square

Rachel was shocked. Harry must have seen her expression and grew concerned.

What year is it?

1893

How?

Rachel felt terrible. He looked inconsolable. He had been in the basement of the university for sixty years. Rachel was silent. She held her questions until Harry spoke.

Why are you here?

Separated from my class tour

How?

Long story

When?

16 hours

Like me soon

Rachel gulped. A sense of dread descended. She had not fully considered that it could happen to her.

What happened to U?

Watched the riot. Girl got attacked. I helped. Lost my group.

Did they look for U?

Harry shrugged.

Never saw them again

Did U see other groups?

He nodded.

Found a group. Followed them to TourPod. Tried to go with them. Ship went straight through me.

What did they say?

Said they'll come back. Rescue me.

Rachel smiled at him reassuringly. She wanted to make Harry feel hopeful again. She was positive that her dad would figure out what to do. He was smart and dependable. He was never the first to jump and generally shied away from taking the lead. But he always kept calm and worked through problems until they were solved.

Everything will be fine. U will see.

Harry's eyes took on a different look as he reacted slowly. Suddenly he didn't seem so depressed.

Rachel started to write his next comment as he pointed at the letters.

N---o---w I h---a-----v-----e   y------o------u

Rachel dropped the chalk.

Harry had a wicked smile.

JOE--1870

The static electric attack had passed, and Joe was furiously patting his hair flat again. As the group made their way toward Montmarte, the artists' village in Paris, Joe tried to understand how he had anticipated the horses that almost trampled Vera. As they crossed the bubbling Seine, he replayed the events. He had known that the thundering horse and wagon was charging through the streets just then. It was like a distant, hazy memory that had suddenly lurched to the front of his consciousness. He felt something coming before it was in eyeshot. It made no sense.

They continued to walk in silence, passing throngs of horses, bicycles, and pedestrians dressed in their finery. The bustle and beauty were only interrupted by the rotting horse carcass that the group had to walk around. They covered their noses to avoid retching. In Paris, thousands of horses dropped dead on the streets and sidewalks every year.

They stopped to admire an old man and his grandchildren busking. He played the organ while the children sang. The oldest of the boys accompanied on a violin. A small crowd gathered. Joe was struck by how vibrant and healthy looking the onlookers were. Despite the primitive medicine available, the physical labor and long work hours that many were subject to and the relative hardship, everybody was well-dressed. The women gathered around were groomed to the hilt. Many sacrificed domestic comforts, preferring to commit what funds they had to enjoy life outdoors. The sun had set. City employees were busy lighting the many oil lanterns that illuminated the intersections. Everything was for sale or hire in the many stores they passed--clothes, newspapers, cooking utensils. Benches on the sidewalks were brimming with gentlemen enjoying cups of wine and ladies gossiping. As they approached the Café Guerbois on Avenue de Clichy, Vera gathered the group around her for new information and instructions.

"We'll be entering the world-famous Café Guerbois in a few moments. It's a busy little restaurant and bar frequented by many of my favorite artists--Degas, Monet, Renoir, Sisley, Cézanne, and Pissarro, among others. We should get a table at this hour. It fills up at around nine. I'll get us seated. When the waiter approaches, I will order drinks and some of the local cuisine. I'll also point out any artists."

Leonard was clearly already searching the tables for celebrities, while Carl, feeling hungry, was obviously scanning the platters, and measuring the portion sizes.

"It's Sunday night, so we might get lucky and see the Batignolles group of artists and writers debating. No overdrinking or mingling."

They stepped inside. The café was busy and noisy. There were neat rows of rectangular tables with white tablecloths running from one end of the room to the other. The large poplar wood bar area situated on the right was ornate and well stocked. Neatly dressed waiters with large moustaches and white aprons circulated while two ritzy ladies manned the bar counter.

Vera approached the maître d' seated in a raised cubicle at the entrance and asked for the five of them to be seated. They followed him to a table, passing lively groups of eclectic patrons as they made their way to the far corner and took their seats. The maître d' bowed politely and beckoned a waiter over to take their orders. Vera ordered a glass of absinthe for everybody and a bottle of pastis.

She described their drinks. "Absinthe is a highly alcoholic, extremely potent drink made from wormwood leaves. It is popular in nineteenth-century France after French soldiers, who had been using it as an antimalarial drug during their war in Algeria, returned. It's sometimes called 'the green lady' because of the many poor souls who fell under its spell, became addicted, and fell into fits of madness. It is popular among the artistic community of nineteenth-century Paris and is considered a symbol of creativity."

Leonard picked up his cup and swirled it, watching the drink slosh around. Fumes seemed to rise from the surface.

"It is rumored that Vincent van Gogh cut off his ear under the spell of absinthe, a warning not to order a second glass," Vera said.

Joe sipped from the greenish liquid. It had a powerful, bitter taste, with a strong hint of sweetness, reminding him of licorice. If he'd had a more developed palate, he would have also detected hyssop, fennel, and coriander.

Joe didn't enjoy it but felt compelled by the situation to drain the small glass. Leonard was gagging a little as he struggled through his helping. The others would have ordered seconds if they could. Joe picked up his glass of pastis, a yellowish liquid mixed with ice that he swished around the cup. He tasted it and decided that he would be happy to stick with that.

The chatter seemed to get louder from the tables near them. Vera indicated for everybody to huddle closer. She pointed to a group sitting a few tables away. "Don't stare. But that's Manet, Louis Edmond Duranty, Émile Zola, and an empty bottle of absinthe over there. I think that things are about to explode."

The waiters returned with five different dishes. Vera told them to place a single dish in front of each member of the group. They placed a bowl of hard bread in the center and stepped away. The bread had been hardening outside of the oven for twelve hours.

Joe took a piece. It hurt his teeth to chew, so he put the remainder to the side. He had a bowl of pureed vegetable soup in front of him. The other dishes smelled glorious, offering steak, fish, and chicken. Joe felt a little unlucky.

Vera helped. "Feel free to swap. Take whatever you like. You'll be getting dinner back on the ship."

As they started to taste their meals, the celebrity table erupted. Manet slammed the table with his fists and leaped to his feet. Duranty stood up defensively but with far less certainty and confidence. Manet was screaming at him. Zola, between them, was trying to calm the situation, but Manet would have nothing of it. His face growing increasingly red, he lunged at Duranty, who ducked for cover and found himself crouching behind his chair as Manet grabbed the empty absinthe bottle.

The maître d' rushed over, flanked by two of the waiters, and demanded that Manet take his seat. All the patrons seemed bewildered and nervous. Vera was sitting on the edge of her seat. Manet stabbed his finger toward Duranty, shouting. He demanded that Duranty face him in a duel to the death. Zola was trying to calm things, but nothing seemed to work.

Manet finally noticed the maître d', who was pleading with him to please step outside until he had recovered from his angry state. Manet gathered himself together, took his hat, nodded indignantly at the staff and patrons within his range, and stormed out. As he exited, he glanced back. Joe thought he smirked.

Vera stared at the group aghast. She could barely contain herself.

"You just witnessed the famous argument between Manet and Duranty. Duranty insulted Manet by publishing a poor review of his work, and Manet challenged him to a duel. Manet will win the duel, wounding Duranty. But they will make amends and remain friends."

Leonard would have been skipping and dancing if Vera hadn't forbidden it. The chances of witnessing this were so slim. Nellie was drumming on the table, positively buzzing. Vera ordered another round of absinthe to celebrate the historical sighting they had just witnessed. And then a third. Everybody seemed to enjoy the sole fillets, so she ordered more and topped it off with rum sherbet and pudding.

CHAPTER 9

The group was animated, no small thanks to Absinthe. Vera settled the bill at the maître d' cubicle, while outside, Leonard attempted to teach Carl the bourrée, a seventeenth-century French folk dance, to the amusement and annoyance of the restaurant patrons seated outside. His bony frame lurched dangerously from side to side. Vera exited, and they followed her through Montmarte, the cobbled, artist-infested neighborhood. They headed to a clearing where Ash would pick them up.

Leonard's footing was unsteady, and he threw his arms around Joe and Carl as they stepped onto the sidewalk. With his head buzzing, he was trying to lock eyes with every lady who passed. The sidewalks, jammed with seating for the many outdoor cafés, were thronged with diners. A gentle drizzle began to fall, forming small puddles that dazzlingly reflected the golden lights from the streetlamps and lanterns that lined the walls. Joe and Carl held on to him, making sure he wouldn't break the ranks and get himself into trouble.

Vera babbled on about the neighborhood, pointing out the more popular restaurants and apartments that housed famous artists or writers. Carl suddenly threw Leonard's arm off his shoulders and spun around wildly, realizing something. Seeing him, Vera's tipsiness passed in seconds. Stone-cold sober, she shifted into command mode.

"Where's Nellie?!" she exclaimed.

Confusion.

"We're going back to the Café Guerbois. Quickly! Keep a lookout. We need to find her."

Joe felt his stomach drop as the breath left his body. Thoughts of Rachel, alone and lost, filled his head. He noticed Vera instinctively reach for a handheld device concealed underneath her jacket. Fortunately, they hadn't wandered far. Carl lurched, trying to steady himself. He comically craned his head, searching up and down the street. Leonard, caught off guard by Carl's exaggerated motions, stumbled and crumpled into a drunken heap. Vera and Joe lifted him to his feet, and they turned back to the café.

Carl spotted her surrounded by a group of young, scruffily dressed sailors with shabby caps. Nellie seemed bewildered, though faintly flattered. Nodding and tittering, she seemed relieved when Carl stumbled into the center, attempting to rescue her.

He took her arm firmly and steadied his balance as he took in his surroundings. Bemused, the sailors exchanged comments and snickered before the largest of them stepped forward, stopping inches from Carl's face. He leaned in toward Carl and spat out an unintelligible comment.

From the outside of the circle, Joe glanced nervously at Vera, who had now removed a concealed gun from her inner jacket pocket.

Carl, clutching Nellie's arm, staggered backward, legs wobbly and head bowed. The sailor stepped forward and, without warning, raised his fist and boxed Carl squarely on the nose, sending him sprawling backward. Just as suddenly, though, the sailor collapsed, pulling a surprised colleague down with him as he fell to the floor. Joe noticed Vera, finger on trigger, had her gun trained on Carl's attacker.

"It's a StunGun. He'll wake up in a few hours with a headache," she whispered.

The remaining suitors took their cue and fled the scene while the colleague lifted his unconscious friend over his shoulder and stumbled away. Nellie crouched over Carl, cradling his head. His hands covered his bloody face. Joe could tell instantly that his nose was broken.

"Help me pick him up. We need to get out of here before the police arrive," Vera commanded.

Joe and Leonard, also now sober, swiftly obeyed her. They lifted Carl and hurriedly staggered away as Nellie trailed, trying to dab his nose and wipe the blood from his face with a dirty cloth.

"Please, people. Is it so hard to stick with the group?" Vera pleaded.

Nellie looked sheepish but still gave Vera an exasperated shrug as if to say she didn't invite the attention. Carl gave her shoulder a squeeze as they continued up the Avenue de Clichy. The group staggered toward the Tuileries Garden and found a quiet spot in the trees. Carl and Nellie sat on the grass, and she tended to his face as he winced in pain. Joe moved toward the Seine as it splashed against the embankment. He quietly pulled out his BioSensor and moved it around under his coat, searching for sign of Rachel. Leonard pointed to the impressive Notre-Dame cathedral spire dominating the skyline, ready to admire it with anyone who would pay attention to him, which was nobody at the moment. Vera removed her PodCom from the inside of her jacket and called Ash. The Crichton promptly landed.

As Joe boarded behind Vera, Ash was already standing in the center of the common area with his voice suppression scanner in hand. The rest of the group charged up the ramp to be the first to have their voices restored. Ash swiped the scanner across everybody's necks as they entered. As the doors closed, Joe's companions wasted no time.

"My hero! How is your face?" Nellie exclaimed.

Carl's ego seemed to be more wounded than his rapidly healing face. Ash brought the first aid nanokit and seated himself across from Carl. He moved the scanner over his nose.

"Why were those guys hitting on you?" Carl asked.

"Did you see Manet shouting in the café!" Leonard shrieked.

Ash put the nanokit away and went to arrange dinner.

"Hey, John. Enjoy today?" he asked Joe, who was standing near the eating area.

"Pretty good."

"We can't have any issues this tour. The last one was a bit of a disaster," Ash casually added.

Joe perked up. "What happened?"

"A girl went missing, and they weren't able to find her."

He folded his arms guardedly, surprised that Ash knew anything about Rachel. "How come the ship couldn't locate her? Or the guide?" Joe asked.

Ash shrugged. "The signal from the tourist isn't very strong. Maybe she moved too far away."

"There's so little to go on?"

Ash continued, "I think that the pilot could have tried harder before leaving. Maybe they didn't have much time."

"Sounds like nobody did anything. I mean--" Joe remarked.

Ash stopped him. "We have to let them do their job. The chances of another tourist finding her are practically zero. And they would just end up the same as her."

"I don't know. I think a bit of effort, retracing steps--"

Ash cut him off again. "Don't go there. Everything must go through the guide or the pilot. Really."

"I mean, somebody has to do something."

Ash smiled. "Nobody has given up yet."

"Did they tell you to look into the missing girl? We're doing the same tour after all."

"No. But we would obviously bring her back with us if we saw her. It's so unlikely."

Joe persisted. "So, maybe we should--"

"It's starting to sound like you came on this tour to find her. John." Ash interjected. He held his stare for an uncomfortably long time before stepping away to set refreshments down on the table.

Was that a veiled warning? Had Ash somehow figured out who Joe was? Maybe Ash was just trying to avoid more disasters on his shift.

Joe sat next to Carl, but he wasn't hungry. Vera was presenting the next set of activities.

"Tomorrow, we jump to April 1874 to the very first Impressionist exhibition at Boulevard des Capucines, where many of the greats were first introduced. You'll have a chance to mingle. We'll then travel to the outskirts and try to catch some of the artists painting their greatest works."

Joe wasn't listening. He glanced up at Ash, wondering if he should have suggested they look into Rachel's disappearance. If Rachel was in Oslo, he should have demanded that the tour go there first.

"After dinner, take some personal time and rest. Place your clothes in the Fabricator next to your beds. New ones will be there tomorrow. Go journal, check your footage, but, most importantly, sleep. Time travel takes a toll, and you want to be fresh."

She was right. Joe felt exhausted. He retired to his compartment and changed into sleepwear, throwing the period costume into the bin where it was deconstructed into neutral fabric for reuse. He opened his bag and took out his VisionPlayer. He peeled his EyeCam off his right eye, placed it into the storage slot, and reviewed his footage, pausing and replaying the events around Charles Gleyre's studio, where Vera was almost trampled by horses. He thought about his premonition and regretted not pulling her out of the way. He hated that he was so passive. He needed clues. Some direction.

Joe lay awake most of the night. Whenever he dozed, visions of ghosts, enraged and wailing as they pleaded to be rescued, jolted him awake. At the first light, he sat up. The sunrise was golden spectacular. He'd seen too many sunrises since Rachel disappeared and quickly turned his attention to the fresh set of nineteenth-century finery neatly presented in the Fabricator by his bed. He was the first passenger in the common area. Ash joined him. He nodded at Joe as he checked the navigation system and the TourPod's cloaking status.

"Coffee?" he offered. "We have one of those DrinkMaster on board."

"Plain black is perfect."

Ash nodded. "I have developed a taste for kopi luwak."

"I've never heard of it."

"It's partially digested coffee cherries, which have been eaten and pooped out by a civet."

Joe grimaced at the thought.

"The beans cost thousands of dollars for a single cup. It's amazing to me that this is basically free. I feel rich drinking it, even though I know it's completely artificial. Pretty much everything today is artificial anyway. That's why these trips are so great. Right?"

He pulled out the two steaming cups and handed Joe one of them.

"Thanks," Joe remarked.

Joe couldn't read Ash. He still thought about the veiled warning the previous day. But otherwise, Ash was very pleasant and professional. Ash seemed to pay more attention to him than the rest of the group, as if he were watching Joe's every move onboard the ship.

Vera appeared, making straight for the DrinkMaster, and sucking down her coffee before acknowledging anybody else. They could hear Carl begging Nellie to wake up and get dressed. Soon the group was assembled, seated, and locked in for their next time jump.

"Good morning, everybody," Vera said. "We have a very busy day planned. In a few minutes, we'll be jumping, so get yourselves ready."

Carl was still touching his nose, while Nellie yawned. Joe made his way to an empty chair at the mess table. He felt Vera's eyes following him and finally met her gaze once seated. She spoke as soon as she had his attention.

"How was the day, John?" She seemed strangely friendly.

"Fine. Fine, thanks. Great." He prayed that was enough as he dropped his eyes, studying the table and moving his coffee cup around. Vera was not done.

"Did you see any artists you love, John?" she persisted.

Why was she singling him out? He looked back up at her but faltered his eye contact as he struggled to remember the names of the artists they had seen at the Charles Gleyre studio. Vera seemed to be studying his face.

"Umm. They were all great," Joe finally responded.

"All great?" she repeated quizzically.

Awkward pause.

"Sisley," Joe blurted out as the name finally came back to him. He met her gaze and repeated. "Sisley was great to see."

Vera seemed skeptical. She squinted at him as the other tourists took their seats and then continued with the day's activities.

"A little bit about the exhibition today. It was organized by Monet, Pissarro, Degas, Renoir, Sisley, Morisot, and several other artists. They held it as a protest and to free themselves from the official national art exhibition known as the Salon de Paris. The salon continually ignored many of these artists, rejecting their submissions every year. So, they decided to hold their own exhibit as a thumb to the academy's nose, rather than as a promotion of their new style. The rest is history. You will see 165 artworks. Perhaps the single most important collection of Impressionist painting in a single place in all of history."

Leonard was shifting in his seat as if he could barely contain his excitement.

Changing tone, Vera concluded, "I must warn you again not to run off with anybody else and to stick with me and your fellow travelers."

Leonard jumped in. "Renoir actually hung many of the pieces himself when the other members of the organizing committee failed to show up on the first day."

Vera offered a strained smile and continued, "After the exhibition, we will make our way back to the ship for a quick jump to Italy 1882 to observe Renoir at work. More to be discussed later."

She turned to Ash, "Are you ready?"

Ash acknowledged, charged up the nuclear propulsion, darkened the windows, and accelerated. A loud crack drowned out the chatter from the cabin. Joe felt a thrilling rush for just a moment, followed by a peaceful calm. Ash glided the ship back into the clouds. They had already arrived.

JETHRO--2130

Jethro reviewed Gater's EyeCam footage from the trip where he'd struggled with Rachel. He watched from Gater's vantage point how Gater had been following Rachel's group through the streets of Oslo. He saw Rachel turn around and notice him. He saw Rachel alert Sara. They both turned around. The teacher headed to the front of the group to alert the guide. He saw Gater speed up and grab Rachel, pulling her backward and into a side street. He fast-forwarded to where Gater had her cornered. She looked terrified. Jethro studied her face, playing the footage backward and forward, looking for an indication that she knew anything about Gater's activities. Jethro ran scan lines across her face, searching her expressions for a sign that she was hiding knowledge.

Gater struck her. Rachel was thrown to the staircase. Jethro watched Rachel strike back with the shard of wood.

Jethro smirked ever so slightly. Feisty girl. He saw Gater grasp her by the throat and throw her forcefully against the wall, knocking her unconscious. He saw an old man descending the stairs with a rifle and how Gater fled the scene. Gater stopped at the entrance to the town square and reached for a transmitter disk from his pouch. The transmitter was a small, sleek titanium device that hummed slightly when he activated it.

Jethro watched him place it against the ground by the corner of a building and how it spun rapidly and then burrowed through the pavement. Jethro scrolled back to the library and selected the footage from London the previous day. He watched Gater plant another transmitter disk in Whitechapel, London. He saw Gater scanning the passing pedestrians, making sure that nobody noticed his activity. He saw

Rachel's group mingling among the locals. Rachel was casually watching the passersby and clearly noticed Gater with the disk in his hands. Gater seemed to stare at her.

Jethro couldn't tell if Rachel's lingering glance was meaningless or if she had noticed what he was holding. He watched Gater follow the group, obviously realizing that they were time tourists. He stalked them all the way back to their TourPod and concealed a tracking device on the underbelly of their ship. He had made enough of an impression on Rachel that she recognized him when she saw him the second time in Oslo.

Jethro closed the EyeCam screens and called Vinod, his chief of operations, into his office.

"Gater was careless," he commented softly as he slowly rolled a wooden baton backward and forward on his desk.

Vinod found Jethro's absence of tone and expression chilling. And he hated that baton. The thought of Jethro using it again terrified him. Strangely, though, in his two years working closely with Jethro almost every day, he had never even seen his expression change. Even when Jethro was threatening staff, or carrying out his threats, Jethro's countenance and tone never changed.

When Vinod thought about it, he had never seen Jethro eat or go for a bathroom break. He had neither seen a single member of Jethro's family nor transferred a friend's call or taken a personal message for him. Vinod had only ever seen Jethro work.

The previous September, he decided to beat Jethro to work. For the entire month, he tried to arrive at the office earlier than him but had never succeeded, even coming in at three in the morning to find Jethro still at his desk.

"Did anybody realize what Gater was doing in London?" Vinod asked, drawing Vinod back to the present.

"Impossible to tell from the footage."

"Do you want us to locate the teacher?" Vinod asked.

"No, it's too risky," Jethro answered. He stood up, holding the baton and tapping it gently into his free hand.

"Even if the girl saw the transmitters, it's unlikely that she would know what they do. Nobody has any reason to suspect anything. The most important thing now is to make sure that our operator license goes through. Once the TTA backs off with the inspections, we can take any decisive action that we need."

"And the father?" Vinod asked, fidgeting with his sleeve nervously.

"If she said anything to him before Oslo, or if the teacher said something, Gater and Shiner will find out."

"We'll have to take it up with Gater again when he is back. We can't have our people making mistakes like this. If Barrett finds out about us now, he will do everything he can to shut it down. It could set us back years."

Vinod agreed as he straightened his glasses.

Jethro approached Vinod and asked about the progress, "How close are we to the World War I tour planning?"

Vinod reported, "The transmitter signal from Sarajevo, June 1914, is very strong. Our ship successfully arrived within one hour of the Ferdinand assassination. We still need to work out some of the logistics for the actual fighting, and we need to get the uniforms, rifles, and ammunition."

"And the Jack the Ripper tour?"

"Gater put up all the Whitechapel transmitters last month. We are ready to take the group."

"And the bookings? How many are confirmed?"

"Every seat has been taken. And we tripled the rack rate," Vinod announced proudly.

"Good." Jethro placed his baton back on his desk. Then he continued, "I want more transmitters up. By month end, I want the Vietnam War, the Sino-Japanese War, and the JFK assassination. And I want transmitters at the Jimmy Hoffa disappearance. You will get it done, no?"

Vinod nodded and shuffled backward out of Jethro's office. When he was gone, Jethro sent a short message to Shiner. *Tell me every move that Gater makes.*

87

Chapter 10

The Crichton hovered for a few minutes, Ash waiting for an amorous couple sitting on a park bench to clear out. He eventually aimed an ultrahigh frequency sound wave at the young lovers, causing them sufficient discomfort to find another park, and Ash brought the ship down to the quiet enclave of the Champs-Élysées Gardens for disembarking.

The passengers filed out; men wearing lounge suits, high-buttoned waistcoats, stiff collars, neckties, and top hats. Nellie wore a tight bodice with lace trimming and a skirt with such exaggerated embellishments that her derriere protruded horizontally.

Strolling along the Rue Royale and then the Boulevard des Capucines, Vera pointed out the high-society, and bustling, fashion stores. Soon, they were in the queue alongside an eclectic mix of art aficionados outside the freshly restored building. Its Belle Époque façade adorned with vibrant stained glass and ornate ironwork shimmering under the Parisian autumn sun. Vera ascended the narrow, marble steps and paid the sixty francs admission, and they hurriedly followed. entering a small, unremarkable exhibition room.

The gallery showcased two hundred artworks, 165 of them presented by the Impressionists. They called themselves the Anonymous Society of Painters, Sculptors, and Printmakers. The word *Impressionists* had not been coined yet, though that was about to change. The paintings were neatly hung on the otherwise bare white walls, and all were for sale.

The crowd inside was small but busy. Most seemed to be curious onlookers, as opposed to interested collectors or art critics. Many of the artists were standing by their pieces, hoping to make a sale.

Leonard could not be contained. He waited for the go-ahead from Vera and jostled off to the closest artwork and moved from there. one painting to the next, never skipping. The most famous painting on display was Monet's *Impression, Sunrise*. Carl and Nellie were immediately drawn to it, particularly since Monet himself was explaining his vision for the painting to a small group of bystanders. Joe's curiosity was piqued by a middle-aged, pompous-looking gentleman who strode around the gallery scribbling notes as he dismissively glanced at the various artworks. Vera grabbed Joe vigorously by the arm, and whispered into his ear.

"That's Louis Leroy, the art critic!"

Joe shrugged, betraying his ignorance.

"He will write a scathing critique of the exhibition, mocking the artists and their paintings. He calls his piece 'Exhibition of Impressionists,' coining the term that stuck."

Joe saw a gob smacked Leonard across the hall, standing next to the painter Pissarro. The artist was haggling with a buyer. He was asking one thousand francs for his painting *The Orchard*. The collector, arms folded loosely, didn't seem that interested. Pissarro was animatedly trying to convince him, pointing to the fine brushstrokes and colors. The collector would not budge, leaving Pissarro exasperated. He offered the collector a withering stare, causing him to back away cautiously. Back at the Crichton, Leonard would tell the group that the painting sold for $25 million in the mid-21st century.

Carl and Nellie cautiously slid right up to Monet as he explained his *Sunrise* to the bystanders. Leroy joined them. Monet was explaining how he was able to depict the frosty dawn as the sun begins to heat up the day. He pointed out how he had chosen to use vivid colors rather than focusing on painstaking details. He highlighted how the luminous hue of the sun infiltrates the rest of the sky while boldly reflecting against the pulsating ocean. He asked his crowd of onlookers if they sensed the eeriness and endlessness of his presentation. Carl and Nellie stood transfixed, mouths agape. Leroy huffed and let off a loud raspberry from his puckered lips, abruptly ending the explanation. Monet glanced at him hatefully and then lowered his eyes, defeated. Louis Leroy had already moved on to ridicule the next piece.

Vera gathered the group together in the center of the gallery. "We'll be leaving in thirty minutes. Please mingle, absorb, and enjoy. You are witnessing the birth of the most influential movement in art history. Be sure to check out Morisot's *Hide and Seek*. It's one of my personal favorites. We will meet by the entrance. And don't be late," she warned.

Joe made his way to the entrance. He stepped outside and pulled his coat around himself to shield against the freshness of the morning. The line of skeptical attendees was still growing. As he scanned the bustling street, he felt a prickle in the back of his head, like the sensation he felt right before Vera's close call with the galloping horses the previous day. The tingling was less acute, but Joe realized that something was up. His hair had begun to bristle, and his fingers stung when he touched them against his clothing. He looked from side to side, searching for danger. Reaching for Milo's BioSensor inside his coat, he activated it. Turning in a circle stealthily and slowly with the device partly concealed, he watched the signal gauge. It was glued to the zero reading. He held it, concealed in his palm, parallel to the ground, bending and straightening his elbow as he willed the indicator to move. A stuffy woman with tiny spectacles tugged on the sleeve of her well-dressed companion as she stared at Joe. Exasperated, and conscious of any undue attention he was drawing, he extravagantly checked his wristwatch and turned his forearm upward. And there it was. The needle moved. Slightly. His pulse raced as he turned his wrist again, and he immediately turned his gaze upward to follow the direction of the BioSensor receiver.

Straining his eyes, he spotted it. It was almost invisible. He knew none of the bystanders would see it. But Joe knew a TourPod when he saw one. And he knew that it wasn't the Crichton. It was somebody else's.

Joe delicately pocketed the BioSensor as Carl and Nellie joined him by the entrance. Nellie, noticing his hair standing on end, reached out to pat it down. Joe blushed as she giggled but quickly averted his gaze when he noticed that Carl had followed his eyes toward the skyline. Vera came out last, dragging Leonard, who seemed outraged, and they all followed Vera down the street as she remarked on the morning's events.

"This is the luckiest group I've taken in months. That was simply wonderful. We'll be taking public transport back to the Champs-Élysées Gardens and jetting off to Italy shortly."

They stood by the roadside waiting for a horse-drawn "bus." A large carriage arrived behind two powerful horses. The men climbed the steep steps to the upstairs carriages, while the women sat in the main carriage. The horses clopped down the street. Joe cast his eyes to the sky every chance he could.

The ride to the pickup point at the Champs-Élysées Gardens was uncomfortable. The men were seated on the open roof of a cramped wagon, the women stuffed inside. The passengers on the roof were exposed to the wind, chilly weather, and anything else that might have blown across the street. The sun had been smothered by a thin layer of clouds and it started to drizzle, making the journey even more miserable.

Remarkably, Leonard had not lost even one inch of his beaming grin. He was still playing the events of the first Impressionist exhibition in his head and seemed to be enjoying the primitive transport experience.

Joe felt every bump and ditch that the horse-drawn wagon encountered reverberate throughout his body. Carl sat on his right hand to try and cushion the shocks with the left fruitlessly hanging above his head to shield against the gentle raindrops. Their omnibus ran swiftly relative to the other horse and bicycle traffic, outpaced only by smaller, private taxi carriages.

Vera sat inside the wagon with Nellie, jammed shoulder to shoulder against twelve other women. She shoved her way through to a window seat, offending several passengers and stuck her head out to holler to the men.

"I hope it's not too uncomfortable up there. All part of the experience. Be ready to get off at the next stop!"

Joe and Carl exchanged relieved glances.

The horses slowed, and the "bus" came to a halt, letting the tour group out. Joe followed behind the rest, searching the horizon for the second ship that he had spotted earlier. The sky was overcast and blocked his view, though he could sense its presence. He knew it was possible that the unidentified ship was following him. If Rachel's disappearance was connected to her tour, Milo had warned him that the perpetrators might come after him too. Maybe they thought he knew whatever Rachel knew. He steeled himself for the confrontation.

They made it to the clearing quickly where Ash waited for them by the Crichton. Joe glanced upward again. The strange TourPod had moved eastward and was now hovering above the tree line, unmistakably following him. He slipped his hands inside his jacket, activated the BioSensor again, and turned it towards the sky. The signal was slightly stronger. Maybe Rachel was inside.

The others boarded and rushed for the refreshments that Ash had put out for them. Joe was distracted, hurrying ahead but failing to even notice the spread of laboratory-grown bison, kale, and cucumber sandwiches. Heading to the pilot's cabin, Ash glanced at Joe as he was tucking the BioSensor into his coat pocket. After everybody was seated and devouring their snacks, Ash took the Crichton up to ten thousand feet. There was a general chatter as everybody commented on their favorite moments from the morning.

"What a fabulous exhibition that was!"

"I'd give my eye teeth to have been allowed to buy one of the paintings," Leonard remarked. He glanced at Vera, who shook her head.

Vera began to update them. "No dawdling. Chop-chop. We're jumping to the Bay of Naples, Italy, October 1881. Renoir painted his girlfriend and future wife, Aline Victorine Charigot, by the sea over a period of several weeks. Up until then, Renoir had mostly painted society portraits and landscapes in Paris. This was a breakaway from subject matter that he considered restrictive. When we arrive in Italy, you'll all go to your compartments, change, and Ash will take us down. I'll give you further information and instructions then."

Nellie leaned over to Joe and asked, "How are you enjoying the tour?"

Joe nodded reflexively. He was never the first person to strike up a conversation. It was an aspect of his personality that bothered him and that he hoped to correct. He'd worry about it after he found Rachel.

"It's been pretty great. What about you both?" He looked up at her and Carl.

"It's wonderful. It's our honeymoon. Not being able to talk on the ground is bumming us out a bit. That's our only complaint."

Carl agreed as he rubbed her coat to make sure it would be warm enough.

Ash chimed in, "We're jumping in five, four, three, two, one."

Joe noted the familiar crackle accompanied by the rushing sensation. The Crichton hovered, stationary – Joe felt like a diver standing on the edge of a cliff, waiting to be pushed. Then the engine fired and they were jetting to Naples at breakneck speed.

RACHEL--1893

Rachel edged backward from Harry, startled by his sudden shift in personality. His wicked grin betrayed his deviant intentions. His delirious, pleading stare told her that she was the eternal companion who would roam the colorless world with him for the rest of their ghostly lives.

Rachel edged toward the door. She would not let another man keep her in this forsaken city. The thought of Gater dragging her away from her classmates surfaced as she shrunk away from Harry. Frozen with terror, flashes of the attack replayed in her head.

"Keep still, or I'll hurt you--badly," Gater had coldly whispered into her ear.

She felt his wiry, steel grip around her shoulders as he dragged her into the entrance foyer of a dreary apartment building and threw her into a corner, blocking her escape. Then he struck her fiercely, pulling her hair out with the back of his hand as she smashed into the staircase.

"Did you see me?" Gater had hissed. "Did you see what I was doing?"

The words echoed around her, filling the silence. Now, Harry's crazed stare as he lurched for her merged with the terrible memory of Gater into a violent, overwhelming kaleidoscope. She was paralyzed.

She felt her body slamming into the banister again as Gater had towered over her. Whimpering, she shook her head as she picked up a large shard of wood from the splintered railing and whipped it across her body, catching him on the cheek.

I fought back. A tiny whisper crept into her conscious. She'd cut Gater with her wild strike. The whisper in her head grew louder, pushing some of the fear aside.

I can fight back.

Gater had touched the wound and rubbed his bloody fingertips together. Then he snarled as he sprang forward and slammed her against the wall and into a black void. She'd woken up to the concerned frown of an old man with a shotgun.

No!

Harry forced Rachel's thoughts back to the present as he lunged at her repeatedly.

Fight.

She picked up a glass beaker and smashed it, the sludgy, gray contents glooping onto the floor by her feet. Holding up the jagged edge, she stabbed at Harry, determined not to lose the fight this time. Face-to-face, they swiped at each other, Harry futilely trying to pin Rachel down while she stabbed at any appendage she could reach.

As his ghostly arms passed through her body, his frenzied eagerness slowed, ultimately giving way to sadness. Harry's shining form grew dimmer. His shoulders sagging, he backed away remorsefully and turned to the side, unable to look at Rachel.

She felt a combination of revulsion and sympathy. Harry's body swayed and rocked ever so subtly as he seemed to fight back tears. Eventually, Rachel hurled the beaker against the wall, shocking him back into focus. Harry slowly turned toward her, wearing a puzzled look. She picked up a piece of chalk, wiped off the board vigorously with her sleeve, and began to write.

I won't stay here with U

Harry came over to the board and pointed at the letters.

I know

We can help each other

Harry looked searchingly at her.

What can I do?

U tried to go back?

He nodded.

Tell me everything U did that didn't work

Harry focused his gaze on her and pointed at the letters again.

Will you help me?

If I get back, I will come for U

His eyes began to well up. He nodded at her, accepting her deal.

I tried to leave Oslo. Walk back to England. Many times. Something always pulled me back.

Rachel wondered if it was a good idea to hear these stories from Harry. They made her feel despondent. Harry continued anyway.

Tried to kill myself. Walked into sea to drown. Can't drown. Same with fire. Can't burn. Stepped in front of wagon. Killed a... ...

Harry stopped himself for a moment and glanced at Rachel.

Jumped off a hundred buildings. Terrifying. Didn't die.

This time Rachel interrupted.

What ideas do U still have?

None. You are stuck. Forever. Like me. Other ghosts too. Must find your own place. Scare people away. Can stay with me.

Rachel shook her head. She knew that Harry wasn't telling her everything. He just wanted her to lose hope and to be his companion.

What other ghosts? Show me.

Harry shook his head.

Too dangerous

Dangerous? But U can't die!!

Demons

Demons?

They tear you apart. Eat ghosts.

GATER--1881

Gater and Shiner hovered above Paris. The tracking device on the Crichton brought them right to it, though they stayed well out of eyeshot. Shiner sat at the mess table sharpening a blade, his StunGun, revolver, and garrote all spread out in front of him, freshly cleaned and fine-tuned. He also had his PocketHolo open. He studied a collection of public information on Joe and Rachel Hasselback. Gater glanced backward.

"Shiner," he called.

"Yup."

"The receiver is vibrating. They've jumped."

"OK?"

"They've gone to Italy 1881."

"So, jump after them!"

They both strapped in for the jump to Naples and were back within eyeshot of Joe's group minutes later.

Gater stood and went to his compartment to put on his ground gear. Shiner followed his lead, doing the same. They both fabricated brand-new, plain black suits that matched the style of the local period. Gater kept on his boots and elected to wear his black trench coat over the local fashion. He proceeded to conceal his various weapons, signal receiver, and other ground tools in various pockets within his coat. Shiner was similarly armed.

Shiner gave Gater a once-over and commented, "You don't think you might be a bit conspicuous with that trench coat?"

Ignoring him, Gater took an additional transmitter disk with him in case they needed to return to Naples, October 1881. They proceeded to the cockpit to monitor Joe's group activities, noting that the TourPod had already begun to hover just above ground level, looking for a suitable place for the tourists to disembark and settling on the gardens around the Fontana della Tazza di Porfido. Gater followed from a distance. Once the ship was below the tree line, Gater guided his ship to a clearing a few hundred feet north and landed. Gater and Shiner quickly swapped their jackets for more period-appropriate ones and then disembarked, jogging through the trees and brush.

Shiner spotted the tour group gathered next to the ship. Vera was lecturing about Renoir's fascination with voluptuous women. They lay low, waiting for Vera to lead them toward the seashore.

Shiner whispered, "Do you see Joe?"

Gater glanced at him, annoyed. He knew that Shiner had already done his research. "Well, of course. He's standing to the left of the guide. With the purple waistcoat."

Vera walked with Leonard keeping pace so that he could hear more about the artistic journey. Joe walked next to Nellie, with Carl lagging slightly between and behind them.

Gater and Shiner followed, crouching as they carefully stepped. Gater was waiting for Joe to drop back. Shiner wasn't ready to strike. He was content to watch them for another day. He wanted to observe the interpersonal relationships between the passengers and to wait for a real opportunity. In minutes, they were at the seaside.

Gater softly smirked, "Now they are the stalkers."

The tourists were all crouched down, clumsily tiptoeing toward the secluded site where Renoir was painting Aline Charigot. He watched as they crouched behind a row of rocks about fifty feet from the renowned artist. Gater and Shiner gave extended blinks, activating the zoom in their contact lenses. They studied Vera, trying to identify where she had concealed her StunGun. They searched every fold and bulge on her outfit, looking for additional weapons.

Gater whispered, "Doesn't look like she's carrying anything else." Gater turned to Shiner and beckoned with his fist, indicating that he was keen to go in, incapacitate the group, and take Joe.

Shiner shook his head. "Wait."

Chapter 11

JOE--1881

Joe sat behind the pile of rocks observing Renoir paint his masterpiece *Blonde Bather*. The backdrop was perfect. Bright-blue crashing waves spilling frothy whiteness onto an unspoiled, empty beach. Alina Charigot, unencumbered by clothing, sat on a soft white blanket staring longingly at the cool water.

Nellie stuck her elbow into Carl's ribs. He was paying too much attention to the attractive, voluptuous, nude model. Joe too had zoomed his EyeCam vision and was admiring the artist's mastery. But he was also looking for unidentified ships in the sky. The prickle at the back of his head had returned. He looked around when, suddenly, Vera gasped. A small group of awkward-looking strangers had descended from the trees just behind them. Dressed similarly to the Crichton passengers, gaping at the perfect scene, they shuffled after their tour leader.

Vera scampered over to them, keeping her head low and out of sight. Another tour group had arrived at the same site. She made a beeline to the leader.

"Oh dear," Vera said. "This is a first for me."

"Me too," Pedro, the second guide, agreed. He was a handsome six-foot Spaniard with a chiseled jaw and a captivating smile.

"Where are you from?" she asked, twirling a lock of loose hair.

"Southern Europe, 2135. We're doing an Impressionist tour. Like you?"

Joe, Nellie, and Carl were trying not to stare at the newly arrived tourists, who were trying not to stare right back at them. They were a group of older tourists: three well-groomed women and a thin, stately-looking man with a neatly trimmed moustache. Nellie beamed and waved her hand. They nodded back. The older man tipped his hat. Most of the group were fixated on Renoir who was still completely focused on his artwork.

Vera said, "We'd better record this venue on the restricted list."

Pedro agreed. He opened his frock coat and removed his PocketHolo. Joe noticed his StunGun and a well-concealed, deadly-looking plasma gun. As did Gater and Shiner.

Pedro shrugged as he scratched his head. "What were the chances? I'll record it now."

The TTA mandated that should two tour groups ever arrive at the same historical tour site at the same time, they should record it immediately. The record would then appear in a global tour operator list of restricted attractions. No further tour groups would be permitted to visit the venue at the same time. In this way, the TTA was able to ensure that historical events would not turn into crowded spectacles.

"Done," Pedro said.

"Let's enjoy this all now," Vera said.

The morning was splendid with crisp air and warming sunshine. The newcomers activated their EyeCam zoom features. Vera flirted hopelessly with Pedro, while Nellie, still fascinated with the newcomers, gestured and gesticulated to anybody that would tear their eyes from Renoir and the busty Alina. Leonard, growing increasingly frustrated by the new tourists blocking his previously perfect view, forgot himself. He steadied himself on the rocky cover as he craned his head, attempting to see Renoir's canvas, and dislodged some loose stones and pebbles. Alina heard the clatter and pulled a sheet up to her bosom. Renoir turned to look and immediately spotted Leonard.

"You! Come out from there immediately!" Renoir barked.

Leonard ducked back behind the rocks and searched for Vera. Vera was scrambling toward him.

"Hey! I saw you. Come out." Furious, Renoir took a few steps toward the rocky outcrop.

Leonard stood up and edged toward him. His eyes had begun to water, and he had a huge grin painted on his face, somehow simultaneously experiencing terror and unfettered joy. He held his hands in the air as if he'd just been caught with stolen contraband.

"Come here." Renoir's tone softened after he saw Leonard, scared, obviously awed by Renoir's presence and harmless. "Come, come. We won't hurt you."

Aline seemed to relax, though she was still covering her heaving bosoms. Leonard approached Renoir a little faster, though he still seemed frozen in every part of his body except his legs. He stopped a few feet away, eyes wide and mouth petrified in a cartoonish grin. Renoir stepped over and began to study Leonard's face. He touched Leonard's chin and turned his head from side to side, scrutinizing Leonard's bony nose and crinkled eyes. Sticking his finger into the cleft of Leonard's chin, her ran it over his creased skin and over his frozen lips and teeth.

"Remove your jacket please," Renoir ordered.

Behind the rocks, Vera and the tourists watched the scene unfolding. She shook her head violently when she heard the request. Leonard immediately complied, letting his jacket fall to the ground.

"Hmm," Renoir commented as he stepped around Leonard, appreciating his tall, thin frame.

"Yes. This might just work. Take your shirt off please."

Leonard immediately began to unbutton his shirt. His hands were shaking with excitement. Joe was startled and turned to see how the others were reacting. Nellie giggled silently and put her hand over her face. Vera, horrified, turned to Pedro.

"Enough," she hissed.

Vera and Pedro both stood up and simultaneously drew their StunGuns as they broke cover and walked around the rocky border onto the sand.

Noticing them, Renoir jerked backward, startled. Alina, his buxom model, covered herself with her sheet again as she let out a shrill scream. Leonard's face dropped.

Without another word, Vera shot Renoir, knocking him out instantly. He crumpled in a heap. Alina climbed up onto her haunches, one arm outstretched to tend to Renoir and the other to protect herself from Pedro. Before she could scramble over, Pedro shot her, and she collapsed back onto her blanket.

"Put your clothes back on and get back with the others," Vera snapped at Leonard.

Leonard's face dropped as he blushed. He knelt to gather his jacket and tie as Pedro administered nanodrops to Renoir's and Alina's upper lips.

With Leonard dressed and back behind cover, Vera explained to the two concerned groups that Renoir and the model would both wake up shortly with slight headaches and no collection of the recent events. The two groups retreated from the chaotic scene and said their goodbyes in the forest. Joe focused again on the prickle at the back of his head. He cast his eyes to the sky, looking for the mystery ship, and then studied the trees and brush, squinting to see if anybody else was there. Confirming that nobody from the group was watching him, he sneakily checked the BioSensor. Nothing. Surreptitiously, he angled it upward. Glancing sideways to check that the others were ahead of him and occupied, he lifted it from his pocket, when suddenly, Vera called over to him. He dropped the BioSensor back as his body jolted with fright. He saw Vera's eyes following his hand in his pocket, and he guiltily folded his arms.

"Are you with us?" she asked. "Don't fall behind." Vera's stare lingered before she turned back to the group and made her way to the front again.

Gater and Shiner had been watching when Pedro and the second tour group arrived. There had been no workable way to stealthily separate Joe from the other tourists. Both groups headed back to their TourPods, with Gater and Shiner still trailing Joe. When they arrived, Ash was pacing back and forward outside the Crichton, waiting for them. Vera told him about the second group, shooting Renoir and Leonard's foolishness. Passing him on the way up the ramp, Joe noticed that Ash was bothered. Hungry and thirsty, but otherwise completely enthralled, Leonard, Carl, and Nellie collected in the central cabin, waiting for refreshments.

Ash stayed back until everybody was inside and seated before walking around the ship to the rear sensors. He crouched, reached his arm as far underneath as he could and removed the tracker that he had positioned there before their initial departure. He squeezed it between his thumb and forefinger, rubbing off dampness from the earlier drizzle against his jacket sleeve. Then he reattached it, cast his gaze at the trees bordering the clearing one last time, and headed back onboard.

Their voices restored, the group chose beverages from the DrinkMaster. The conversation was even more lively than usual. Leonard tried to explain the thrill of being so close to Renoir. All Nellie could do was scream with laughter. Joe didn't participate, sipping habitually at his plain black coffee. He sensed danger almost every moment they were outside the ship. He knew that he was being watched. He had to convince Vera to take the group to Oslo to see Munch. And he had to meet the men on the mystery ship.

"Well. It seems like you enjoyed that. Some more than others," Vera remarked.

Leonard fell silent and blushed. Nellie chimed in about handsome Pedro and the elegant tourists. Carl was quiet as usual, though clearly not impressed by Nellie's Pedro comments.

"I will warn you once again that any scenes, any wandering off, any misbehavior cannot be tolerated. Ordinarily, we would have to lock you in a compartment for the rest of the tour, Leonard."

Leonard sat with his head bowed, while Carl gave him an encouraging bump on the shoulder.

"Never mind. In a few minutes, we will be jumping to Les Lauves, southern France, 1904, to follow Paul Cézanne. He painted some of the most wonderful Impressionist landscapes from his studio and the fields, meadows, and riverbanks surrounding Aix-en-Provence. We will take a short stroll from the center of Aix-en-Provence up to his studio and then, if we have time, via the Bridge of Trois-Sautets toward the Montagne Sainte-Victoire."

Leonard, hoping to redeem himself, pointed out Cézanne's reclusive lifestyle and dependence on his father.

Vera offered a forced acknowledgment and continued, "This will be a long outdoor outing with a short stopover at Cézanne's studio, if time allows. Remember not to wander off." Strangely, she glimpsed at Joe.

RACHEL--1893

Rachel paced between the laboratory tables. She knew her best chances of running into another TourPod group were by the National Museum or on Ekeberg Hill. But she also knew that the chances of another tour arriving within the next few hours were infinitesimally small. She glanced sternly at Harry, who withered under her gaze. Eventually, she stormed over to the board, spat on it, and violently wiped the contents clean with her sleeve. She glowered at Harry again and grabbed a piece of chalk.

Take me to other ghosts NOW!

He shook his head meekly.

Too dangerous

NOW! I will help U

You don't understand. Aren't a ghost yet

Understand what?

Only place for me is here

Others might know stuff. We will come back here

Harry's shoulders slumped, defeated. He acquiesced.

Fine

Rachel didn't wait. She beamed at him and skipped over to the big wooden door to jerk it open. Her hand passed straight through the handle. She looked up at Harry worried. He gave her a shrug as if to tell her that it was inevitable. Rachel grabbed at the handle more frantically, getting impatient and jumpy. Harry watched her, hiding a smirk. Rachel stopped and gave him a withering stare. Harry controlled himself. He moved over to the board and pointed at the letters.

B---- R ---- E------A-------T----------H-------I---------N----------G

S--------L-----------O------------W----------S

I--------------T

D------------O---------------W--------------N

Rachel calmed herself. She took a few deep breaths and slowed her heartbeat. She remembered the yoga lessons and emptied her mind. When she felt completely calm, she reached for the door handle again and opened it. She gestured to Harry to hurry and ran out into the corridor. Harry followed her more reluctantly. Rachel and Harry went up the stairs and waited at the top to make sure that the passage was clear. Rachel was worried that she would run into the police. Harry, though he was a ghost, was almost visible at times. They had to be careful.

When the passages were clear, Rachel ran. Harry always seemed to keep up, though he moved slowly. They got to the exit door quickly, and Rachel yanked it open. A young student was about to enter. He stepped aside and apologized for blocking the doorway. Rachel rushed past. Harry followed, smirking quickly at the man. The young man shrieked and fainted. Harry looked at Rachel and shrugged.

They retreated behind a bush. Rachel indicated for him to lead, and he set off toward Christiania Square in the center of Oslo.

BARRETT--2130

Yulia buzzed Barrett's office. Milo was waiting in reception. He was swiping through the adverts displaying the many tour options and commenting loudly.

"Joke."

"Boring."

"OK, this is interesting!"

Barrett swiped with his palm, activating the intercom. "Yes, Yulia?"

"Mr. Morton to see you," she said, keeping a nervous eye on Milo. He had just taken a handful of her mints.

"Send him in please," Barrett instructed, "and please bring us a jug of Celery Soda."

Milo didn't wait for Yulia and walked over, pushing the door wide open.

"Good to see you again Dan. I see you're doing well." Milo winked while glancing at Barrett's heavy midriff.

"It's been a few years, Milo. Nice to see you too," Barrett responded deadpan. "Take a seat."

They both sat, chewing on mints.

Barrett joined the TTA at the beginning, when there were a handful of operators and a limited volume of tours. He was the first compliance officer charged with performing regular reviews on all the operators. Every three months, he would accompany a tour, checking their safety standards.

Morton Tours was consistently his least predictable inspection. No two tours were ever the same. The passengers were usually wealthy, unsuspecting retirees. Milo always took the tourists right to the edge of some calamity, eruption, feast, stampede, party, tsunami, or invasion. He was an innovator who always managed to find the best spots. His clients were mostly satisfied, when they weren't horrified and threatening to sue.

Deep down, Barrett believed the tours were safe, though he suspected that Milo hadn't disclosed all his equipment and instruments to the TTA. The Morton TourPods also always seemed battered. He didn't know how they never fell apart. He'd given Milo plenty of warnings but hadn't ever cited Morton Tours for a serious infringement, until the smuggling embargo surfaced. Up until that scandal, he had trusted Milo, even liked him.

Barrett started, "I really appreciate that you came."

Milo thought for a while. "Oh, you know. I left a lot of good friends here. Great to see everybody."

Barrett almost choked. Nobody had challenged the TTA more than Milo Morton. In the end, he'd been detained, fined, and expelled for smuggling broken swords, arrowheads, figurines, pottery shards, ancient toiletries, even food back to the present. They'd never seized anything that a serious collector would have considered precious. But he had broken a central time-traveling law. Milo had argued that other operators and tourists were also bringing back mementos. In the end, he couldn't fight them, and he couldn't keep hiring lawyers to defend every new accusation they threw at him. Milo had very few friends at the TTA, and the resentment was entirely mutual.

Milo got to the point. "The father of a girl who went missing on a Time International tour came to see me."

"Interesting. You're talking about Rachel Hasselback?" Barrett commented.

"He asked for my help."

"What does he think you can do for her? What can you do?"

"I don't know. But I'd like to try to help him find out what happened to her."

"We all want to help," Barrett replied. "Just don't make any problems for me," he added.

Milo brushed the slight off. "Did you hear anything new about her that you are allowed to share?" Milo asked hopefully.

"Why would I tell you?"

"What happened with me was a long time ago. I'm just trying to do right by the father."

Barrett didn't respond for the longest while. He took another mint and sucked on it slowly as he studied Milo. Milo stared back at him.

"You know. You broke my trust. I always defended you."

Milo had no comeback. Silent, he looked away. Barrett sighed.

"I only have suspicions. But we have no facts or even real leads," Barrett finally said.

He was tempted to say more. Nobody knew time travel better than Milo. Milo looked up, searching for a lead. Anything.

"What do you know of Dark History Tours?" Barrett eventually asked.

"That's Jethro Wenger's new operation," Milo answered. "He was bad news back then. I heard he might be connected to this?"

"I've noticed some remarkable coincidences. Did you ever come across him? Jethro?"

"Oh yes," Milo confirmed, "but not in a way you would ever guess."

Chapter 12

Rachel and Harry headed toward Christiania Square in the center of Oslo. The walk should have been ten minutes, but Harry was clearly struggling, frequently stopping to catch the breath that he no longer had. Rachel had no time for empathy. She grew frustrated, occasionally gesturing violently, though she always backed down, remembering that she was dependent on Harry to introduce her to ghosts, who would hopefully give her more ideas than he had.

They kept to the alleys and passageways wherever possible. Rachel lifted a notebook and pen from the open briefcase of a bank clerk who was taking a late-morning nap on a park bench along the way. She would be able to communicate with other ghosts without speaking.

She tore out the used pages and put them on the bench next to the peacefully dozing man, making a mental note to atone by volunteering at a shelter or something back at home...if she ever got home. Harry asked to take a last short break as they rounded the final corner leading into the old town square.

Graceful buildings bordered a large courtyard and a gleaming bronze fountain. She felt a rush of homesickness, wishing she was fountain spotting with her family. This would be fountain number ninety-five. At the far end, Rachel noticed the Gamle Rådhus. The restaurant premises were large and easily identifiable. The building was built in 1641 and had served as the town hall for over a hundred years before being converted into a fire station and then, a church. It had been a restaurant since 1856. Rachel opened her new notebook.

Almost there?

Rachel smiled impatiently, hinting to Harry that he could rest as much as he liked in a few hundred feet. She continued to write.

Where did U learn about breathing?

Agnes

Agnes?

Will meet her now. She knows things

Why don't you practice?

I did. A few years. Helps but doesn't stop you from ghosting. Gave up

Rachel felt sad for Harry again. It must have been hard for him to be alone for so long. She wondered how long she would be able to hold on before disappearing.

How long has Agnes been a ghost?

More than 250 years

Rachel was shocked and dropped her pen. She scrambled to pick it up to continue writing, but Harry was already standing. He nodded to her, and they continued to the old restaurant. Rachel waited until the maître d' had been called away from the entrance and slunk in with Harry, almost invisible, leading.

Harry guided her through the large facility, sticking closely to the side walls and curtains. They got to a dark, crooked staircase, and Harry headed down. Rachel gulped and followed slowly. Harry waited for her in the basement passage and then headed to a heavy, green, dusty door at the end of the passage covered with peeling wallpaper. The musty air had the overpowering scent of lavender, as if somebody had tried to hide a terrible odor. Harry glanced strangely at her and passed straight through to the other side. Rachel slowly advanced until she was right at the other end of the corridor.

The door was locked and bolted with the key inside the keyhole, turned sideways. She unlocked the door hesitatingly, pushed it open, and stepped inside, closing it softly behind her.

MILO--2130

Milo and Barrett sat back down in Barrett's office with their beverages. Barrett had chosen a Lebanese sahlab topped with shredded coconut and pistachios. Milo had selected a Da Hong Pao tea. The original, when located, cost hundreds of thousands of credits. He had picked up a taste for it on his various tours to ancient China. Fortunately, the DrinkMaster replicated the taste of most drinks almost identically at a fraction of the cost. Milo told Barrett about his past dealings with Jethro.

"I met Jethro Wenger around eight years ago. I'd put together a tour that covered oppressive regimes and controversial leaders throughout history. It was action-packed. I called it Brutal Dictators. We covered four regimes over a sixty-hour period. Starting with Fu Sheng, the cruel leader of the Chinese Qin dynasty, we jumped forward to explore ancient Rome under Caligula, jumped again to check out Russia under Ivan the Terrible, and then ended with Oliver Cromwell's dogmatic rule over England. The tour was popular, a best seller for me."

Barrett was impressed. "You always had a knack for designing original programs. I think that's missing these days."

Milo continued, "Jethro Wenger booked to come with the second or third group that I took. Strange guy. His politeness seemed very rote and learned, not genuine. He was stiff. I had a sense he was hiding behind his manners, like a bedsheet concealing a volcano."

"That's him," Barrett agreed as Milo paused to sip his coffee.

"He was courteous but intense. Never wasted a word. On the TourPod, I could never tell if he was enjoying himself or hating every moment. And he was with a super-friendly group. Three wealthy Mexicans. Very fun and engaging. They were just disappointed that I didn't take them to see Porfirio Diaz. They brought some amazing tequila on board. Genuine stuff. I don't believe Wenger even touched a drop off it."

Barrett commented, "I can't picture him drinking with friends. Or having friends."

"The tour went pretty uneventfully. We witnessed a public execution in China. Pretty horrific, actually. Fu Sheng's soldiers boiled a man alive for saying the word *'lacking'* in the town square, which apparently reminded the emperor of his missing eye. I believe we all turned our faces and left as quickly as we could. Except Wenger, who didn't even flinch. I remember him saying how important it was for commoners to respect their leaders. I don't think he enjoyed Caligula. We passed by an orgy. The Mexicans were fascinated with the openness and the sexual immorality. Jethro seemed disgusted."

"Interesting choice of activity Milo…"

Milo shrugged and continued "Ivan the Terrible was explosive. We followed him and his army as they began the siege of Kazan and saw his erratic mood swings and rash executions. His routine politeness made it very difficult to tell, but I think that Jethro admired the siege tactics.

"But the interesting part was the Cromwell leg. We arrived just after the execution of King Charles. We spent some time in London watching a parliamentary debate followed by the shooting execution of Leveller Lockyer. We didn't stay long enough to witness the actual execution, and nobody seemed to mind except Wenger, who tried to convince me to stay longer. He didn't put up a fight or anything, and I didn't find it strange that he wanted to see the guy getting shot. It is kind of interesting or important to witness history, both good and bad."

"So, what stuck in your mind?" Barrett asked.

"He seemed so completely comfortable and in his element during that part of the tour. While I was following the map on my PocketHolo, he just seemed to know the way. The locals automatically stepped out of his path, without looking up at him or talking to him at all. It was just so strange. All tourists feel awkward and a little uneasy during the ground trips. It's the first and only time I ever saw somebody who seemed to fit in so well."

Barrett seemed perplexed. "What do you make of that?" he asked.

"I don't know. I asked him about it when we were back on board the ship. He just shrugged it off. He said he enjoyed England the most and had always found the Cromwell period very fascinating. He said that he was a student of history and had studied it extensively, which I guess makes sense. I came away not trusting him. He gave me the creeps."

"You know that he is heading up Dark History Tours. Do you think he is up to anything illegitimate now?"

"It wouldn't surprise me. But, from what I've heard about him since, I think you would have a very hard time proving that he was breaking any rules. No loose ends. He runs a very tight ship."

"Thanks, Milo."

JOE--1881

Joe, hoping to catch Vera alone, hung around the common area awkwardly while the others went to change into their newly fabricated early-twentieth-century costumes. She picked up on it quickly.

"How are you enjoying the tour, John?" she asked.

"Great. Thank you," Joe answered.

"We've had some luck with the artists we've seen!" she exclaimed.

Joe nodded as enthusiastically as his mood allowed. He could think of nothing but Rachel, though. The clock was ticking. He had less than two days of touring to go before they would have to head back home through the wormhole. All he wished was to get to Oslo in the same timeline as Rachel.

"Are you looking forward to the next ground trip? Paul Cézanne is one of my favorite artists and a real recluse. We'll hopefully get up close. What's your favorite of his works?"

Joe was sure she was probing.

"Sounds very exciting," he responded.

Vera leaned in. "And don't tell anyone else, but we'll be heading to Arles after that to see van Gogh. You like van Gogh?" Vera whispered.

Joe deliberately sat up and pumped his fists, feigning as much excitement as he could muster. Vera, unblinking, was waiting for any response that referenced art or culture.

"Um, Vera." He hesitated.

"Yes, dear," Vera replied. She sat up and tilted her head toward him.

"I was really hoping to get to Oslo to see Munch."

"He certainly was an interesting character, but why?"

Joe took a deep breath. Part of him felt that Vera was already suspicious. Surely she had seen him using the BioSensor. Anyway, it was just a matter of time before he would have to come clean.

"I'm sure that you heard about Rachel Hasselback, the girl who went missing on last month's tour. Apparently, Oslo was the last place that she was ever seen."

"Yes. We were deeply saddened that she disappeared. And so...?" Vera sat back, folding her arms. She was going to make him say it.

"I would really like to see if we can find her and bring her back."

Vera stared at Joe. It looked like a light just turned on in her head. He could tell that she was putting the pieces together. Her tone changed. "Your name is not really John Holtzman, is it?"

"I am Joe, Rachel's father."

"You lied to come on this tour? Why?"

"I signed a document that said I wouldn't try to find Rachel by myself." Joe lowered his eyes. Vera dramatically stood. Her face had started to flush.

"And are you trying to find her by yourself, Joe?"

"No. They said they would try to find her. I'm just trying to help."

"Are you sure?"

Joe realized that Vera was not sympathetic. He should not have told her who he was so quickly. He had to make Vera feel completely in charge. He needed to seem harmless. He had to try and reel this back before she decided to punish him.

"I am sure. I won't break away from the group. I am just doing my best to be a father."

Vera paused before leaving Joe with a warning. "I'll need to ask Time International and the TTA about this. If you do anything I don't approve of, I will have you locked in your compartment until the end of the tour."

Joe didn't answer. His jaw stiffened, and he met her gaze.

"We'll need to search your bag again," she continued.

Joe realized quickly that if Vera or Ash searched his bag and found any of Milo's paraphernalia, they would lock him up for the rest of the trip. Finding Rachel would be entirely outside of his control. He'd almost certainly lose her forever. But if he showed her that he was cooperative and harmless, maybe she would empathize with him.

"I'll save you the trouble." Joe submitted. He pulled the BioSensor out of his coat pocket and placed it on the table. Vera immediately grabbed it and picked it up.

"This is a receiver coded to pick up Rachel's genetic signal within a one-mile radius. It's supposed to even detect biomaterial that she left behind. I picked up a signal briefly in Paris, but nothing since."

Vera turned it over in her hands. Her stance seemed to soften as she examined the device. "Where did you get this?"

"I bought it from a scientific hobby shop," Joe lied.

"I will be confiscating this for the rest of the tour."

"I understand." Joe cleared his throat and continued. "I just want my daughter to be found. It's really the main reason that I booked to come on this trip. Can we go to Oslo?" Joe asked.

Vera shut the BioSensor off and turned toward her compartment.

"We'll see. If there is time. If we do, it will be the last stop on the tour."

Joe stood up, thanked her, and hurried to his compartment.

"Assuming the TTA doesn't instruct me to detain you," she added as an afterthought.

BARRETT--2130

Barrett opened the Dark History Tours compliance report once Milo had left. Agent Chen prepared the assessment, though she reminded Barrett that it was incomplete. She was still waiting for information and answers to several questions. Senator Pearson had put pressure on him to submit a positive report and stressed that he wanted their application for an operator license to be approved without any issues.

Barrett scrolled to the summary of findings.

TourPods: Excellent
Fleet consists of fifty-two ships. Forty-five of them comfortably seat groups of up to six passengers. Seven smaller vessels seating up to three passengers complete the inventory. Vessels are assembled using the latest graphene, titanium, and nano-compounds. Onboard navigational and operating systems are all brand-new FaceMart 10.1 systems. Nuclear propulsion in all the engines is generation 6.

Safety: Excellent
All ships are coated with MarvApp triple nano-shielding. Cabins include proprietary state-of-the-art depressurization and stabilization technology. Tethering devices are all new-generation Tesloft Prime-matics. Voice suppression, germ suppression, and tracking systems are grade A.

Crew: Very good (PENDING)
(a) Pilots: Suitable experience. No record of serious accidents or breaches of law. High percentage of pilots were combat pilots (awaiting war records).

(b) Tour guides: Majority of the tour guides certified by Time Obscura. The college is very new. Insufficient record to make a formal

assessment.

(c) Operations personnel: All seem experienced, well-trained, and capable. Insufficient background history available on the reconnaissance crew and security and response teams (awaiting personnel and qualification reports on several key personnel).

Regulations: Very good (PENDING)
All interviewees are highly familiar with the TTA guidelines. All licenses and clearances are current. All reporting is up-to-date. Updated tour itineraries have been requested but have not been presented.

Other items and comments: PENDING
During test tours, guides did not seem completely familiar with the itineraries. Accompanying personnel (usually reconnaissance or security crew) broke away from the excursion plan at times and were unaccompanied. We were unable to inspect all equipment.

Barrett had been half expecting a damning report and was somewhat relieved with the overall findings. The lack of information that they had on many of the staff concerned him. He knew very little about the college that had certified many of the guides. The point that bothered him the most was that certain crew on parts of the supervised tours had been unsupervised.

Barrett decided to perform a last review of a live Dark History tour. He knew that Jethro would be very angry, and he was sure that Pearson would create problems for him. The other issue was the report deadline. He had to present it at the latest the day before the Compliance and Oversight Committee, which gave him a maximum of two days to finalize it. Barrett considered sending Agent Chen to supervise a second tour. It would probably be a waste of time. The guides would just conceal any illicit activity from her again. He thought about going himself. He simply didn't have the time, and besides, he was too old and unfit. The guides would run circles around him. Then, another thought crept into his mind.

Milo Morton. They would never be able to scam a scammer. He could try to convince Milo to do the final review for him. It would be a massive risk. Barrett was sure that the Compliance and Oversight Committee would be skeptical of any evidence that Milo uncovered. And he might also pull some stunt on the side that could cost Barrett his reputation. Though, if Dark History were up to anything illicit, or were connected to the latest disappearance, Milo was as good an option as any that he had to uncover it. And Milo would get to the truth faster than anyone else.

Barrett's phone started to ring. He hadn't decided yet, but whatever he did, Barrett had to move quickly, and carefully.

CHAPTER 13

JOE--1881

Joe was agitated. He threw his old clothing into the Fabricator and slammed it closed. The panel automatically updated to the tour's next destination and displayed the date, 1904, and location, southern France. The flashing green sensor indicated it was calculating the appropriate "men's style." Then a blue light began to flash and glow as the machine whirred gently, manufacturing a period appropriate outfit.

He aimlessly fiddled with his VisionPlayer. Missing Oslo would mean almost certain failure. Rachel would be lost. His mind raced as he thought about his confrontation with Vera. Maybe he should have been more aggressive, somehow forced her to take them to Oslo next. He reached for the door panel to open his compartment door when he overheard Vera and Ash.

"He's been lying to us the entire time. Keeping him on is a huge risk," Vera whispered.

Ash asked in a hushed voice, "Think he knows something?"

"No idea. What if he tries something in Oslo? Or before?"

"No way of knowing. Chances are he won't get an opportunity."

Vera's voice was firmer. "I want to confine him to his compartment.

Still waiting for HQ to guide me."

"Interesting… Seems like a no-brainer, given that he faked his ID."

"We can't give him an inch of freedom. I think Oslo is out of the question."

Joe had heard enough. He suspected that Ash knew more about Rachel than he let on. And Vera would rather sabotage any hope of finding Rachel than risk another surprise on her tour. His clothes were ready, and the other passengers had started to assemble in the common area. Joe put on Milo's stained vest, grimacing as he did so, and then slipped on the newly fabricated suit. He felt sick with worry and steadied himself on the sideboard. Then he dropped the tiny vials into his pockets and joined the others.

Ash's gaze was on him constantly. He avoided eye contact, went straight to his launch seat, and secured himself. Nellie took her seat next to Joe and asked him if everything was OK.

Vera, beaming, readied the group. "In a few moments, we will be jumping forward to 1904. I won't repeat the program again except to tell you one more exciting piece of information. One of you is going to accompany me to Cézanne's studio to meet the man in person. It's only fair to draw lots to decide who that will be. And don't worry if you don't win. There will be more special opportunities."

Vera passed around a small pouch. Each of them pulled out a small metal tag with a symbol. Vera then held up her own tag. Leonard had the matching one. He pumped his fist in the air and whooped. Ash dimmed the lights, and they jumped forward with a loud crack.

RACHEL--1893

Rachel stepped into the creepy room at the end of the basement passage. She pushed the sickly green door closed behind her, making sure to leave it ajar while allowing her eyes to adjust to the darkness and immediately recoiled at the smell. Stale wine, old spices and rancid cooking oil had filled the room with a rancid stench that was almost visible. The space was cavernous, the walls unplastered, exposing the original stone bricks. There were small circular windows beneath the ceiling letting thin rays of light enter from the outside sidewalk level. At the far end of the room, Rachel could make out jutting partitions that served to divide the back of the empty area into small stalls. Harry stood in the middle of the room facing away from her.

She mouthed to him, "Harry. What is this?" and scraped her feet on the dusty floor.

Harry turned his head gently toward her. He nervously put a finger up to his mouth to silence her and then gestured for her to wait.

It was uncomfortably quiet until Rachel recognized a faint rattling sound from behind a partition. The noise gradually intensified, and she shuddered when she recognized it was chains shaking. She edged back toward the door.

Harry retreated and came to stand beside her. A ghostly woman inched slowly from the rear of the room and began to advance toward them. Harry mouthed, "Agnes," to Rachel.

Wearing a subtle, confident, though unwelcoming smile, she seemed timeless. Small and rake thin with long black hair, Agnes had sharp, jutting features, seemingly carved by her solitude. Rachel was terrifying. She willed herself, her throat and her feet not to betray her terror by screaming or fleeing. She couldn't betray her fear, or Agnes would destroy her. Harry did not budge. He was rooted to the spot and shaking.

Rachel greeted Agnes, giving her a timid wave. Her hand weighed a ton.

Agnes's stony expression remained fixed.

Rachel tried again, this time writing in big letters in her book:

Hello. I am Rachel. Please help me.

Agnes moved to within a few inches of them and then stopped. Rachel waved her book subtly toward Agnes, partly to make sure Agnes didn't float right through her but mainly to show that they could communicate.

Agnes stared straight through Rachel and then finally looked down at the book.

Rachel wrote again:

Hello

Then she opened the book to the page where she had written out the alphabet.

Agnes pointed out her *Hello*.

Rachel continued writing.

I am lost.

Agnes pointed at her letters.

Yes

I am disappearing.

Agnes looked her over.

Yes

I am from America.

Sweden

I got here yesterday.

260 years

Rachel stared at her. Apart from still being transparent, she began to look normal. Maybe even more normal than Harry, and friendlier than expected. Although, something about her seemed off. She had a distant look in her eyes, as if she was looking past Rachel's face and not at her. Rachel guessed that 260 years in a basement would do that to a person.

Agnes had arrived in Oslo as part of a tour of great city fires. Oslo had been largely destroyed in a blaze in 1624. Agnes, a widow, had been separated from her guide in the turmoil and confusion. She had been in Oslo ever since, mainly haunting the building that currently housed the Gamle Rådhus restaurant. The building had a history of activity dating back to shortly after the fire. At one time it had housed prisoners, in this basement, awaiting their beheading. That explained the chains still attached to the stone walls. The Oslo locals, suspecting that the basement was haunted, imagined the chain rattling came from those prisoner ghosts. Very few people ever plucked up enough courage to enter the room. Rachel wanted to learn what she could from Agnes, and to go very far away as soon as she could.

Chains rattling. It was U?

Yes

Ghosts can't touch things. No?

Agnes didn't respond. She closed her eyes and started to breathe slowly. Rachel could see her thin chest rising and falling as if her lungs still worked. Her forehead creased as she focused. Then her eyes flashed open, and she flung out her hands, shoving Rachel across the room with one explosive move. Rachel fell back against the door, slamming it shut.

Rachel was devastated. She hastily put her hands up in front of her to protect against another attack. But Agnes hadn't budged from where she stood. She watched Rachel and began to snicker silently. Rachel was confused as Agnes shrugged and dropped her hands to her sides, signaling that she was not going to strike again.

Rachel picked herself up, dusted herself off, and still shaken, walked steadily back to face Agnes. Agnes pointed at her book, which was lying on the floor. Once Rachel had recovered it, Agnes started to point at the letters.

Breathing and concentrating stops ghosting

The hierarchy had been established. Agnes fixed a steely, unblinking stare firmly on Rachel's face, waiting for Rachel to ask her questions. Rachel was shaking. She knew she was broadcasting her fear, but she persevered.

R U a demon?

Agnes shook her head.

What are U?

Lost travelers become ghosts. Slowly disappear forever over time. Stay in one place. Weak ghosts

She glanced at Harry.

Pathetic. Can't talk, can't touch, fade away. No power. Less than an insect.

Must keep your strength. Only thing left is terror.

Can U become a person again?

Harry seemed insulted by Agnes's slight against him. He began to strut with his chest pushed outwards boldly, seeming to crave respect and their attention. Neither Rachel nor Agnes paid him any notice. Rachel's question got his attention, but Agnes answered first.

Heard stories. Never met anyone who did

Did U try?

Tried going inside people

What happened?

Nothing. They get scared. Just passed through them.

What R demons?

Agnes blinked for the first time since Rachel met her. She paused, and her lips tightened.

When a traveler is murdered, their soul is released and cannot settle. Vanishes rapidly. Can enter another body first. If it does, creates a demon. A person possessed.

What happens to them?

They change. Unpredictable. 2 minds in 1. Can go mad. Some just starve and die.

R U scared of them?

Most are evil. And powerful.

Powerful?

Agnes was enjoying the attention she was getting. Her eyes seemed softer. She slowly told her story.

Lars and Lilly Norstrom were with me. Got separated from group during Oslo fire. He caught fire. Horrible. Lilly and I - ghosts. Together for years in yellow building across from square. Strange man came. Lilly recognized Lars inside. Said he was drawn to us.

Agnes shuddered.

Not Lars anymore. Ripped her into pieces. Devoured. I got away. Found this basement.

What happened to Lars?

She shrugged.

I stay here. Hope he left Oslo

Rachel understood now why Harry didn't want to leave his basement at the university. But she still felt no closer to understanding how to stop the terrible transition from happening to her.

BARRETT--2130

"Yulia," Barrett called, "Please get me Jethro Wenger from Dark History Tours."

Barrett needed to lock in an urgent Dark History inspection that would be back before Thursday. Barrett steeled himself for the inevitable resistance.

Jethro promptly jumped on the line.

"Superintendent Barrett," he acknowledged, "What can I do for you?"

"Hello, Jethro," Barrett answered. "There are outstanding items on your application, and we are running out of time."

Jethro sighed impatiently and answered, "Yes. Vinod has your list. You want references and technology specifications. We'll get them to you just as soon as we have them and will look forward to a positive recommendation from you. Is that all?"

"No, it's not," Barrett answered. "I need to conclude this inspection by Thursday afternoon, or I can't give a recommendation."

"That will be a big problem for me and my partners," Jethro stated. He reached for his wooden baton and began to roll it up and down his desk.

Barrett continued, "Maybe we can get comfortable with all the open items with one final tour inspection. It will have to be this week."

"We have nothing to hide, Superintendent Barrett. Send someone tomorrow morning." Jethro hung up.

Barrett thanked Jethro and suggested a time before he realized that Jethro had already terminated the call. At least he had agreed. Now he needed to get Milo on board.

"Yulia. Please get me Milo Morton. Oh, and a Columbian Hacienda El Roble coffee. The Melbourne roast. With lukewarm Nakazawa milk."

"No problem, Milo is on the line," Yulia responded.

"Dan?" Milo greeted, sounding like he was in a rush.

"Milo. Is this a convenient time?"

"Not really. I'm in my submarine."

"Look, I need a big favor. It's about Dark History."

"OK?" Milo answered.

"Their application for an operator license is up for approval. I have a supervised tour inspection scheduled, and I need you to do it."

"What. Why me?"

"Because I think they are hiding something. It's going to be hard to catch them, especially when we are not sure what we are supposed to be looking for. You have the fresh eyes and distrusting nature that I need."

"I am flattered, but I'll pass. Is that all?"

"I wouldn't ask if I thought somebody else could do it."

"It's not for me. The TTA doesn't need me. They made that clear already," Milo responded.

Barrett rose to meet Yulia as she entered with his coffee. Realizing this would not be an easy negotiation, he softened his voice. "What's it going to take to get you on board with this?"

Milo paused and considered. He swung the submarine sideways as a school of colorful fish swam past. "They can apologize to me, clear my name, and compensate me for all my costs and losses."

"That's not going to happen," Barrett responded.

Milo shrugged. "Well, what then?"

"Help me for the sake of the girl and her dad. The inspection might shed light on her whereabouts."

"Barrett. I'm a trader...with a grudge against you. Sentimental motives?"

"You still owe the TTA sixty thousand credits in fines and penalties.

The TTA will eventually come over and claim it from you, "

"You bastards could try," Milo retorted.

Barrett sat back at his desk and put both hands on the table.

"Look. This is what I can do. I will get your debt written off in full. But I am asking you because we were once colleagues. And because you can make a difference for this family."

Milo stared at Barrett silently. He accelerated the submarine and swerved upward, sending a stream of bubbles in its wake.

"Plus, a tour fee of three thousand credits a day."

"Fee!" Barrett retorted. "You haven't led a tour in forever."

Milo reached for the screen as if to terminate the call.

"But not one credit more." Barrett gave in.

Milo smiled.

"When is the inspection?"

"Tomorrow morning."

"What!" Milo yelled.

Just then another call for Barrett came in. This time from Senator Pearson.

"Sorry, Milo, I must take this. I'll send you the details and credentialing," Barrett muttered and disconnected the call.

"Senator Pearson. How are you?"

Senator Pearson was in no mood for niceties. Jethro had already called him to complain about the additional inspection.

"Barrett. I've been told that you have created additional requirements for the Dark History Tours application. Would you care to explain why that is?"

"Senator Pearson. There are still some outstanding elements in the compliance report, and I don't want to delay my report to the Compliance and Oversight Committee. I am trying to finish the job as quickly as I can by arranging for an additional inspection where we can hopefully get all the answers we need."

"Well, it didn't sound like that to me," Pearson snapped. "There better be no delay in your submission. And I expect a positive opinion."

Barrett countered. "I will provide a factual report, Senator Pearson. I am sure that I will be able to recommend them for approval, if they follow all the regulations and guidelines."

Pearson concluded the conversation, "If Dark History isn't approved this Friday, Jethro and his partners will be very disappointed, and it will reflect very negatively on you and your career." Pearson disconnected.

"No more calls, please, Yulia," Barrett implored.

CHAPTER 14

Ash hovered over the Bay of Naples long enough to ensure that Gater's ship had picked up their tracking signal. Then he jumped the Crichton to 1904. It crackled over the South of France an instant later, and before long Ash found a remote field surrounded by olive and fig trees, not far from Cézanne's studio and home. He brought the ship down, and the group all unlocked their seat straps. Joe was used to the jumping already. He didn't feel woozy and got up quickly.

As Nellie paraded through the common area, admiring her purple-and-white-striped dress, Leonard grunted and sluggishly stood. His body was struggling to keep up with his exploratory joy. Carl gulped down the last of his snacks and absently bumped into Nellie's ornamental hat complete with an oversize bow. She cursed affectionately as she straightened it.

The men were all dressed in formal, drably colored three-piece flannel suits, starched white shirts, and brightly colored neckties, with small bowler hats. Joe's kept falling off, and he couldn't steady it on his head. He was too anxious given the uncertainty around the Oslo leg and couldn't keep still for long enough to get used to it, though he wanted to wear it incase his hair bristled again. His bowtie, choking him whenever he moved his head, constantly reminded him that he was running out of time. Ash scanned all their necks with the voice suppressor and then Vera hurried them out of the Crichton, which promptly shot up to hide above the clouds. Vera pointed out some interesting facts about the region while they stood in the fields surrounding Aix-en-Provence under an azure sky. The air was sweet with the scent of blooming lavender, mingled with the subtle hints of olive oil and ripe figs carried by a gentle breeze from the nearby town. Deep green cypress trees swayed gracefully around them. As soon as they set off toward the center, Gater and Shiner brought their ship down behind a thicket. Vera was immersed in her soliloquy, and her group was too busy listening to even notice.

"If you look to your left, you will see the great Montagne Sainte-Victoire, a feature in many of Cézanne's landscapes. He felt himself to be a part of the forests, valleys, and countryside blooming with almond and olive trees. He could never stand to leave for too long. It was also here in 102 BCE that Gaius Marius, the Roman general, routed the Teutons in the Battle of Aix. But that's for another tour, which Time International would be very happy to take you on."

As Joe watched Vera's mouth moving, he felt that prickle at the base of his neck. His hair started to bristle and sting against the felt hat. Even his arm hairs began to rise. His fingertips felt like they were on fire. He was being followed. He reached for the tiny vials in his pocket. Touching his clothing created static sparks, and he quickly pulled his hands out.

The group made their way toward the town center. The wide streets were lined with leafy sycamore trees. As they strolled, they passed elegant mansions and the impressive Fontaine de la Rotonde with its bronze sculptures.

The smells of freshly baked pastries and hot coffee from the bustling cafés were irresistible. Vera insisted that they all take a quick seat at Les Deux Garçons, Cézanne's favorite spot, and enjoy an early afternoon snack.

Joe painstakingly swallowed his rice-and-apple gateau in three mouthfuls and was ready to continue. He wasn't particularly hungry but had to concede that it was better than anything he had eaten back home.

Vera sensed Joe's impatience but managed to ignore him as she continued to enlighten the group for another fifteen minutes that felt like an hour. They finally set off, this time up the hill toward Cézanne's studio. Joe was walking alongside Leonard, who still had pastry crumbs and cream stains covering his waistcoat and was feverishly trying to tidy himself up.

Joe, feeling the strange buzzing sensation, glanced behind him. And there they were. A few hundred feet behind them, and heading up the hill, he spotted two figures. One was freakishly tall and pale, just as Sara, Rachel's teacher, had described. His suit was dully colored, and he wore a waistcoat and necktie. Just his shoes and overcoat were oddly modern. The second thug was shorter and less conspicuous, having gone through greater pains to fit in.

They were following him. Joe felt it in his bones. He wondered if they had followed Rachel. Had she spotted them too? Did they snatch her when she fell behind? Joe's mind began to race. If he lagged behind, would they grab him? He would finally know what happened to Rachel, but how would he ever find her? Maybe they would take him onto their TourPod, and she would be there as well. If she wasn't on their ship, she was likely to still be in Oslo. And he would be helpless and useless to her stranded here on the outskirts of Marseilles, France. He glimpsed behind him again, long enough to see that they were now much closer.

JETHRO--2130

Jethro left his office and rode down the escalator to a spacious open-plan floor filled with modern office cubicles. The whole area gave off a blinding whiteness. Employees sat hunched at their desks answering calls, recording conversations, and placing bookings.

Nobody dared look at Jethro, not because he wouldn't tolerate them interrupting their work. Most of the employees preferred that he not notice them. Jethro shuffled quickly through the array of cubicles toward Vinod's glass office at the end of the rows. Vinod hastily stood up as he entered and sat again only after Jethro was seated.

Jethro began, "Vinod, have you made all of the arrangements for the TTA inspection?"

"We'll be taking an agent with us on a composers' tour that we arranged. Beethoven, Mozart--"

Jethro interrupted him abruptly. "Are all the transmitters in place? All the ones I want for now?"

"Almost, sir. We have a few more trips planned, and they will all be done."

"I wanted them in place already." Jethro's voice was steely calm, but his impatience and dissatisfaction were immediately apparent. "And you are wasting precious time on a *composer* tour?"

"I'm sorry, sir. I just thought that this itinerary would be inconspicuous. Better not to take risks."

"Vinod, you need to do as I say. What still has not been done?"

Vinod opened a HoloScreen and scrolled quickly. His hand shook as he reached the bottom of the list. Jethro sat, unblinking, looking straight ahead.

"It's just Jimmy Hoffa, the Boston Strangler, John F. Kennedy, Osama bin Laden, Nanjing, and the Chmielnicki pogroms. Those are the only events that you wanted where we haven't got signals planted."

"Well, I suggest that you discard this tour and continue with our plans. I don't want to have to do this myself."

Vinod jumped to attention and immediately activated his SmartGlove. "Not to worry, Jethro. I will fix it immediately."

Jethro stood up. As he made his way to the door, he turned and offered a final thought. "And make double sure that this TTA agent sees and suspects nothing. If he causes any problems, I will handle it. You just do your job."

With that, he left the office, leaving the door open behind him.

GATER--1904

Gater and Shiner were a few hundred feet behind Joe's tour group when they arrived at Cézanne's studio. They crouched by the side of the road behind a large crop of garrigue and watched. The group had gathered around Vera, as she told them how she and Leonard were going to knock on the front door, posing as a husband and wife. They would ask Cézanne about his next exhibition, hoping to be invited into his studio.

She positioned the rest of the group by the large north-facing window, which would offer them the best view into the studio and the artist himself. She advised them to duck low and stay hidden. Gater and Shiner watched as the group split up, leaving Joe, Carl, and Nellie alone, and unarmed. Vera and Leonard were promptly let inside by Cézanne.

Gater turned to Shiner. "Now! Let's go."

The pair edged forward toward the studio Gater could tell Joe was trying to find them, his head jerking from side to side. He was slowly shuffling forwards as if his legs were thousand-pound bags of flour.

"I'll go get Joe. You take care of the other two," Gater instructed Shiner.

"What if something happens to the other two? No way," Shiner countered.

"Well, what do you suggest?" Gater shot back.

"Wait for them to head back. They will pass us on their way to the front door. If Joe lags, we'll grab him and knock him out."

"And if he doesn't?" Gater responded.

"Then we will wait a little longer till a better opportunity comes up," Shiner calmly replied.

"Better than this!?" Gater sounded incredulous.

"Yes. This isn't a clear opportunity. He is with half his tour group. The only difference is that the guide isn't with him."

"He already knows he is being followed. How many opportunities do you think we'll get?"

"I don't think he suspects anything," Shiner stated rather condescendingly.

"You are mad!" Gater whispered harshly, doubting his professionalism. He was surprised that Shiner hadn't noticed Joe looking for them.

Shiner glowered at him coldly and Gater stared right back.

They continued to argue as the sun set, with Gater getting more and more impatient. Shortly afterward, Vera and Leonard reappeared. Leonard, eyes glazed over, looked stupefied. Vera, holding his hand, led him out.

"Dammit!" Gater seethed. "This is your fault."

Vera called out, and they regrouped. Carl and Nellie gathered around Leonard. They followed Vera past the studio to a clearing behind a thick forest of olive trees. Gater and Shiner crept after them. Shiner had miscalculated their return journey, thinking they were going to head back down the hill. They watched from behind the trees as Ash brought the Crichton down and the group gathered around the entrance as the ramp lowered. Gater alternated between glaring at Shiner and watching Joe as he slipped away yet again.

JOE--1904

Joe was the last to board. He looked from side to side as Leonard steadied himself on the ramp. Stopping halfway up, Joe swung around. He crouched down, peering through the brush and growth, until he locked eyes with the blackest set of eyeballs he'd ever seen. They were unblinking, unapologetic. Joe froze. It seemed like a terrifying eternity before Gater stood up so that Joe could see him clearly. Gater nodded and smirked, letting him know that he was coming for Joe. Joe stared for a few moments longer and then hurried onboard.

Vera was waiting for him to enter. "By the way lovey, we aren't going to Oslo. Best say your goodbyes tomorrow in Arles."

RACHEL--1893

Rachel had no more questions for Agnes. She realized that Agnes could not stop her from turning into a ghost. She wrote.

Thank U, Agnes. I am going now.

Where?

To find a tour group

No

Rachel smiled. She imagined that Agnes had enjoyed her visit and wanted her to stay a little longer. She'd made a strange friend.

Must go now before it's too late

Agnes sneered, and Rachel's heart began to speed up.

You aren't going anywhere

The air around her got cold again. Rachel shuffled into a more defensive position, getting ready for another attack.

What do you mean?

You closed the door

It's not locked

Look

Rachel walked to the door. There was no door handle on the inside. She hadn't shut it behind her when she entered. But she had jolted the door closed when Agnes pushed her into it. *Dammit!* she thought. Rachel felt all around the door, trying to identify some secret way of getting it open. She looked backward at Agnes again, vengefully. Agnes stared at her, gloating. She stormed over to Agnes.

HOW DO I OPEN THE DOOR?

You don't

HOW?!!!

Only opens from the outside

Rachel walked around the room pushing against the bigger stones that she saw, hoping for a secret exit. Nothing was a secret handle. Maybe prisoners from days past had dug an exit. She walked to every corner of the room and scratched the cement, kicking at the dirt, looking for a trap door. Nothing. She saw a dilapidated, dust-coated table, and pushed it over to the wall underneath a window. Standing on the table, she was still at least a foot too short to reach the windows. She marched over to Agnes again and wrote.

There must be a way!

Agnes flapped her hands, mocking Rachel. Rachel went over to the door. She banged and thumped until her fists were bruised and sore. Eventually, she realized there was no chance that anybody would open it. The only thing she was achieving was confirming to the locals that the basement was haunted. Rachel was trapped. She collapsed at the door and cried for the first time since Gater attacked her. She held on to the door, her shoulders heaving as she sobbed.

Agnes stood motionless in the center of the room watching Rachel cry. Harry moved over to stand beside her. He crouched down next to her and sat silently. Rachel stopped crying. She gazed at Harry sadly. He looked wretched. She picked herself up and walked over to Agnes.

U knew this would happen.

Agnes locked eyes with Rachel and slowly shook her head.

I will get out.

You have a home here now

Rachel marched back to the door and positioned herself in a lotus stance. She thought of Joe, Daniel, and her home. Then she cleared her mind of everything else, pushing her panic and helplessness to the side. She focused on nothing except her body. And she started to concentrate as she breathed deeply.

CHAPTER 15

JOE--1904

Back on board, Nellie immediately cornered Leonard about his experience with Cézanne in his studio and what he was painting. Carl asked if there were any nude models in the studio, for which Nellie gave him another withering stare. The group gradually gravitated to the mess table, and Ash set out meal packs and drinks for dinner. Meanwhile, Joe sat alone, tormented.

He finally had a clue. He'd seen Rachel's attackers. Or at least suspects linked to her disappearance. They had even taunted him. He knew that he would have to confront them. They terrified him, but he had no other options. And now, Vera was doing everything she could to keep him away from following the lead. He considered alerting Ash or Vera, given the danger that the brutes might pose to the whole group, but didn't trust them. He would just need to be prepared and draw them away from the group.

As everybody ate, Vera prepared them for the next excursion.

"After an early dinner, we will be heading to Arles, northwest of Aix-en-Provence. We arrive around mid-February 1889 to experience the life of Vincent van Gogh, who moved there the previous year. We'll be visiting several of the locations where van Gogh painted his masterpieces then heading to his home called the Yellow House. And...after drawing lots, one of you will accompany me to van Gogh's rented bedroom."

"Awesome!" Nellie exclaimed.

"Leonard, unfortunately, we can't include you in the draw this time," Vera concluded, giving an overly exaggerated frown. Leonard slapped the table and groaned.

The group finished the meal and retired to their compartments to ready themselves.

While his new clothes were being fabricated, Joe pulled his EyeCam off his iris and inserted it into his VisionPlayer. He scrolled the footage of Gater, searching for clues. He zoomed in on their faces as Gater and Shiner crept behind the group as they proceeded up the hill toward the studio.

Joe noted the pair were snapping at each other. Their clothing had no labels, patches, or unusual markings. Gater's coat did not look like it was made in the twentieth century. The fabric looked too sleek, and there were no buttons. The cut of the cloth was modern. The bulges under their coats betrayed concealed weapons. Joe scrolled to Gater revealing himself. He fixed on Gater's sneer and the cold, dark eyes set against his pale face. This was certainly the man that Rachel's teacher, Sara, had described to him. There was no doubt in his mind. This man was his key to Rachel.

Vera called for the group to reassemble. Joe, realizing he'd lost track of time, grabbed his clothes out of the Fabricator, almost dropping his VisionPlayer. He buttoned his shirt all wrong and ran out of the compartment still holding his shoes.

MILO--2130

Milo cursed under his breath throughout his predawn commute to the Dark History launch base in Sweet Grass, Montana. His tour was scheduled to depart at 7:00 a.m., which meant leaving his cottage in Vermont at 5:00 a.m. How had he allowed Barrett to persuade him? The money helped, he quickly concluded.

He arrived at the impressive marble and steel entrance at 6:00 a.m., plenty of time to explore before the departure. He hadn't taken three steps when a guard stopped him.

"Can I help you, sir?"

Milo flashed the TTA badge Barrett had sent to him. The guard scanned it and admitted him.

"You are early, Mr. Morton. Please wait here. Somebody will come and fetch you shortly."

Milo stood in the cavernous white-and-silver lobby. It was still dark outside. A series of shooting stars streaked across the inky black sky, their silvery light reflecting in his eyes and casting brief, mystical glows around the room.

A second guard came for Milo and accompanied him through a series of passageways toward the waiting area bordering the departure gates. Milo, trailing slightly behind, spotted a TourPod hangar through a side passage. He called to the guard.

"Sorry. I'm feeling a little dizzy. Can you hold this?"

The guard hurried over, and Milo abruptly shot him with his StunGun. He carried the guard into a restroom stall, pulled his trousers down, and sat him on a toilet seat. Opening one of his vials, he rubbed the contents under the guard's nose. The guard would wake up in an hour or two, not remembering where he was or how he got there.

Milo hurried back to the passage and crept into the terminal. He climbed down the stairs to the hangar floor and made his way through the rows of vessels. They were the most modern and sleek that he had ever seen. He ran his hands against the sides of a six-seater TourPod near the back of the hangar. The smooth, shimmering compound was unlike anything he'd felt before. His fingertips felt almost electrified.

Milo opened his bag and took out a small lock disabler. It emitted a low pulse as he scanned it against the base of the ship, revealing the central security system. He adjusted the frequency and attached it to the hull. The pulse intensified until the ship's hatch slid open.

Milo climbed aboard and activated the torch on his SmartGlove. The interior was modern and luxurious. It reminded him of a SlingShot bullet. Efficiently designed, it lacked the warmth that he had tried to produce in his Morton TourPods. The nuclear propulsion core housing was significantly larger than those he saw on other ships. He noted every intricate signal receptor and mapping device on board. This meant that the navigation system was also more advanced. Strangely, there were coffin-shaped containers installed in the rear. Black and covered with an opaque glass casing, each was large enough to hold a man.

Milo hurriedly checked that his EyeCam was recording when he heard somebody enter the hangar. He leapt out of the TourPod, landing awkwardly and stifling a groan. Rolling onto his back, he shuffled underneath to retrieve his lock disabler. The footsteps grew louder as the men approached. Moving steadily and carefully, Milo deactivated the pulse and pulled the device off the underbelly in the nick of time. The hatch slid closed moments before two maintenance workers turned the corner.

Milo lay still until they passed and then crept out, climbed back up the steps, and snuck back into the administration block. He headed to the waiting room and nonchalantly took a seat, moments before the departures supervisor came to fetch him.

"Mr. Morton, please follow me."

Milo clutched his bag and followed her to the departure lounge. He was introduced to the tour guide and an 'operations specialist'. The guide, Wanda, a short, stern-looking woman with beady eyes and a puffy face, extended her hand and shook his stiffly. The operations specialist, Dmitri, had shaved blond hair and a squashed nose from, Milo imagined, years of fistfights. He was built like a chest freezer.

Wanda invited Milo onboard. She and Dmitri followed right behind him as if he were a convict being led to his cell. Milo knew when he was being escorted very well, and he noted it strongly in Dmitri's mannerisms.

As Milo boarded, he glanced at the windows surrounding the departures hall and caught a glimpse of Jethro watching intently.

GATER--1904

Gater and Shiner sat in the cockpit of their ship studying the Crichton as it hovered in the distance. The signal from the tracking device was strong and clear, and they were ready for the next jump. The heavy silence between them was tangible. Gater's every muscle was tense as he played the wasted opportunities over in his mind. He was disgusted by Shiner. They would never get as good a shot at Joe as they had been gifted at the studio in Aix-en-Provence. Shiner sat sharpening a blade as he eyed the monitors. After a few moments, the Crichton vanished in a blue crackle.

"They jumped," Shiner said. "Arles, March 3, 1889."

Gater was silent, setting course without offering Shiner any warning. Their TourPod jumped before Shiner found his seat, crackling as they disappeared, and leaving Shiner to frantically steady himself against the console as the ship reappeared. Shiner glared at Gater as he glanced over to the navigational screens to confirm they had arrived at the correct period. He then fixed the guidance system on Ash's transmission and accelerated toward its position, stopping a few miles short to make sure they weren't seen. Shiner picked at his fingernails with his sharpened blade.

Shiner broke the silence. "They're obviously going to see van Gogh. Let's get ready."

Gater, noting that Shiner was preoccupied with his blade and the navigation screen, felt for the fist-size piece of lead pipe that he kept in his pocket. As Shiner turned to activate the manual navigations, Gater, clutching the piping, swung the back of his fist at Shiner's face, catching him on his jaw. Shiner tumbled backward, raising his arm to protect himself from a further attack as his mind reeled.

Gater jumped on top of him and slammed his fist into Shiner's cheek.

This time, Shiner collapsed onto the floor. Gater stepped around and grabbed him around his chest, slipping his arms under Shiner's. He dragged him across the floor and threw him on his bed. He pulled out a ream of steel wire and wound it around his body and the bed multiple times.

Then Gater wound the wire around Shiner's feet and tied his hands to the bed posts. Feeling confident that Shiner was secure, Gater busied himself, fabricated clothing for the Arles mission. He heard Shiner stir as he was strapping on his shoes. Gater concealed his weapons in the pockets and lining of his trench coat and boldly stepped back into Shiner's compartment. Shiner was groggy but awake. He glared at him.

Shiner gasped, "What the hell?!"

"I'll deal with Joe myself."

"Are you crazy?"

"I'll free you when the job is done," Gater responded.

"You'll regret this."

Gater, rolling his eyes, turned around, and headed to the cockpit. Joe's tour had descended to a clearing near the Rhone River, not far from the Yellow House. Gater followed and guided his ship behind a row of trees.

RACHEL--1893

Rachel, stuck in a miserable, dreary, and haunted basement, was running out of time and energy. She kicked weakly at the door as she racked her brain. Her fingerprints, smudged into the dust, already covered the dirty wooden surface. She stared at her useless hands. Her right hand was still corporeal. She placed it on the door and pushed ineffectually against the green paint. Her left hand was dematerializing. It was now more ghostly than real. She held it up to the door and slowly extended her arm. Her fingertips reached the door and passed through, only stopping when they reached halfway through her palm. She yanked her hand back, terrified at how quickly she was disappearing. She breathed deeply until she was confident that she could feel both of her hands again. It was getting harder to keep herself together.

Agnes pointed at her notebook. She wanted to say something. Rachel picked up her pen and turned to the alphabet page.

Save your energy

Why?

I will teach you to be a powerful ghost

I DON'T WANT TO BE A GHOST

She grimaced at the alarming thought and knew she needed to come up with a plan. Fast! She had to get that door to open. She stood and leaned against it. From the inside, there was no door handle. She bent and looked through the keyhole. The door was still unlocked. She needed somebody to twist the knob. But she knew that nobody would come near the haunted room. Not after her hysterical banging.

She was the only one who could open the door. Her left hand had started to fade away again when Rachel had an idea. She placed her hand by the latch and slowly started to move it through the door. First up to her fingertips, then up to her finger joints. Then again up to her palm. She figured her fingertips were next to the door handle.

She had no real way of knowing without grasping anything with her hand. If her hand was still flesh and blood, she would need to extend it to grasp and turn the handle. Feeling even more frustrated, she pulled her hand back. Agnes shook her head. Harry offered a reassuring smile.

Then Rachel had another thought. If she could accelerate the dematerialization, she could stick more of her arm through the door. Then, if she could restore her hand, she might be able to turn the door handle and free herself. The plan was risky. She shuddered at the thought of her arm becoming a part of the door. If she went too far, she might turn into a ghost even faster. The process might become irreversible. There were no other options. She kicked at the heavy wood causing Harry to jump at the loud thud. If breathing deeply and steadily slowed the process, the opposite might work to quicken it. She started to breathe more rapidly.

Rachel huffed and puffed, all the while concentrating on her left hand until a faint numbness began to creep through her fingertips. She shut her eyes. Agnes, watching curiously, inched towards her. After a few minutes, Rachel glanced at her left hand and reached for it with the right. Her whole arm past the elbow had turned ghostly. Her eyes swelled with tears. She'd gone too far.

Dammit! She had no time to backtrack. She reached for the door at the height of the handle again. Her fingers passed through with ease. Then her palm. Then her wrist. A little more. She second-guessed her position and moved her hand farther to the right. And then a little to the left.

Silently observing, Harry suddenly perked up. He shuffled over to her and waved to grab her attention. Then he stepped through the wall to the other side. Poking his head through the door, he began to guide her, ducking back and forward, all the while gesturing, until her hand position was correctly aligned. Then he stepped back into the basement with a thumbs up. Now came the hard part. Rachel had to reverse the process so she could turn the handle. She squeezed her eyes closed and began to take deep, slow breaths.

Agnes seethed. She glowered at Harry as she tensed her body.

CHAPTER 16

JOE--1889

Carl pulled the winning disk and won the honor of accompanying Vera to van Gogh's bedroom. Nellie begged him to trade with her as they disembarked.

"Please! We'll get whatever you want for dinner for a month when we're back." She pulled at the card as Carl clutched it firmly. He only conceded after Nellie, gazing deeply into his eyes pleadingly, wrestled it out of his hand.

Joe disembarked behind Leonard. They stood in the clearing behind a set of trees separating them from the Arles train station. A frosty wind blowing across the treetops. Through the leaves, the scent of coal and oil mingled with the cool dusk air. Workers in soot-streaked overalls move sluggishly through the fading light as the sound of metal clanging against metal drowned the chirping and trilling of the birds.

Nellie pulled her jacket tighter around her body, though Joe could tell she was enjoying the freshness. All clothing back home was temperature and climate-resistant. Most people had never felt uncomfortably hot or cold before.

He heard a steam train approaching, and they all moved closer to the station for a better view. A gritty, black blur thundered past, spewing copious amounts of swirling gray-and-white smoke: carriage after carriage, never-ending, filled with gloomy passengers returning from markets, factories, and farms.

The conductor blasted his whistle to clear the track as the train ground to a halt. Joe smothered his ears with his hands as the screeching grind of the train's wheels fought against the metal tracks.

Vera appeared as the passengers burst from their compartments clutching bags and suitcases.

"Quite a difference to a SlingShot, eh?" She chuckled.

"We'll progress through the center of Arles to the banks of the Rhone River, where we will visit the location where van Gogh painted the famous *Starry Night* over the Rhone. After that, we'll head to the Yellow House where van Gogh rented a room and painted three hundred of his most famous artworks."

They set off alongside the train track, passing groups of locals buttoning jackets and checking watches. Life seemed grimmer in Arles than in Paris or Aix-en-Provence. Vera explained that Arles had once been a major port on the Rhone and a thriving town. When the railroad replaced the river as the major vehicle for trade, the town was forgotten.

Hungry children approached them, pulling on their clothing as they begged for a coin. Prostitutes, some of them pregnant, stood around the entrances to crumbling buildings. A pack of scruffy, stray dogs draw near. They sniffed at Joe's clothing, and he moved away, avoiding their matted fur and gaunt frames. The dogs whimpered and retreated, dull and clouded eyes fixed on him and the group.

Vera commented as she walked, "Animals always behave strangely around us. As if they know we don't belong in their world."

No sooner had she explained animals when a cacophony of howling dogs and laughing children arose, drowning out the chirping crickets and the dull, thumping hiss of the stationary train. The howling intensified until it became impossible to ignore.

Joe turned and noticed a pack of disheveled mutts of all shapes and colors encircling a strange figure lurching backward and forward on all fours. The street children were shrieking with hysterical laughter.

Then Vera shrieked, "Leonard! Where is Leonard?"

Joe edged carefully toward the dogs, though they were focused on an unlikely distraction. Leonard, in the center of their circle, and on his hands and knees, was face-to-face with a skeletal mutt, growling softly and unpredictably. Seemingly well versed in dog etiquette, he bowed his head, allowing the dog to sniff him from top to toe, which the dog did with cautious alacrity, making its way around to Leonard's rear. Leonard swiveled his body around mimicking the dog. The two were circling each other, head to hindquarters, as the surrounding dogs bayed, while the children screeched.

Clutching her StunGun, Vera was already on the PodCom, alerting Ash that Leonard was missing. Joe tapped her on her back, and she turned around briskly. He pointed to Leonard and the dogs. Vera took a few steps toward the strange spectacle.

"Leonard Lambert!! Enough!"

Leonard, clearly startled, lurched upward, and struggled to his feet. The howling stopped as the dogs reassessed the stranger in their midst. The trust had been broken, and they began to growl menacingly. Leonard waved his hands soothingly as he glared at Vera, who had ruined his spectacle. The growling erupted into a feverish cacophony of barking and snarling. Leonard grew pale. He cowered as he searched for a way out, the dogs advancing, the circle around him steadily shrinking. A scrawny black-and-white mutt with one eye and a missing ear leapt forward, sinking its teeth into Leonard's left calf. His face contorted into a twisted anguish as he wheeled around, trying to shake the dog off. More dogs leaped forward and joined the scene. Leonard collapsed to his knees as the pack grabbed at his clothing.

Vera shouted into the PodCom, "Ash, where are you?"

Ash responded moments later, "I see him. I'll handle it."

Joe looked up as the Crichton appeared, hovering fifty feet above Leonard. The children scattered as the dogs snarled and howled A light flashed briefly as the ship emitted a high-frequency blast of noise, inaudible to all but the dogs. They let go of Leonard's clothing as they shook, ears pinning back against their heads, bodies tensing as they whined. Leonard collapsed, face first in the grimy mud. Wailing and cowering, the mutts retreated, and the remaining children scrambled off. As the last of the dogs scampered away, Nellie and Joe hurried over to him. Vera concealed her StunGun as she strode behind them.

Joe crouched down and recovered Leonard's glasses while Nellie wiped mud from his face.

"Are you injured?" Vera barked unsympathetically.

Leonard pointed at his left calf.

"Well. Roll up your pants. Let's see."

Leonard sat up, and Joe noticed a glint of satisfaction in the upwards curl of his mouth.

"It's bleeding. You'd have rabies already if not for the treatment we gave you when you boarded," Vera muttered accusingly.

Leonard grimaced as Vera prodded roughly at his wound. She pulled a thin metal rod from her coat and waved it slowly over the bloody tooth marks. It emitted a pulsating blue glow that seemed to soothe and pacify him, while simultaneously knitting the worn skin together. In minutes. Leonard was on his feet, shaking his head at his misfortune. Joe and Carl steadied him, and they climbed back onto the pavement. Vera snorted as she took the lead.

"We've lost valuable time. Please keep up with me," she commanded and strode ahead.

They followed her to the Arles Obelisk with its small fountains in the center of town. The streets along the way were dusty and uneven. The houses and shops were less ornate and more simply built than those of Paris. The group was subdued, taking in the poverty and depression. They pushed on and arrived at the banks of the Rhone as the last rays of dusk disappeared behind the houses. The river curved to the right and gently flowed off in a winding path. Riverside structures lined the dark-blue water. The sparkling, golden reflection of the moon, stars, and lanterns illuminating the lapping tides and the shore stirred thoughts of van Gogh's masterpiece. His portrayal of the scene was even more striking.

It was colder at the river's edge. The group collected tightly around Vera as she spoke about van Gogh's portrayal of the glowing stars. Standing and listening, the prickle at the base of Joe's neck reappeared. He sensed the crooked mouthed man watching him again. Joe felt for the vials in his pocket and wondered what reaction they would have if he used them. He had never struck another person and hadn't even been in a scuffle since his early school days. His mouth went dry as his mind raced. When would Gater make his move? Gater was two hundred feet away crouched behind a cart, watching them as he fiddled with a length of garroting wire.

MILO--1975

Standing in the main cabin, sandwiched between Wanda and Dmitri, Milo noted that the Vonnegut, Dark History's TourPod was a different make and model than the ship that he had examined earlier. Having spent the best part of twenty years in time ships, flying them, crashing them, and repairing them, he could tell that this vessel was less sophisticated. There were similarities. However, only a lazy inspector would have confused them. As he entered, he ran his hand against the outside hull. The protective nano-compound seemed more in line with TTA regulations but was less dense than the other model. Wanda directed Milo to place his bag in a compartment and to take a seat for liftoff, which he dutifully did.

Milo pulled out his PocketHolo and turned to Wanda. "Where are we going today?" he asked.

"We're finalizing a twentieth-century music tour, covering Memphis, San Francisco, Detroit, New York, and Seattle." Milo noticed that Wanda would not make eye contact with him as she guardedly answered.

"Great."

The takeoff was unremarkable, and Freddy, the pilot, steered the ship out steadily. The nuclear propulsion fired as expected, creating a wormhole, and the pilot accelerated steadily. Milo barely noticed the familiar crackle as they jumped through time. He scrutinized the navigation systems and tried to take a mental inventory of all the equipment that he saw on board. The ship steadied and began floating through the clouds as they headed toward Detroit.

Milo unclipped his seat lock and stood.

He glimpsed at the navigation and mapping system: DETROIT, JULY 30, 1975.

"Should I go to my compartment to fabricate an outfit?" he asked.

"Yes, of course," Wanda quickly responded. "Before you do, we'd just like to go over the rules."

Dmitri walked over and stood on the other side of Milo. The way Wanda and Dmitri were bookending him was threatening and made him wary of any sudden movements.

"After landing and the nanodrops, we will exit the ship. Stay by my side as I go through all the safety checks. After you observe that all our equipment is functioning on our short excursion, we will reboard. No wandering off or interacting. Leave everything as you find it. Understood?"

Milo smiled. "You're the boss." He headed to his compartment and took off all his clothing, minus a graying vest and orange boxers. He pulled a pair of bell-bottom denim pants and jacket out of the Fabricator as well as a corduroy button-down shirt. He cringed and put them on. Then he opened his bag and began to prepare for the ground excursion. Milo concealed his StunGun in the inner pocket of his jacket. He had a small handgun with lead bullets, typical of the twentieth century, as well as a micro receiver that could pick up faint signals even across time waves. Milo took out a few vials containing nanodrops and stuffed them into his top pocket, followed by a packet of chewing gum, a notebook, and a pen.

He rejoined Wanda and Dmitri in the common area.

"Detroit, 1970s? I don't remember that being a highlight in world music history."

Wanda jumped on the question. "Maybe you never heard of Motown," she retorted condescendingly.

"Sure," Milo answered, "but Motown Records had left Detroit by then. What's there to see in 1975?"

Wanda and Dmitri glanced at each other, neither attempting to respond.

Milo knew they were up to something else. "I mean, I could understand if we came to see Led Zeppelin in Detroit. But that would be in about '77. Why don't we try to do that?"

"We have our program, Mr. Morton. And we will be sticking to it," Wanda returned curtly.

"Yes, but it doesn't sound very well put together, does it? If you want to take music tourists to relive '75, why not visit the CBGB club in New York?"

Wanda glanced at Dmitri as she grabbed her bag. The Vonnegut commenced its descent for landing and disembarkation.

If Milo could keep them on the defensive, they wouldn't ask him if he had any weapons or equipment on him. They would never let him take anything with him on the excursion. If they felt pressured, they might also make mistakes. Changing topic, Milo asked about the ship and its technology.

"When was this ship built?"

"August 2127. At Nokia Airlabs. You already have all of the records."

"Are all of the ships the same?" Milo continued to press Wanda.

"Yes. Again, you already have all our fleet records."

"Do you have any newer or updated ships in the fleet?"

"Our fleet was bought in August 2128. We've given you the documentation." Her shoulders tensed as she adjusted her glasses, glaring at Milo impatiently. Her small ears were turning red.

Milo could not read Wanda. She might have been unaware of the hangar filled with upgraded ships. She was on edge, stabbing at the ship controls as Freddy piloted the Vonnegut over Detroit. The ship landed in a clearing in Bloomfield Township north of the city.

Vera stated, "The famous singer Aretha Franklin lived in Bloomfield. We're going to scout out the area and to finalize the Detroit tour."

Milo followed as she and Dmitri disembarked. Dmitri looked absurd. His stocky frame and bulging muscles were crammed into a denim pantsuit and pastel-orange shirt. Milo asked what equipment they took with them on ground excursions. Vera showed him her StunGun and PodCom, plus a small first aid kit. Dmitri ignored Milo, who then repeated the question. He pulled out a PodCom and waved it in front of Milo's face. Milo, nodded and then peeked over as he casually dusted off his shoulder, catching a glimpse of a more ominous-looking, metallic object under Dmitri's floral-print denim waistcoat. One was a gun. The other, a circular flat device, he had never come across before.

RACHEL--1893

Goose bumps formed on Rachel's skin as the temperature steadily dropped. She kept her eyes tightly shut, too scared to move her hand even slightly. All her effort and energy was concentrated on her steady, deep breathing. If she could keep her heart rate slow and think only of getting her left arm working, she was sure she could open the door. She willed her fingertips, her nails, knuckles, palm, forearm – everything to make her arm whole. She visualized the bones and flesh taking shape. She pictured her forearm getting longer and longer, as molecules formed into muscle and tissue. She imagined her wrist – seeing the veins turn blue as the blood pumps through.

She tried to imagine her fingers wrapping around the handle on the other side of the door. The wood surrounding her arm seemed to thicken and tighten as her solidifying arm displaced it. Slowly, the sensation returned. A squeezing around her wrist and a coolness against her palms. She touched a smoothness, possibly metal, and opened her eyes again. Her arm, grotesquely perpendicular to the door, completely stuck, as if it were a part of the wood. She glanced at Harry and gulped. He nodded at her reassuringly, and she twisted the knob.

Meanwhile, Agnes's face had turned an ashen grey. Her irises rotated to the back of her head, leaving only the white of her eyes glowing. The air around her turned colder. Agnes was going to try to stop Rachel from leaving the basement and was wasting no time. She frantically twisted the doorknob as far as it would go. Then she stepped backward, pulling the door open as she moved. A gust of dry air from the passageway blew into the frosty basement. Rachel felt a massive sense of relief and a rush of invigorating energy. She readied herself to charge out of the room. She had to free her arm first, though. She needed to ghost it again. The whole process in reverse, while Agnes was clearly about to send some explosive energy her way. Short shallow breaths. And quickly.

Agnes suddenly charged forward, slamming into her, forcing Rachel forward and pushing the door backward toward the frame. The push was powerful and almost threw Rachel off balance. Her arm, still stuck in the door, was the only thing that kept her standing. She dug her heels in, slowing the momentum. Somehow, the door remained slightly ajar. But she knew that she could not withstand another blow like that.

Agnes collected her strength again, forcing her eyes back as she readied herself for yet another attack. Rachel, whimpering softly, tried not to panic. She steeled her mind and continued to pant. Harry, spectating from the side, knew that if Agnes could force the door closed, probably wounding Rachel in the process, Rachel would be stranded forever, with hideous Agnes, her dead gray skin and her glowing white eyes. Rachel was losing focus. She was running out of time and she knew it. Her arm was stuck. There was not even a micron's distance between her flesh and the compacted wood surrounding it. She couldn't get it unstuck fast enough and started to tug on it painfully with the other arm.

Blood began to drip as her skin turned red from the friction. She stared helplessly at Harry, her eyes filled with tears and terror. He turned back to Agnes and jumped in front of her, distracting her, crossing right through her and filling her face with his own. Waving his arms, he gritted his teeth, snapping his mouth open and closed. A flicker of confusion shot against Agnes's creased face. Her tightened mouth slackened into a momentary gape. He had forced her to lose concentration. Harry flailed about, crossing through her again and jumping up and down. Agnes hissed at him.

Whatever he was doing, it was buying Rachel time. She squeezed her eyes shut and forced herself to hyperventilate, imagining all the bones, tenders and flesh in her arm disappearing. It was starting to work. She lost sensation in her fingers and then her palm. Harry, however, was growing tired. His bouncing had become less animated as he wheezed for breath. Agnes, ignoring him, had started to gather strength again. Rachel, pushing Agnes out of her mind, imagined her blood drying up and vanishing. Harry had almost collapsed by now. Her arm, strained and reddened, slowly began to inch backwards. Rachel quickly and forcefully twisted it and yanked it, trembling slightly, towards her, leaving a gaping hole in the door.

Agnes's eyes suddenly flashed, and her body exploded with intensity, slamming into Rachel again. She sent Rachel flying with such power that she crashed straight through the damaged, weakened door. She landed on the passage floor outside the basement room with a dull thud.

Shaken and winded, she gasped for breath as she lay amid the shards of wood. Raging white fire seemed to burn behind Agnes's eyes. Rachel picked herself up, marched toward Agnes, and walked straight through her to pick up her notebook and pen. She leaned over to Harry, with a weary smile, and gestured for him to follow her as she stepped back again through Agnes on the way out of the basement. Harry followed.

As she glanced over her shoulder, she saw Agnes gathering energy for yet another attack. This time, even the chains hanging from the walls had begun to rattle. Rachel picked up her pace and bounded up the stairs to the upper floor of the restaurant, and to safety. She stopped only once to turn around and mouth, "Horrible witch!"

CHAPTER 17

Leaving the Vonnegut behind, Milo, Wanda, and Dmitri headed to Telegraph Road, a nondescript stretch of tarmac running parallel to Minnow Lake. Tranquil, calm, with the odd waterfowl, but mostly quite nondescript, Milo had to wonder again why they were here. He took general notes about the Dark History Tour processes. Freddy had been good. The Vonnegut was camouflaged well in advance of touching down. They made sure to land unseen and safely. The pilot had quickly flown away and was hovering nearby in case of any incidents. Milo could not fault anything in the execution so far. He was, however, very bothered by the actual itinerary and continued to quiz Wanda.

"So, this is a real destination in the Twentieth-Century Music Tour?"

"Of course," Wanda shot back, and turned away from him, clearly irritated with his questions.

He persevered. "I don't understand why we didn't come to Detroit in '65 during the height of Motown."

"I wouldn't know. Let's see, shall we? Maybe we will change the tour," she answered dismissively.

They walked along Telegraph Road until they arrived at a small restaurant with an ordinary, white and red sign - The Machus Red Fox. A minimalist, clean white building with a pointed red roof, it offered steaks and cocktails, mostly to travelling salesmen. The American flag hung proudly from the portico. As they approached, they passed a collection of Fords, Pontiacs, and Chryslers in the parking lot.

"Lunch?" Wanda offered.

"Sure," Milo accepted, "if we have time. Isn't there something to see here?"

"We've learned that Aretha Franklin used to frequent this restaurant. We're just checking that."

Milo rolled his eyes. He didn't buy it at all. Following Wanda and Dmitri in, he took a seat with them in one of the booths. The large, dimly lit interior with draped velvet curtains was surprisingly elegant. A waitress came around to take their order, and Wanda presumptively ordered the special for all three of them. Milo glanced around. The tables were mainly empty. There were small groups of businessmen spread out, hunched over their bloody steaks. He noted a particularly animated discussion in the far corner. Speaking like mob bosses, the patrons were heatedly arguing a point. Milo thought it best to keep his head down. He knew there had been a strong Mafia presence in Detroit and did not want to draw any attention to himself. Dmitri abruptly jumped up and hurried towards the exit.

Milo, surprised, turned to Wanda. "Where is he going?"

"He's just stepping outside to have a cigarette."

"It's 1975. You can smoke inside."

"Maybe he forgot."

"Maybe I'll go and join him," Milo answered and jumped to his feet.

"Wait," Wanda exclaimed after him as the waitress approached with their drinks.

Milo hastened out and spotted Dmitri on the porch surrounding the restaurant, as he was rounding the corner. Following at a slight distance, he saw him crouched down by a drain pipe, holding the strange, paper-thin metallic disk from his coat. Dmitri placed it at the corner where the pavement met the wall. He squeezed it, and the span like a saw blade, burrowing itself into the ground. Clearly satisfied, Dmitri jumped to his feet surprisingly quickly and turned, freezing when he saw Milo watching him.

"Hey, Dmitri," Milo greeted him. "What are you up to over there?"

Dmitri opened his arms innocently as if he had nothing to hide. Then, grinning, he strutted over to Milo like an old buddy.

"It's nothing. I'm running some tests to make sure that our immune boosters will work."

"What does that even mean, Dmitri?" Milo replied as Dmitri gradually advanced toward him.

"Oh, you know. Just some tests," Dmitri said dismissively.

He casually slipped his right hand behind his denim jacket, reaching for a weapon. Milo, seeing his hand disappear, realized that Dmitri was going for a weapon. He calmly reached behind his back to grab his own. As he grasped the handle, Wanda grabbed both his arms. She was impressively strong and held him firm as Dmitri pulled out his StunGun. He approached so closely that Milo could smell the garlic on his breath, and then extended his apelike arm, aiming straight at Milo's face.

JOE--1889

Vera had to holler to grab Leonard's attention. Standing by the Rhone at nightfall was entrancing but also icy. Nellie was freezing, and Carl urged Vera to get moving. A swarm of mosquitoes rose from the river, and they were mercilessly attacking the group. Eventually, Vera sauntered over to Leonard and shook him from his deep contemplation. Certain that Gater was watching and waiting to pounce, Joe's imagination was running wild. He needed to take the initiative this time.

The group left the riverbank and wandered down the Rue Marius Jouveau toward the Yellow House. Carl and Nellie held hands while Vera pointed out the history of Arles and the famous sites. Joe followed quietly on his own, considering the possible outcomes. His stalker was the obvious key to finding Rachel.

He quietly dropped back farther from the rest of his tour until he was trailing a few paces behind. Clutching a vial between his fingers, he scanned the surrounding streets and buildings. The prickling feeling behind his eyes intensified until he had an overpowering urge to turn. His hair was standing on end. Joe turned around slowly, his heart pounding as he scanned the dimly lit riverbank. Like a spreading ink stain, Gater emerged from the shadows of the trees, his black figure looming just a few feet away, eyes gleaming with violent intent, he rapidly approached. Joe, anticipating an attack, threw his glass vial down in front of his charging attacker. It landed on a clump of soft mud and failed to shatter. *Dammit!* Joe thought as Gater caught him and twisted him into a neck lock.

"I guess you came for your daughter," Gater taunted him.

Joe writhed and flailed, trying to free himself. Gater's grip was unbudging and firm. He was going to choke Joe unconscious. Joe, gasping for air, spotted the tiny glass vial a short distance to his right.

"You're in the wrong place," Gater teased. "You're supposed to be in Oslo, aren't you…"?

He squeezed tightly again. Joe gagged and slammed his elbow into Gater's side, over and over again, but it didn't seem to have any effect. As he struck, he lurched his body forward, managing to inch closer to the vial.

"You'll never find her…" Gater whispered.

Joe's sight began to cloud over. He needed to free himself. Urgently. Joe was so tired and weak at this stage, his arms felt like rubber. Slamming his fist upward, he managed to connect with the side of Gater's head. The blow achieved nothing except to take Gater by surprise. Joe felt Gater shift slightly to protect himself and quickly dropped all his weight by throwing his body forward and lifting his legs. Gater staggered forward to steady himself

The vial was now within reach, and Joe stomped on it, remembering at the last second to shut his eyes. The glass shattered, emitting an audible *POP*. A blinding white smoke quickly filled the air, swallowing the both of them in a cloud. Gater shrieked as he loosened his grip. Joe quickly squirmed and crawled away from the haze. Gater was blinded, and he hunched over, his arms waving in front of him to grab Joe as he screeched.

Joe turned, waiting until Gater's side was sufficiently exposed and charged into him, knocking him over. As Gater bundled over into the river embankment, his coat opened, exposing its contents. Joe caught sight of various metallic objects and weapons. Joe seized the opportunity and jumped on him, grabbing at whatever he could. As he scrambled for clues, Joe's mind started to race. He now knew for certain who had attacked Rachel. He was also certain that she was in Oslo. He had confirmed that Gater left her alive. And he grasped that, somehow, Gater was able to find her again.

Up ahead, Vera shouted back, "Who is coming up with me to van Gogh's bedroom? Was it Carl or Joe?" She turned and noticed Joe's absence. Immediately stopping the group, she gathered the tourists together.

"Again!? Where is Joe? Who saw Joe?"

Leonard, Carl, and Nellie shrugged, almost in chorus, as they scanned the tree line. Just then, Vera heard Gater, blinded and shrieking, as Joe grabbed for his weapons and gear. She sprinted and quickly found them mid-struggle at the river's edge.

"Stop!" she yelled as she drew her StunGun.

Seeing her with her StunGun drawn, Joe jumped backward to give Vera a clear shot at Gater. Gater, realizing the danger, immediately dived into the river moments before Vera fired. He disappeared beneath the water. Vera marched up to the river's edge, StunGun fully extended in front of her, poised to fire again. Joe quietly concealed the shiny objects he was able to take from Gater as he moved alongside her.

Vera ordered him, "Get behind me, Joe! Who was that guy? Was he a vagrant?"

Joe shrugged as he retreated and then headed back toward the group. Nellie and Carl immediately came over, concerned, patting him gently on the back. Leonard had a wild, excited look in his eyes, but also seemed a little jealous that Joe, and not him, had been attacked by a real-life nineteenth-century criminal.

Once Vera was calm and collected, they advanced again toward the Yellow House. Joe fingered the new gadgets hidden in his jacket. The main piece of equipment seemed to be a receiver or transmitter that fitted nicely in his hand. The others were a compact, but extremely strong baton and a small, titanium cylinder the size of his thumb. Squeezing and rubbing the new tech, he felt somewhat closer to Rachel.

RACHEL--1893

Rachel and Harry crept up the stairs leading back to the restaurant. The chains from the basement fell silent. Harry seemed unusually pale and dim. He smiled weakly at Rachel as they entered an empty room. The tables were all set, and many of them had half-eaten plates of tasty-looking food. Some chairs had been knocked over.

Eerily quiet, Rachel could not see a soul. Nobody at all. Just lots of delicious food. She knew she needed to replenish her energy, but strangely lacked any semblance of an appetite. She took a roll and a piece of fish on the way out. Casting a glance backward, she saw the maître d' trembling under the counter.

Of course! The crashing noises from the haunted basement. That will clear out a restaurant.

Harry turned to the cowering man. He whimpered as he tucked his head even tighter under his arms.

Outside again, Rachel wrote in her notebook.

I'll take U back to your spot.

Harry pointed

Thank you. Weak

As they left, three policemen arrived at the Gamle Rådhus, though none of them seemed keen to be the first to enter. She and Harry headed through Christiania Square, stopping to rest at the fountain and then, to Rachel's dismay, almost every block thereafter.

Rachel had been stuck in Oslo for approaching two days. Her left hand and forearm were flickering again. Harry looked as sickly as she could imagine a ghost looking. She wanted to get him back to safety and then she would go back to the museum to wait and watch. They progressed street by street, with Harry, barely visible, keeping to the shadows. Drawing no attention, they were soon back at the university. Sitting on a bench close by, resting one final time, Harry gestured for Rachel to open her notebook and started to point.

I didn't tell you everything

About what?

About becoming human again

What do U mean?

Harry told Rachel one final story. He reminded her of the time he had been trying to kill himself. Harry had tried everything. Nothing had worked. Harry had returned to his laboratory one evening, feeling desperate and despondent, when he heard a large wagon approaching. When the thundering horses were too close to evade him, Harry stepped in front of them. The horses reared up and tried to swerve at the last moment. The carriage jackknifed as the driver lost control. The carriage wheels snapped off and rolled to the side of the road. The driver was flung from his seat and landed headfirst with a gory crunch. When the dust settled, Harry heard a man whimpering from inside the carriage compartment. He nervously approached. The passenger, an old man, was struggling to free himself from the wreckage when he caught sight of Harry.

His mouth dropped wide open, and his eyes bulged out of their sockets with fright. Already weakened from the accident, he grabbed at his chest, as his heart began to fail. Choking and gasping for breath, he was in the throes of death. Harry put his arms out to help. After they passed through the dying man, Harry noticed a satisfying tingle in his fingertips. He drew one hand back and was startled to find that his thumb had become fleshier. The very life force that left the dying man, invigorated Harry.

Realizing what had happened, Harry fell on the man and restored his whole body. Thrilled, and full of hope, he immediately ran to the obvious time tourism hotspots, searching for a tour and a TourPod that could take him back. None came. And his body began to dematerialize swiftly thereafter. Harry finished telling her about his most successful haunting and paused. Rachel began to scrawl questions furiously.

How does it work?

You touch a dying person

Any dying person?

Sitting on the park bench, Harry told her everything that he knew. He figured out that he could become temporarily human again if he was around dying people precisely when their life was leaving them. So, he hung around hospitals. It was hard to time the moment precisely, and he tried to be discreet about it.

He made an ethical and practical decision not to haunt the operating rooms, which were generally full of surgeons and nurses anyway. He mostly waited near emergency rooms and hospices until he spotted a very ill person. Then he would locate their ward and bed and wait nearby until he sensed they were taking their last breaths. Harry told Rachel that he always felt terrible about the process. He often found himself apologizing and explaining to the terrified dying person that he was there to ease them through their final journey. Harry realized that it usually made matters worse for the suffering, and now mortally terrified, patient. In most cases, the process didn't work.

What makes it work?

You have to scare the person to death

I must kill them?

If you don't, you can't absorb vitality

Why did U stop?

It takes a toll

Conflicted, Rachel didn't know what to think. Something was amusing about picturing Harry bumble and apologize his way through the haunting of a terminally ill pensioner. But how could she ever do that? She would only eat lab-grown meat because she considered the slaughtered variety murder. And now, unless she was rescued very soon, she would have to kill a person to even stand a chance of going home. It seemed impossible. She would worry about it later. Right now, she still had time.

Harry, move it! Let's get you safe.

She pushed Harry to get going.

CHAPTER 18

The water was icy, and the current was ferocious. Gater thrashed his way back toward the riverbank. He sensed a large river barge was heading toward him. He tried to listen for Vera and the tour group. He knew their next site would be connected to Vincent van Gogh and wanted to find them quickly. His eyes were still burning, but the effects of the blinding gas had started to pass. The lights glowing from the street were still dim and shadowy. He ducked his head underwater and rubbed them again when he resurfaced. Blinking feverishly, the blurry lights began to take more shape. Just in time. The river barge captain blared his horn and screamed for Gater to get out of the way. Gater ducked underwater, narrowly avoiding the rusty hull, and swam furiously. He pulled himself to shore using a tree branch.

Breathing heavily, as he sat on the riverbank, he took stock of his equipment. He pulled out his laser gun, StunGun, garrote, PodCom, knuckle duster, PodCom control for the ship, karambit knife, Pocket Hologram, two transmitters…and that was all he had. Where was his TimeLocator? And where were his graphene baton and Universal Key? Gater's blood began to boil. No time to rest. He needed to find Joe before they got back to their ship. This time he would kill him. And anybody else who got in his way.

Gater took out his Pocket Hologram and searched for popular van Gogh tourist sites. He set off quickly in the direction he assumed that the tour group was heading. There were only two likely sites: the Yellow House or the Arena. The Yellow House was much closer. In fact, if Gater didn't run, he might miss them. So, Gater ran.

JOE--1889

Vera led the group toward the Yellow House. She explained how van Gogh had hoped to turn his room into a studio that he would share with Paul Gauguin, the great French Impressionist painter. Gauguin had come to stay with him for a while. They painted together, producing some masterpieces, but the relationship was tumultuous.

Gauguin never trusted van Gogh or his brother, suspecting them of exploiting him for his money. Van Gogh was greatly distressed when Gauguin decided to leave the Yellow House. He followed him out, brandishing a razor. Distraught, van Gogh returned to his bedroom and severed off part of his left ear. He wrapped it in paper and sent it to his favorite employee at the local brothel, a pretty, young cleaner known as Gabrielle.

Not surprisingly, and extremely responsibly, she forwarded it to the hospital where he was being treated. They were not able to reattach it. He returned to the house and was back and forth between his rented room and the hospital constantly after that.

Before they arrived, Vera left them with one delectable tidbit of information, "Between you and me, they say that Carlton Ming, the famous collector from New York, got hold of the ear before it was incinerated. If you are ever invited to view his private collection, he might show it to you."

She drew their attention to the building. It was not hard to notice.

There was a team of police and a hospital wagon standing stationary on the street outside. Angry residents were buzzing around, flailing their arms and pointing at protest signs. A large, angry woman and a meek, thin man stood at the front of the crowd of locals, facing off with the police. The woman was stabbing a page full of signatures with her chubby index finger and yelling.

"You need to take him away. We've collected thirty signatures. He's a redheaded madman!"

"Please, sirs. He clearly needs help. If the hospital can cure him, he is welcome to come back."

Standing on the fringes, the police seemed to resent the confrontation. The small group of citizens had started to chant, "Remove the redheaded madman! Remove the redheaded madman!"

The chanting got louder. Passersby interrupted their evening strolls to stand and watch. The crowd grew. A window in the building above the loudest participants silently opened and a bucket full of dirty water splashed on them, eliciting shrieks. The occupant, van Gogh, then screamed at the rabble below.

"They're trying to poison me. They are the criminals! Not me!"

The large woman looked up at him and yelled angrily. The crowd grew and got louder. More of the protesters turned to the police, heatedly demanding that they do something immediately. Van Gogh reappeared at the window. He was hurling down dirty rags, empty paint jars, and more buckets of water. He started singing loudly to drown out the chants from the demonstrators.

Vera turned to her group, amazed. She shouted to them so they could hear her, "This is incredible. Van Gogh is going to be evicted. We are going to see it! This is history in front of our eyes!"

Leonard wore his usual dumbstruck face. Nellie was a little frightened and had curled up against Carl. He was enjoying his protector role. Joe glanced up and immediately moved away and to the side, separating himself from his group. He reached into his coat and removed the graphene baton that he took from Gater earlier.

The scene was so filled with chaos, screaming, singing, and dirty water that none of them noticed Gater's arrival. Except Joe. Joe sensed him getting closer and positioned himself to ambush Gater before he could reach anybody else. He spotted him cautiously creeping and hiding behind the corner of the building.

The police would be a deterrent. Gater would have to be cautious to avoid them. Joe watched as he made his move and quietly started to follow. Gater drew his StunGun. Joe quietly drew near to him. As Gater took aim, silently and deliberately striding toward them, Joe sprinted and brought the baton down on his shoulder. Gater took his shot while simultaneously trying to twist out of the way of Joe's strike. He connected, snapping the bone with a crunch. But not before Gater's shot brought Vera crashing down and unconscious. Nellie saw Vera collapse and turned to find an enraged Gater, injured and seething. Carl instinctively pulled her backward to position himself between her and Gater, who now let out a loud cry and swung his gun around. He caught Joe on the side of his head, instantly knocking him out. Nellie wriggled out of Carl's grasp and ran to call for help. She slammed straight into a largest, and very bewildered policeman. He turned to face her, and she gestured wildly at her group. Gater was now standing over an unconscious Joe and Vera, his gun extended and pointing at Carl and Leonard.

The policeman blew his whistle shrilly, drawing the attention of all the other policemen present. Gater shot the StunGun, instantly knocking Carl unconscious. Leonard stood frozen with terror. Two policemen fumbled uselessly for their revolvers. Another policeman threw his arms to his sides, not knowing where to run first. Three older, more experienced policemen pulled their guns out. One yelled, "Halt!" The demonstrators were silent. Even van Gogh had stopped singing.

He pulled out his karambit knife and crouched over Joe.

The police chief yelled again, "Halt!" and fired, wounding Gater again in his already broken arm. Gater cried out. Hearing a loud gunshot, the onlookers shrieked and ducked. Gater leaped up and ran, disappearing into the trees. The policemen yelled and pointed and then stood back conferring. Their suspect was gone, leaving only a thin trail of blood. Two of the policemen walked over to Joe, Vera, and Carl. Nellie had also run over to check on Carl. The onlookers began to chatter excitedly.

And then, van Gogh began to scream again, "He was coming for me! He was coming for me!"

The protesters, reminded of the crazy artist in their midst, started to chant. Several of the policemen stepped into the building, heading up to van Gogh's bedroom. He sang and threw more paint tins out of his window. The police chief pulled Nellie and Leonard, the two conscious witnesses, to the side to begin interrogating them. His deputies were carrying the limp bodies of Carl, Vera, and Joe to the hospital wagon.

"Did you recognize that man?"

Nellie shook her head.

"No?"

She shook her head again. Leonard, still shocked, was silent.

"Why did he attack you?"

Nellie shrugged.

"Why did he attack you?" the policeman repeated.

Nellie shrugged again. Leonard just stared, mouth agape.

"Can't you talk? I am asking you questions?"

Nellie tried to indicate that she couldn't talk.

"Are you both simple? Are you unable to speak?"

Nellie waved her arms animatedly, trying to indicate that she could. Leonard started shaking his head, playing over the events of Gater pointing a gun at him.

The police chief turned to a deputy. "They are mental cases. Put them in the wagon as well."

The policeman who had entered the building returned with Van Gogh. Clearly feeling defeated, he was subdued. He bowed his bandaged head, glancing sideways at some of his neighbors, offering a weak apology. The police marched him to the hospital wagon and put him inside with the tour group. The police chief walked around to the driver.

"Best take them to the insane asylum. To Saint-Paul de Mausole asylum. They are all nuts."

The police chief slapped the horse on its side gently, and the wagon set off on its two-hour journey.

MILO--1975

Wanda stood behind Milo, firmly gripping his arms behind his back in a lock. Dmitri loomed before him, StunGun extended, lips curled in triumphant glee.

"You saw something we didn't want you to see," Dmitri said ominously.

Milo arched backwards to gauge Wanda's strength. He could almost reach one of his nanotech vials. Extending his fingers, he touched his pocket.

Milo asked, "We're not here to see Aretha Franklin, are we?"

Dmitri shook his head as he grinned. "No, we aren't," Wanda added.

"This is about Jimmy Hoffa, isn't it?"

They were both quiet.

"He was the famous trade union boss. He disappears today. His body was never found. His murder was never solved. Nobody has ever figured out what happened to him. Is that what you are doing here?"

Dmitri asked, "Should I shoot him now?"

Milo continued, "You want to bring groups to the scene of the crime. You've placed a transmitter by the restaurant, so your TourPods can travel right here. To watch the crime?"

Dmitri smirked at Wanda. Milo was puzzled. Was there more?

Milo needed time. He could just about touch the vial with his middle finger. If he could get it between the mid finger and his index finger, he would be able to grasp it and use it.

Milo commented, "You know…I think you're doing it wrong."

"Doing what wrong?" Wanda asked. She gripped him more tightly.

"Well, the way you are doing it, you're going to have to plant a transmitting device at every site you want to visit. It will take years to do." He almost had it…

"Who the hell do you think you are? Wait. Dmitri. He's wasting time. Shoot him now."

Milo grasped the vial with the tips of his fingers. He pulled it out of his pocket and squeezed as hard as he could, cracking the glass. The gas crackled as it reacted with the air, releasing a blinding, thick gas that engulfed Wanda and Milo. Wanda began to cough as Dmitri's meaty hand reached for his eyes.

She relaxed her grip long enough for Milo to break free. He pivoted behind her back to the parking lot as he reached for another vial from his pocket. Pulling a handful out, he searched through them as he sprinted. Wanda lay sprawled on the ground hacking, but Dmitri was already in hot pursuit. Milo found a pale-blue gassy mix. Dmitri, an athlete, was considerably faster and catching up to him fast.

Milo shoved the other vials back in his pocket and pushed the blue one against his clothing forcefully until it cracked. The solution soaked a small part of his jacket and then rapidly spread to cover his clothes. To Dmitri's shock, Milo began to disappear. The solution made the sunlight bend around him. It looked like he was wearing his background. Perfectly camouflaged. Dmitri could make out Milo's head as it bobbed up and down with his gait, but even that was tricky.

Milo reached the first row of cars and ducked. He crouched down while pulling his jacket collar up over his head and ran along the rows. Dmitri advanced slowly, scared to pass him. Milo was cars ahead of him now. He approached a red Ford Gran Torino at the end of the third row, slowly opened the driver's door, and silently climbed in. Pulling out his Universal Key, he placed it against the ignition. Then he waited until Dmitri was closer. Paranoid, Dmitri made his way up and down the rows of cars, scrutinizing every patch of gravel and looking under each hood.

He rounded the corner and entered the row of cars in front of Milo's row. Milo started the ignition and pumped the gas pedal, creating a growling roar. Dmitri startled, looked up, unable to distinguish which car had roared to life. He approached cautiously, squinting through all the windshields. As he got close enough, Milo floored the accelerator. The car screeched forward, speeding into Dmitri and ramming him into a Chevrolet shorty van. Dmitri groaned. Blood seeping from his mouth, his head flopped to the side.

Milo ducked back into his seat, glancing around nervously to see if anyone had witnessed the event. Dmitri's eyes closed as he choked. Now, to find Wanda.

He headed back to the restaurant, stopping to let a topless Chevrolet Caprice filled with shady mobsters drive past him. He calmly walked around the restaurant to the side where he'd left her. She was standing inches away from the corner with her StunGun drawn, eyes still puffy and bloodshot, waiting to blast whoever came near her. Wanda hadn't seen him yet. He quickly stepped back around the corner and began to taunt her.

"You sure you want to do this, Wanda?"

He heard her jerk to attention. She shot her StunGun carelessly in his direction, missing him completely. Milo figured she had planned to stun him unconscious and leave him here to fade away.

"I'll leave you alone if you put your gun down," he pressed. She shifted about nervously, squinting down the passage. Milo adjusted his position so that he could see her better. He watched as she carefully approached the corner, pounced forward, and wildly shot another blast from her StunGun into thin air. He crept behind her as she stood, confused. Then he strolled up to her from behind, took hold of her head with both hands, and rammed it against the metal awning. It made a dull clunking sound, and she collapsed to the floor, lifeless. Milo leaned over and checked her breathing. She was still alive.

Now, how would he get home?

CHAPTER 19

JOE--1889

Joe stirred and groggily opened his eyes. His right cheek and ear thumped with a dull pain. He grabbed the side of his head to ease the throbbing. He was lying on the floor of a wooden wagon, covered by scratchy, brown sack cloth. Propping himself up on his elbows, he looked around, shielding his tender right eye. A very drunk man sat opposite him, clutching a wounded arm. Next to him was one of the policemen from the Yellow House demonstration.

Carl was lying next to him, still out cold, and Nellie was cradling his head. Vera was flat on her back. She lay at the back with her head rhythmically bumping against a side panel as the wagon wobbled and rocked over the uneven gravel road. A small puddle of drool bubbled from her mouth, darkening the corner of the stiff, light-green blanket that somebody had wrapped around her. Leonard sat on a bench with his typical stunned expression, his eyes staring straight ahead and occasionally darting to the side.

Following his eyes, Joe cast his attention to the back and noticed van Gogh sitting downcast, head bowed in his hands. Can't be. He blinked and took a second look. Vincent van Gogh was definitely in the wagon with them. Leonard gawked at him for the fiftieth time. He was giggling.

Had Vera been awake, this would most likely be the highlight of her entire life as a tour guide, and she was sleeping through it. Van Gogh groaned softly and raised his eyes. Joe held his gaze. He seemed tortured, betrayed, and deeply depressed. Joe nodded to him and smiled weakly. He felt an indescribable urge to offer hope. Joe would have told van Gogh that some of his greatest works were yet to be painted. That he would recover and be happy again.

But Joe knew that van Gogh would take his own life in little over a year. That he would never really know love or even tranquility. Joe understood why the TTA mandated that time travelers have their voices suppressed. If Joe were to tell van Gogh what lay ahead for him, that he would be known as one of the world's greatest artists posthumously, would it change his life? Perhaps he would have committed suicide earlier? Would he stop painting? Would he change his life and deprive the world of some of its greatest artworks?

But by talking to him kindly, maybe Joe could make a tortured soul a little bit happier. Milo told him that no scientist had ever conclusively discovered the effects of changing the past. People used to believe in the butterfly effect. That killing one butterfly could irreversibly alter the future, destroying timelines. But nobody really believed that anymore. Current wisdom states that if van Gogh were to stop painting, somebody else's artworks would hang in the great museums where his used to hang. They might even be the same paintings with a different signature in the bottom corner.

The real reason the TTA didn't want tourists speaking to the locals was so as not to frighten or torment them with crazy stories and predictions. And so that the tourists would be locked up in insane asylums and then into ghosts. And, here he was, on the way to an asylum…

Joe and van Gogh studied each other for what seemed like hours. van Gogh seemed desperately lonely, and Joe was happy to provide the companionship, even if it was with a shared silence. The wagon violently shuddered over a ditch, disrupting the moment and van Gogh slowly lowered his eyes, refocusing on his upturned palms.

The wagon slowed, with the sound of a metal gate unlocking. Guards waved the wagon driver through into a walled compound. The horses neighed and started trotting forward again. Carl stirred, though Vera, who had caught the force of Gater's StunGun directly in her face, was still completely unresponsive.

The wagon came to a stop, and some orderlies from the asylum unbolted the wagon door and swung it open. The passengers ravenously snorted in the fresh air as they stood up to stretch. Joe helped Carl to his feet and then, with Nellie, steadied him to the back of the carriage. All the sentient passengers climbed out into the frosty grounds, while two orderlies went in to fetch Vera. Once they were assembled, the Chief Psychiatrist, Marceau, a stern-looking man with red hair and a scar down his left cheek, offered a curt welcome.

"You are now standing in the central courtyard of Saint-Paul Asylum. An orderly will shortly take you to your dormitories. You must immediately go to sleep. If you do not go to sleep, we will administer drugs and treatment to help you fall asleep. Tomorrow morning, you will be woken at 6:00 a.m. to be showered and deloused. You will then be evaluated by a psychiatrist and your treatment prescribed. If you are rowdy, you will be placed in a solitary cell and restrained until you are quiet. Is that understood?"

The orderlies then forcibly steered the new patients toward the wards, separating Nellie from the rest of the group. She resisted passionately, sobbing as she tried to re-join Carl. The orderlies grabbed her firmly and pulled her toward the women's section.

The men were herded indoors and upstairs. Groaning, snoring, and the occasional stifled scream polluted the otherwise deathly silent passages. They halted in front of a dull metal door, guarding the silent holding cell within. The orderly unlocked the door and gestured harshly for everybody to enter, to find an empty bed, and to shut up.

Joe wandered in and found himself a creaky, stained mattrass in the far corner. Van Gogh followed him in and wordlessly took the bed closest to his.

MILO--1975

Wanda lay motionless, still clutching her StunGun tightly to her bosom. Her brightly colored, crocheted, woolen lantern hat had fallen off her head and lay on the floor next to her oversized Dooney & Bourke zebra-print bag.

Milo crouched and opened her bag, emptying the contents onto the floor. He sifted through the pile of knick-knacks. She had bright-pink lipstick, a large, leopard-print wallet containing US bank notes from various decades, a mirror, a switchblade, a plastic spider, loose coins, a packet of bubble gum, tweezers, a pocket processor, a fake moustache, a small bottle of whiskey, a hammer, a PodCom, and a small book of Nepalese poetry. Milo helped himself to a stick of her gum and took her PodCom, raising it to his mouth.

"Vonnegut. Hello. Are you there?"

Freddy answered him almost immediately.

"I'm here. Who is this? Dmitri?"

"No. Its Milo, the TTA agent. Wanda was injured. It's a long story. She is with me. She is going to be all right. Can you come fetch us?"

"Sure. What happened? Where is Dmitri?"

"Dmitri is sorting out a problem. Just come now. Meet us at the back of the Machus Red Fox restaurant. It's clear. I'll tell you everything. Just hurry."

Milo disconnected. He put Wanda's possessions back in her bag, keeping only the PodCom and slung her over his shoulder. After considering, he pocketed the poetry book as well. Then he walked to the back and waited for Freddy, who arrived moments later. The Vonnegut was well camouflaged. Milo could only tell it had arrived when he opened the hatch and stepped out. Freddy lingered nervously by the entrance.

"What happened?" Freddy said, blocking Milo's way onto the ship.

Milo started to explain. "Wanda tried to pay the restaurant with bills that haven't been printed yet. It got ugly. The Mafia guys who run the place cornered her and took her to a back room. She took a huge blow to the head when she pulled out her StunGun. Dmitri saved her life. He is just taking care of the last of them. He will be here any moment."

"OK," Freddy acquiesced. He was shifting from side to side. Milo could sense his distrust. "But wait." Freddy continued, "Is Dmitri still inside the restaurant? Should we go in and help him?"

"Yeah," Milo agreed, shrugging and fast running out of patience. "It's your call."

He lowered Wanda onto the floor. Then he pulled out his StunGun and shot him.

Freddy wounded and offended, gave a last, sorrowful gaze, and then collapsed onto the floor. Milo tucked his StunGun back into his jacket and leaned over again to lift Wanda over his shoulder. He staggered a little as he carried her onboard. Throwing her down onto her bed, he tied her down firmly with graphene cable. Then he went back out through the hatch.

While grabbing Freddy's arms, he noticed three of the restaurant patrons from the parking lot staring at him.

Oh great. Just perfect.

Two heavyset, hairy men wearing oversized watches approached him cautiously. The ship was heavily camouflaged, though the entrance was open, and the ramp was extended. To a pair of seventies-era mafiosi, this weird silver tongue extending from a dark orifice must have resembled the cover of a heavy metal album brought to life.

Milo rose quickly. Reaching into the Vonnegut, he found the control console by the entrance and swiped the hatch shut, simultaneously retracting the ramp. The two men froze in their tracks, bewildered. Milo approached them grinning, as they tried, faces screwed up in thought, to process the spectacle. He reached them with his arms wide open.

"Hi," he greeted.

Their jackets strained open, barely containing their bulky frames, exposed gleaming gold chains against their hairy chests. The grips of their guns subtly protruded from beneath the fabric.

"What's goin' on here?" the larger man, wearing a white suit, asked.

"Who is dat guy on the floor there? And what was dat thing?" the other added.

"Well," Milo began, "that's my friend over there. I think he ate something that didn't agree with him, and we were just getting some fresh air."

The two men looked uneasily at each other.

"He looks pretty bad. Looks like you iced him."

"I don't like it," the other cautioned his friend, moving his jacket aside to expose his gun.

"Dat looks like one of dem UFOs!" the hairier thug exclaimed, pointing at the faint, shimmering Vonnegut.

Milo smiled reassuringly. As he surreptitiously reached for his StunGun, he tried to keep the situation calm. "Everything is fine. My friend is fine. Look over at him. He is just lying down to do some breathing exercises."

They arched over to look more closely at Freddy on the floor, giving Milo the gap he needed. He pulled out the StunGun and blasted a wave at the two heavies. They both collapsed weightily onto the ground. Milo pulled out another handful of his vials and searched through them, finding a light-yellow one. He cracked it open and poured a tiny amount of nano-solution onto each of their lips. It quickly ran into their mouths and disappeared, erasing their short-term memories.

Then he ran back to attend to Freddy, who was painfully heavier than Wanda. He reached into Freddy's pocket and searched for the PodCom so that he could open the hatch again. Milo dragged him onboard by his feet, cursing apologetically as Freddy's head bumped against the ramp and then against the common room table.

Milo threw him onto the bed and secured him. Then he hastily jumped into the cockpit chair to report to Barrett. He activated the navigation and communications systems and left a message.

"I am coming in soon. You'll need to do a bit of cleaning up. I have an unconscious pilot and tour guide on board. I had to leave one of their guys behind. It's going to get a bit crazy for you to deal with."

The Vonnegut blasted off with a whoosh and a crackle. He'd head back to Dark History. But he needed to take care of some personal business first. Good that he was alone.

RACHEL--1893

Rachel saw Harry all the way to the basement of the university science building. When they were outside his room, she pulled out her notepad. She had to take a few minutes to get her hand working again, before writing to him.

I will come back for you. Whatever happens.

Harry looked older and fainter, though his chin was up, and he seemed more confident. He pointed at her table of letters.

Glad I could help you. Have a good life

He offered Rachel a smile. Rachel drew nearer to him as if to hug him. It was impossible.

She stepped back, cupped her hands together in gratitude, and wiped a tear away from her eye with her filthy sleeve. Then she turned and headed back along the musty corridor as Harry floated through the walls and back to his dark corner of the laboratory. More than anything, ghosts were lonely. While Agnes's isolation manifested itself as a desperate rage that sustained her, Harry was sinking into a depression and would ultimately fade away. Rachel would not judge either of them.

She sprinted out of the building. Her ghosting was happening much faster now. She had to wait until students opened doors for themselves and then slip out behind them. The left side of her face had lost all its sensation. Both of her feet were shimmering. Her left hand, which she had restored moments ago, was already ghosting again. Rachel bolted through the exit door and back onto the street, heading to the center of town and the museum where she was sure future tours would come. Before she had covered a hundred yards, a man across the street called out to her in a high-pitched, nasal voice.

"Excuse me. Hello there!"

Rachel turned. He had already started to cross the street and was fast approaching her, taking unusually wide strides. Rachel held out her arms, conveying surprise. What did he want? The man seemed creepy. His voice was shrill and stuffy, like his nose was blocked. She instinctively backed away. He persisted.

"Yes. Thank you and sorry to inconvenience. I couldn't help but sense that you might be able to help me find somebody."

Rachel shrugged and gestured, conveying to him that she wasn't from there.

"Ahh yes. You're not from these parts. Well, neither was I. You see…I heard there is an old man that, shall we say, haunts the halls of this university. And I'd like to find him."

Rachel froze. Could he be talking about Harry? She stared at his face trying to work out what he knew. He stared back mockingly, mouth smirking and slightly agape. He was an unremarkable-looking man with a neat beard, a monocle over his left eye but there was a darkness that seemed to lurk deep within him like a noxious gas.

"Lars Norstrom is the name. And I sense we have something in common. You see, I could smell you from all the way over there. I think you were on a tour just like me. And you got stranded here, just like me. Only, my tour left me here to die. And you still seem a little bit alive."

Rachel's heart sank into her gut. Lars was the demon Agnes had told her about. The monster that she and Harry had been hiding from. He was the tourist in Agnes's group who was killed in the fire. Agnes said he had possessed somebody. That he was a demon. He liked to tear ghosts apart. She looked past him, for a gap to get far away. Lars read her mind immediately.

"Oh, don't worry. I am not here to see you. You see, you're way too fleshy for me. No. I'd like to surprise the old man with a visit. I'll find him anyway if you won't do me the kindness of taking me to him. But if you won't, I am sure I will bump into you again soon. And I doubt I will be this polite and gracious next time."

Rachel pulled out her notebook and indicated that she couldn't talk and needed to write to him. He nodded respectfully.

"Yes of course. What is it you'd like to say?"

The old man is gone. I can take you to Agnes.

Lars looked annoyed for a moment. A raging fire seemed to well up inside of him. He quickly suppressed it as he turned back to Rachel, politely.

"Agnes. I've not seen her in ages. Yes. She would be a delightful treat."

CHAPTER 20

MILO--2130

Milo gently steered the Vonnegut toward the terminal building, glancing backward at Wanda and Freddy, who were still out cold and securely tied to their beds. Milo cruised in and followed the docking drone as it directed him to an empty bay at the back of the cavernous hangar. He inserted his external drive into the navigation system and scrolled to the trip log.

It took him a few minutes to override the password protections and firewalls before he downloaded the travel history.

He searched through Dmitri's compartment and found a bag. Rifling through his equipment, Milo found another time transmitter disk tucked behind some horrendously sharp and jagged blades. He stuffed it in his bag, making sure not to damage the frozen tubes he had hidden in the false bottom. Before disembarking, he found two more yellow vials. He went over to Wanda and Freddy and sprinkled the contents onto each of their lips. As the doors opened, he was met by Vinod and two Dark History ground crew.

"Welcome back, Mr. Morton. How was your inspection?"

Milo continued to walk, answering only when they were behind him.

"Very interesting. Thank you. Your pilot and tour guide are still asleep. I'm not sure where the security guy got to."

"Asleep? How do you mean?" Vinod queried him and craned his head to look inside the Vonnegut. Milo didn't hang around.

"We logged another jump, to ancient Greece, Mr. Morton…"

Milo called over his shoulder as he left the hangar. "Must be a technical glitch."

He caught a Bubble to the SlingShot station and quickly made his way to Barrett on the ninetieth floor of the TTA headquarters in Rochester, New York. Shadows lengthened as the day waned, painting the peaceful city with an amber and deepening light. It was late Thursday afternoon. He thought about Joe and Rachel as the elevator climbed. She didn't have much time.

"Yulia, how are you?"

She glanced up from her ClipScreen, pleased to see him.

"Hello, Mr. Morton. Superintendent Barrett is in his office. Do you want a drink while I let him know you're here?"

"Thank you. A tall black Finca El Injerto please. With a touch of warm buffalo milk."

Over Yulia's objections, he passed her, knocked, and barged in. Barrett showed him to a seat in his cluttered office.

"I got your message Milo. Seems like things got out of control?"

Milo took out his PocketHolo and dropped the time transmitter disk on Barrett's desk.

"We arrived in Detroit 1975. The tour guide told me that it was a music history tour, even though there wasn't anything interesting going on in 1975 Detroit. It didn't take me long to realize that they were there for the unsolved Jimmy Hoffa kidnapping and murder. I saw their security guy burying one of these at the site where Hoffa disappeared."

Barrett picked up the disk and turned it over in his hands. It was paper-thin and made of graphene. Completely flat, it had no markings or indentations.

"The security guy caught me spying on him and attacked me. I might have killed him. I also knocked out the guide and pilot. I could see they were up to something that the TTA doesn't know about."

Barrett was pulling and bending the disk with both hands and grunted as he tried to twist it. He resolved to send it to the lab to be examined.

"These things are interesting. I think they let you lock onto a specific transmission so that you can navigate directly to events. I could have used these when I was in the business," Milo added.

Barrett's eyebrows arched.

"This alone is a clear breach of regulations. Specifically, 5.1a, which outlaws the use of any nonapproved technologies that will allow a navigation system to target a specific historical event. If they have been planting these transmitters all over the place, and all through time, they put the entire time tourism franchise at risk."

Milo agreed. "But I got a feeling that there was more going on. I can't explain it. The tour guide and security guy were looking at each other like they were enjoying a secret that I hadn't figured out."

"Fine," Barrett responded, "I can only report facts. If we find out more, I will update the Compliance and Oversight Committee. Thank you, Milo." Barrett stood up and offered his hand.

Milo took it firmly. "I think a little added danger pay is in order."

"First, let's find out how much damage you did," Barrett retorted.

JOE--1889

Joe lay in his bed until he was certain the orderlies had left. The door was locked. Fortunately, nobody had thought to search him. He still had Gater's weapons and gadgets.

Carl shifted around in his bed with his head in his hands, distressed over Nellie, who had been separated from the group. Leonard was fast asleep and snoring rhythmically. Joe looked over at van Gogh in the bed beside him, who lay stiffly on his back with his eyes wide open. Joe took

Gater's receiver from his pocket. Flipping it around, he studied it briefly and activated the screen. It displayed a meaningless list of numbers, scrolling options, and 4 dimensional maps that he could not make head or tale of. He put it back in his pocket and took out the small, flat titanium block.

Joe squeezed the sides, causing a small metal tube to emerge from the center. It was a Universal Key—he'd seen these before in Milo's office. Perfect for breaking everybody out of the ward. He arched up and looked around, wondering if anybody else saw it. He needed a plan. And coming up with plans wasn't his strength. He was better at following them or analyzing why they wouldn't work. He thought of Doctor Marceau as well as all the orderlies and guards. The dormitories surely were a maze filled with locked doors and unstable, unpredictable patients. The location was remote, and the gates would be guarded and bolted shut. As he thought about the mess he was in, Vera and the galloping horses flashed through his mind. He had hesitated too long in Paris and Vera was almost trampled under a wagon. He could not procrastinate again.

Joe threw the blanket off and rose to his feet. He looked at van Gogh, who was watching him lazily. Carl saw Joe on his feet and climbed unsteadily off his bed. Joe motioned him to wake Leonard. Then he walked over to van Gogh, now sitting upright. Joe smiled reassuringly. They nodded at each other, and van Gogh lay back down and rolled onto his side, facing away, to sleep.

Joe felt the prickle at the back of his neck intensify. His hair was standing on end so severely it felt like it was trying to escape his scalp. He saw dreamlike visions of the asylum guards shuffling around the grounds and felt the strongest premonition that the corridor on the other side of the door was clear. By holding the Universal Key in front of the lock and squeezing gently, the central tube extended into the keyhole, turned, and swiveled. The internal bolts clanged softly and retracted. Carl and a groggy Leonard joined him. Joe twisted the handle and slowly opened the door. All clear. They hurried out. With prickles running down his spine, he reached for his baton, holding it firmly.

With each step that Joe took down the passage, the tingling intensified. His fingertips felt like they might explode. Small sparks flew off his hands when he touched them to his clothing. After running two hundred feet, he couldn't continue. Something was clearly wrong. Leonard, huffing, grabbed him by the shoulder – forehead creased with concerned limes. Joe shrugged. Maybe they were going the wrong way. He turned around and gingerly stepped back toward their ward. The prickling began to subside. Joe sped up to a jog, and Leonard and Carl, clearly confused, followed him. Groans and sobbing from behind every locked metal door that they passed made Carl shudder. They were heading even deeper into the dormitory section and away from the exits. The passages ahead were clear. They came to a staircase. Joe paused and faltered. Then he led them up to the next level. His prickling and sparking were manageable.

As they ran, Joe noticed that the crying and shrieking from the dormitories were now all female. He had found the women's section. As they rounded a corner, they ran into an orderly pushing a female patient strapped onto a gurney.

Dumbfounded, the orderly searched for his whistle and blew it shrilly. Carl skidded, lost his footing, and crashed into the wall. Leonard froze. Surprising himself, Joe sped up, baton raised, and brought it down heavily onto the orderly's head before he could put his whistle to his lips and blow again. He collapsed in a heap next to the gurney. Patients behind the doors began to shriek louder as they heard the commotion in the passage. The bound patient moaned, her eyes staring vacantly ahead.

Joe motioned for Carl and Leonard to follow quickly as he continued down the passage. He let the tingling in his spine guide him. As they passed a rusting blue door, the prickles intensified. Joe came to a stop and turned around. Nellie was nearby. He headed back to the door.

Pulling out his Universal Key, he swiped it over the lock and squeezed it. The door opened effortlessly. Nellie, red-eyed and sobbing on a filthy mattrass, rushed to Joe. She saw Carl standing behind and embraced him tightly. An ancient-looking woman with a toothless cackle started to bang her fists against the metal frame of her bed.

Vera, by the grim, barred window, sat up, groggy and bewildered. Joe hurried over and helped her out of her bed. She slipped her shoes on and wobbled out of the room with them, hanging on to Joe's arm. Banging, yelling, and the clattering of boots on the stone floors told Joe that the asylum guards were approaching. They would be heading this way imminently. He motioned for Leonard, Carl, and Nellie to step back into the room and locked the door. Moments later, the door handle rattled and shook as the guards tested the door, searching for the culprits who had attacked the orderly in the corridor. The old woman began to shriek and wail. Nellie hurried over and covered her mouth firmly. The guards outside hesitated and tested the door a second time. Finding their room locked, they moved on.

Joe waited until it was quiet again and reopened the door. Then he led the group toward the stairwells, through a heavy steel door and out of the building, ducking to avoid guards as Carl and Leonard supported Vera, who was still slipping in and out of consciousness.

The full moon illuminated the cold, muddy courtyard, framed by the sad, gray dormitories. Scrawny, naked trees shivered and swayed in consonance with the stinging predawn breeze. Joe led them to a cove between the buildings, and they huddled against the bare walls, watching a macabre display in the courtyard. A circle of wretched, tired men in gray rags were assembled in a circle, marching slowly one behind the other. Like the walking dead, eyes vacant, mouths agape and drooling, they trod slowly onward, getting nowhere. Joe took Vera's PodCom and transmitted an emergency signal, hoping that Ash would pick it up. Then they waited, hiding and ducking for cover when guards passed.

After several eternal minutes, Vera's PodCom vibrated. Joe spotted the well-camouflaged Crichton up above as it gently descended. He timed their run carefully, holding the group back as he sensed guards approaching. When the passage was clear, he hurried the group forward, and they boarded. Ash closed the hatch and glided upward. They were safe for now.

SHINER--1893

Gater had tied Shiner securely to his bed. His wrists were bound and fastened above his head, and his legs and torso were wrapped and tied to his cot with graphene cable. The only way he would be able to free himself was if he could wriggle a hand from its tight binding. He pulled and twisted his hands downward, cutting the flesh, until blood from his wrist lubricated his skin. He cupped his palm by bending his thumb toward his baby finger, shrinking his hand size as much as he could, and tried to force it through the wire binding.

Again, and again he tried to jam it through, gritting his teeth each time. The pain was excruciating. He paused to steady his pulse and remembered all the bones he had broken in his life. He had lost count. This was nothing. Shiner steeled himself, and then he screamed and jerked his hand downward with as much force as he could muster. His hand broke free, though he left a chunk of flesh behind, still gruesomely attached to the graphene wire. Shiner lay in agony for a few seconds. Then he reached over to unfasten the rest of the cable. *Gater will pay with ten times as much flesh*, he thought.

Once freed, he hurried over to the medical cupboard, dripping blood behind him. With shaky hands, he disinfected the wound, applied a healing agent, and scanned it with the FirstAid rod, watching impatiently as the flesh knit back together. Then he headed to the cockpit to locate the Crichton. It was twenty miles northeast. A PodCom was missing from its cradle. Shiner reasoned that Gater must have taken it, and he was still in Arles. He tracked the PodCom easily. Gater was moving slowly away from the city center toward the river.

GATER--1889

Shot and bleeding, Gater collapsed behind a thicket near the Yellow House, consciousness slipping away. Fortunately, the police had not followed him and he regained consciousness unmolested. He made a tourniquet from his torn jacket to bandage his arm. Then he hurried to the city outskirts.

At a clearing surrounded by old mulberry trees, he pulled out his PodCom and summoned the DualPod, directing it to his position. He surveyed the area again as the ship approached, making sure he was alone. The heavily camouflaged ship gradually descended until it was hovering almost overhead. Gater entered the landing sequence, but the ship didn't descend. Strange. Gater was losing his patience. He calmed himself and punched in the sequence a second time. Yet again, the ship was unresponsive. He smacked the PodCom against his thigh and started to enter the sequence a third time when a red bar on the screen flashed, indicating the connection was lost. A pang of concern shot through Gater's gut as he rebooted. Something was going on. He glanced up at the ship as it finally descended and turned. The camouflage veneer faded as the DualPod glided down towards Gater, bringing him face-to-face with Shiner, seated in the cockpit.

Shiner grinned at Gater as he held the ship in place. Gater glowered at him.

"This is no time for games, Shiner. Land the ship and let me in."

Shiner sat back, mockingly offended. "We are way past playing games, Gater. You could have killed me. I was lucky to free myself."

Gater baulked. "Killed you. What are you talking about? I had to sideline you so that I could get my job done. You were perfectly safe on the ship. Now, let me onboard!"

"And did you deal with Joe yet? Is he dead?"

"I came close. The police interfered, and he got away. Now stop wasting time so I can finish it."

"You still couldn't kill him? I guess the guys overrated you."

"Enough!" Gater yelled, losing his temper. "Let me on board now!"

"You still haven't apologized for tying me up and forcing me to tear off a piece of my palm."

Gater scowled. He could taste the hatred. Shiner locked eyes with him coolly, betraying no emotion.

"It looks like they aren't in Arles anymore. I will find him. If I have time after I have finished the job that you couldn't, I might come back for you. But maybe not."

Gater pulled out his plasma gun hopelessly, threatening Shiner. Shiner derisively saluted, laughed, and steered the DualPod back above the clouds. He locked in on the Crichton and shot off with a whoosh, leaving Gater mid tantrum in the dreary clearing.

As he watched the ship disappear, Gater knew that Shiner wouldn't return. He would not have if the roles were reversed. He needed to hitch a ride with another TourPod. Something nobody had ever succeeded in doing before. His hatred would drive him. He would not fail. And Shiner would meet his wrath.

CHAPTER 21

RACHEL--1893

Lars stank of malevolence. Beneath his well-groomed exterior and his slow, well-measured stride, Rachel sensed a wickedness bursting to escape. He kept no more than a yard of sidewalk between them at all times.

Rachel led Lars down Rosenkrantz Street toward the city center. They would be at the old restaurant where Agnes was hiding within ten minutes if she kept up the pace. Lars didn't seem rushed, though she sensed his excitement at tormenting Agnes.

"I haven't seen Agnes for two hundred years," he exclaimed with a yearning. "I expect she will be so surprised to see me."

Rachel knew the horror he would bring. She recalled, Agnes recounting how Lars had devoured her friend. Demons fed on ghosts, among other things. Lars seemed to have a particular appetite for her now.

Rachel had no warm feelings for Agnes. She had tried to trap Rachel in her basement and keep her there forever. But she didn't want to bring Agnes into harm's way. Agnes may have been selfish and cruel. But she was lonely, not evil. Bringing Lars to her basement would doom her to suffering, torment, and a gruesome end. Rachel decided to lead Lars away from Agnes as well. She knew he could sense ghosts. His powers to find them were not strong, but he would know if Rachel was leading him astray. Rachel did not want to make him any angrier. She felt stuck.

"How long have you been here, Rachel?" Lars asked.

She held up a finger.

"Well, you're still mostly flesh and blood. So, I am guessing you mean a day." He squealed. "Ooh, you will be a ghost soon too."

Rachel glanced at him. Being alone with Lars was the first experience in this entire ordeal that truly terrified Rachel. She dared not antagonize him, so she lowered her gaze and focused on moving forward. She had no plan or destination, but she knew she could not 'live' with herself, if she brought Lars to Agnes. She had to lead him away. She headed straight, passing the intersecting streets that ran toward the center and the restaurants. Walking swiftly, and with false purpose, she led him further and further away. The lamplights were on now and their glow cast long, haunting shadows on the cobblestones. Bundled-up pedestrians hurried past, their breath visible in the frosty dusk.

"Rachel, I am not sensing that we are near Agnes. Normally, I get the faintest feeling. It's no stronger now than before."

Rachel shrugged. She indicated to Lars that they would be there soon. Lars reached his hand out and placed it on her shoulder to stop her. His grip was icy cold. He stared at her for a moment and Rachel caught a red glimmer behind his eyes.

"I do hope that you aren't leading me on a wild goose chase. You wouldn't want to be alone with me if I don't get what I came for." Lars paused and then leaned his head back and let out a bellowing laugh. His mouth was pitch-black with small, pointy teeth; his tongue darted outward as he lowered his head back and regained composure. He caught his breath and then waved Rachel onward.

"Let's continue now. I am just hungry. That's all."

The sun had almost set, a final reddish glow lingering. Rachel headed forward again with Lars close behind her. She could hear him breathing, a soft, rasping heave that seemed to suppress a faint, whimpering cry. They passed a group of sailors. Rachel thought for a moment about running toward them. They would surely protect her from Lars, if they thought he had taken her against her will.

Lars must have sensed her plan and placed his icy hand on her shoulder again. Rachel pressed on, each step amplifying the creeping terror that clawed at her insides. She could feel they were approaching the coast. They would soon arrive at the Pipervika Harbor. Lars would surely realize that she was not taking him to Agnes, and he would kill her. Painfully. She had minutes to escape. With each step, she scanned the sidewalk for something she could use to attack him. If she could catch him by surprise and knock him over, she might be able to run for help.

They neared the water's edge, and Rachel's frantic search had yielded nothing. It was now or never. Lars loomed menacingly behind her. He was about to ask her where Agnes was again. Probably for the last time. She glanced sideways as though looking for where they were going while lifting her leg. Then she drove the heel of her shoe into his foot. He yelped and grabbed at his throbbing toe, giving her seconds to run. That was all she needed. She sprinted to the water's edge and dived in. The water was paralyzing. The impact and the iciness knocked the breath out of her. Regaining her senses, she thrashed her arms as fast as she could. She had wanted to find rocks or a boat to hide behind. Pausing to glance behind, she saw Lars follow her into the water, giving her no chance to search. Sinking deeper into the frigid waters of the harbor, her face numbed as she swam beneath the shadowy hulls of moored boats. The cold bit into her flesh, each stroke taking her further from the surface and deeper into the dark, silent depths. Rachel swam for her life.

JOE--1889

Everyone collapsed into chairs around the mess table in the ship's common area. Nellie, usually the first to break the silence, was slow to speak, struggling to articulate her ordeal. Even Vera had no words to describe how close they had come to being lost forever.

Joe's shirt was filthy, and blood-soaked. His face was caked with dry blood and mud. He stumbled to his compartment to clean up. Vera watched him go. When she was sure he was changing, she jumped up and locked his door. Nellie, Carl, and Leonard recoiled, surprised. Joe spun around, squeezing the handle to free himself. He heard Vera attempting to calm the others. Even Ash stopped preparing beverages, waiting for her to explanation.

Nellie jumped up. "John saved our lives! He even saved your life!"

"John is really Joe Hasselback. His daughter went missing on a previous Impressionist tour. It is my feeling that he endangered us while trying to find her. I have locked him in his cabin for the duration of the tour. Let him explain himself to the TTA."

Carl objected, "Yes but we would have died there in that asylum."

Vera took a moment as she prepared her cup of coffee, "It's complicated. He lied to get onto this tour. Clearly, he is trying to find her, and it could have gotten us all killed or worse."

Leonard weighed in, "He did nothing wrong. I saw it all. He got us out of the asylum. How can you be so ungrateful?"

Vera pulled her coat tightly around her. "The attacker in Arles was after Joe. Not us. We were all put in danger because Joe is using us. I will not risk that dangerous man coming after us again."

Nellie cried, "You are being cruel. You'd be wallowing in a loony bin right now if not for him. I for one am lodging a complaint and will defend John…. Joe to the end." She jumped up and stormed into her room.

Leonard added, "All of us will."

Ash turned to Vera. "A quick word?"

They both stepped into Vera's cabin, leaving the others ranting and outraged in the common area. She sat on a quilt she had draped across her bed. Soft, ambient lighting cast a gentle glow on the metal walls. A faded photograph, a worn paperback, and a single, wilted flower in a glass vial were placed next to her paisley cabin bag. Once the door was closed, Ash challenged Vera.

"Joe had his sights set on finding his daughter. That's clear. But there is no way that he had anything to do with the attack earlier."

"How would you know?" Vera asked, while sipping at her coffee.

Ash noted the photograph was of Vera's cats. "I heard a little bit about his daughter's disappearance. It's normal to want to find missing loved ones, especially when they depend on you. I know a little bit about the effort to find her. I can assure you that there was nothing in the world that Joe could have done to help the attackers find him."

"He is a danger to us all."

"Look… Let me go in there and talk to him. Find out if he is up to something. He isn't going to hurt anybody on the tour," Ash offered.

"I suppose." she puffed.

Ash headed to Joe's cabin, offering the group a small, assuring smile as he passed them, and knocked on Joe's door before unlocking it. Joe was shirtless, with a thin green strap over his throbbing eye. He looked up at Ash, dejected and bleak. Ash closed the door behind him and stood over Joe, studying him for a moment. Uncertain, Joe reached for the remaining vial in his pocket. Finally, Ash spoke.

"Milo Morton contacted me recently."

"What!?" Joe said as he flung his dirty clothes in the Fabricator.

Ash activated his SmartGlove. "He called me before the trip and told me to keep an eye on you. He told me that he left you a message about me."

Joe shook his head. "No, I don't think so."

Ash put his foot up on the chair. "That's Milo for you. I used to fly with him. We were in the Space Force together. I worked for him for a few years. I was with him when they closed his tour operation down. We've shared quite a few beers together. I bet you'll find a note from him in your pocket when you are back home. Anyway… Some nasty guys are after you."

"Who?" Joe touched the bruise against his face and recoiled slightly.

"Another tour operator called Dark History Tours. They were probably the ones who attacked Rachel. I think they want to kill you."

"How did they find me?"

"Oh. I know somebody at their company. I put a tracker on our ship so that they could follow us."

Joe stood up alarmed. "You did what?"

Ash held his hand up, displaying a holographic picture of himself and Milo posing in front of the newly built Egyptian pyramids. Joe squinted at the picture.

"Milo wanted to keep them close. He felt that the only hope you had of ever finding Rachel was if they take you to her. So, I made sure that they could follow us."

"What do they want with me? Why would they possibly want to hurt Rachel?"

"Milo sent me a message a little while ago. He reckons they are doing something illegal with the time tours and Rachel must have seen something. And they obviously know. He thinks they want to leave her stranded here to ghost, or to kill her."

Joe took a fresh shirt from his bag. "Well, I need to find her. She is alive. I can feel it."

"That's tricky. You think she is in Oslo. Right?" Ash prompted.

"Yes. Wait…" Joe said.

He opened his old, crusty jacket to dig out the equipment he took from Gater and found the device that displayed maps and number lists.

"Know what this is?"

Ash took it and turned it around in his hands a few times. He activated it and studied the menu. He scrolled through the options and selected a mapping function. Then he looked up at Joe and grinned.

"This is exactly what we need."

SHINER--1889

Shiner blasted off, leaving Gater fuming. He disconnected Gater's PodCom and deactivated his PodCom, leaving him completely stranded. Then he locked onto the Crichton and rocketed over to the outskirts of Saint-Rémy-de-Provence, hovering over the Alpilles Mountains. He spotted the ship three miles to the north and waited for it to jump again while sending an update to headquarters.

Urgent update for Mr. Wenger. There have been significant developments. The target is within sight. Guidance is requested.

Vinod confirmed receipt of the message almost immediately and forwarded it to Jethro. Shiner moved over to Gater's compartment while he waited for his new instructions. He opened Gater's bag and emptied it onto the bed, sifting through Gater's stuff. Blades, changes of underwear, SmartGlove, a key, a thin gold chain with a gold disk displaying the letter *S*, a bag of toiletries, a bottle of black grease, and toothpicks. Shiner picked up the gold chain and put it in his pocket. Just then, the call from Jethro came through. He went to sit in the cockpit and connected.

"Well, sir. We followed the target several times during their ground tours. We established that the guide was armed and the members of the group were untrained civilians. We were able to get close to them but not close enough. On the second excursion, Gater decided to prematurely attack without exercising caution. We would have been seen, and it was my feeling that the mission would have been compromised. I stopped him."

As Jethro listened, he picked up a seventeenth-century metal torture device shaped like a pear from his desk. There was a key handle at the one end, which he began to twist. Shiner watched, losing focus.

"Continue," Jethro urged.

"Back on board the ship, Gater attacked me. He restrained me in my cabin and attempted to complete the mission on his own. I escaped and located Gater on the ground in Arles, France, 1889. He had failed and was injured. The target, the father, escaped. I left Gater behind and found him again. I am currently 3 miles from their TourPod."

Jethro took a moment to process the progress report.

"Is Hasselback in your sight?"

"The ship is, yes," Shiner responded.

"You have a maximum of one day to complete, by my calculations. Before he returns."

"Yes, sir."

"We can't have him back here, asking more questions."

Jethro turned the key again, causing metal spikes to push out from the sides of his device. "They'll have two, possibly three more stops. That's if they even continue the tour."

"Right," Shiner responded. "One more opportunity. I will complete the task, sir. Should I try to find out if he knows anything first? Or just eliminate him?"

"We have nothing to learn from him. Deal with him accordingly."

It was clear to Shiner that things had spun out of his control. "Yes, sir."

"You need to get it done, Shiner. No mistakes. If others are in the way, deal with them too. There can be no witnesses."

Shiner began to look busy, swiping at the navigation screen. "Absolutely, sir."

"You understand that you cannot fail?"

The metal spikes gave off a clanging sound as a chain shot to the width of the room. Jethro started to twist the key handle, retracting them.

"Yes, sir," Shiner confirmed nervously. "And what about Gater? Should I have killed him? Should I go back for him? How must I deal with that, sir?"

"Don't kill Gater. You won't like him if he's dead," Jethro responded coolly.

"I don't follow, sir…"

Jethro paused. He seemed to look straight past Shiner, as if he were looking far away or far back into his memory. Finally, he responded.

"Travelers who are killed in a time where they do not belong, never find peace. Like ghosts, they are homeless. But ghosts are harmless and fade away. If a traveler is killed, well…his energy can attach to a person, possessing them. And then you get a demon."

The spikes of his torture device were now fully retracted, and Jethro placed it back on his desk.

"These cursed demons spend their years searching for an end to their misery. They grow hungrier and more impatient as they hunt for a place or time that they can finally rest. They may search for millennia, alone, angry, tormented, seeking revenge, wanting others to suffer as much as they suffer." Jethro paused.

Shiner gulped.

"You don't want that from Gater, do you?" Jethro concluded.

"No, sir."

"I would recommend that you leave him where he is to eventually ghost away, for your sake."

CHAPTER 22

Barrett turned the time transmitter disk over and held it up to his ear. He tapped it a few times, wondering if it would elicit any auditory clues. Getting nothing out of it, he sent it down to the TTA laboratory for analysis. Then he connected Milo's data dump from the Dark History facility to his computer and scrolled through the visual feeds, starting with the fleet of ships from a hanger.

Barrett's team had never seen ships like these before. The nuclear propulsion systems were more sophisticated than anything he was even aware of. It didn't mean that the ships themselves were fundamentally illegal. But the fact that they had never been presented to the TTA for inspection was highly problematic.

Barrett noted this in his report and then moved on to the evidence that Milo had collected on the supervised tour. Barrett could not find any flaws with specifications and features onboard the Vonnegut. The tour guide, Wanda Lambert, was polite and organized. The tour agenda was peculiar, though Barrett wasn't required to express an opinion on that. The pilot, Freddy Benson, was adequately experienced. The takeoffs, time jumps, and handling of the ship itself seemed entirely safe, secure, and professional.

Barrett next reviewed the footage of Dmitri planting the disk in the pavement by the restaurant, as well as the ensuing attack. He had noted Dmitri's excessive selection of weaponry, including arms that were not typical of the job or in line with regulations.

Barrett paused, a nagging unease creeping into his mind. He had a few hours to finish the report and then to present his recommendations the following day. He knew full well that his honesty would annoy certain members of the Compliance and Oversight Committee. With a sigh, he opened Agent Chen's half-done compliance report and dove into his work, the coming confrontation hanging over him.

DARK HISTORY COMPLIANCE REPORT AND RECOMMENDATIONS

Summary of Findings by Superintendent Dan Barrett

Tour ships: Excellent
A new fleet of tour ships was identified. This fleet has not been presented to the TTA for inspection. Preliminary speculative findings indicate that it contains advanced and undisclosed technologies.

Safety: Excellent
Onboard safety was satisfactory. Security personnel are excessively armed.

Crew: Unsatisfactory
(a) Pilots: Suitable experience. No record of serious accidents or criminal activity. High percentage of pilots are combat pilots. Combat records have not been submitted.

(b) Tour guides: The majority of the tour guides qualified at the Time Obscura Institute. The institute was established in 2127. School curriculum and operational manuals not yet submitted. A tour guide participated in the attempted assault of a deputized TTA agent. Recent events suggest issues that require extensive further investigation.

(c) Operations personnel: Most personnel seem very experienced and well trained. Insufficient background history was provided on the reconnaissance crew and security and response teams. Security staff assaulted a deputized TTA agent during a supervised visit. Further extensive examination will be performed to determine if this was an isolated incident from a rogue officer or a systemic issue.

Regulations: Inconclusive
All interviewees were highly familiar with the TTA guidelines. All licenses and clearances are valid and current. Updated tour itineraries have been requested but have not been presented. Staff were found to be performing suspicious activities at visiting sites specifically prohibited by the TTA guidelines. Further investigation must be performed to ensure that this was isolated behavior and not approved by Dark History management.

Other items and comments: Inconclusive
During test tours, guides did not seem completely familiar with the itineraries that were submitted. Accompanying personnel (usually reconnaissance or security crew) were seen to deviate from the itinerary and at times were unaccompanied. They were seen planting unknown devices at a site. One of these devices is in custody and is being analyzed.

Overall recommendation: The Dark History Tours operator license should not be approved at this time.

The application decision must be suspended pending the following:

- *Further investigation of the suspicious ground activities*
- *Detailed background checks of the tour guides and security personnel*
- *Inspections of the new fleet*

Barrett completed his recommendations and sighed deeply. He knew his reluctance to approve the application would elicit criticism. He might find himself the target of a disciplinary action and possibly a smear campaign. Before submitting it to the committee, Barrett called Yulia.

"Yulia, please get Helen Yates from Time International Experiences."

Yulia put a call through to the managing director of Time International. After a few moments, she was on the line, and Barrett got straight to the point.

"We have a theory about Rachel Hasselback's disappearance.

"That's great. How can we help?"

"You are currently running a similar tour that her father is on. It's on the Crichton. It was supposed to go to Oslo 1893."

"OK…"

"It's imperative that the current tour takes him there. Would you reach out to your guide and make sure that the tour heads there?"

Helen agreed and Barrett disconnected. Then he sent his report through to the committee and waited for the backlash.

GATER--1889

Gater limped back to the center of Arles, heading south. The Yellow House would be crawling with police and enraged neighbors. He checked his holographic map as he ran, noting alternative places of interest. He needed to find another tour group. The Café Terrace, the site of van Gogh's famous *Café Terrace at Night*, was a good bet. Keeping his injured arm steady, he hustled and got here quickly. Gater waited at the northeastern corner of the Place du Forum, where van Gogh once set up his easel. The once vibrant café awnings seemed to droop ominously. Street lamps flickered, casting ghostly glows on the weathered facades of the surrounding buildings. Gingerly, and wincing with every jerk, he pulled out his PodCom. Shiner had blocked communication with his ship. Gater wondered if he could pick up a TourPod on another wavelength. The chances were infinitesimally remote. He swiped through, listening carefully. Other than the earliest garbled radio transmissions, Gater picked up nothing. TourPod frequencies were highly specific and hidden, preventing exactly this kind of hacking. He stabbed at the controls again. Maybe, somehow, a TourPod would pick up a signal from him. Nothing.

Gater maneuvered an empty barrel into place and sat watching, alert to any groups who didn't fit in. The café was popular. Throughout the evening, the small round tables outside were fully occupied. Elegantly dressed couples, arm in arm, glided past Gater as he sat, silently focused and seething. Listening intently to the endless French conversations that filled the street, he waited for the telltale monolog of a tour guide. Exhausted and lightheaded, he pinched at his wounded shoulder to keep himself alert. The pain meant that he had not started ghosting. He knew it was only a matter of time.

After a few hours, the crowds started to die down, growing his sense of unease. Gater pulled out the PodCom again. As he impatiently swiped through the dead frequencies, he caught the faintest foreign murmurs from down the street. The words sounded Japanese. He jumped up and stumbled into the thoroughfare. Approaching from the south, he saw tourists slowly heading toward him. Gater hurried over and quickly identified the tour leader, a tall man with a bowler hat and necktie. He jumped in front of them, blocking their path. A small, elderly lady in the group gasped.

"Please. I'm a tourist like you. Call your TourPod. I need to get back, or I'll die."

The tour guide stared in disbelief. Nobody moved.

"Now!" Gater yelled.

The tour guide reached into his jacket. Gater feared he was going for a weapon and immediately softened his tone.

"Please. I just need to tether to a ship while I still can."

Keeping his hand on the grip of his StunGun, the guide asked, "How did you get here?"

"I was mugged and separated from my group. The criminals left me for dead by the river. Please. I'm running out of time."

Keeping his eyes on Gater as the tour group nervously huddled behind him, the guide pulled out his PodCom.

"Gracie, you're not going to believe this, but I found a lost tourist who needs to tether before he ghosts. Can you come down here?"

A voice over the PodCom responded immediately, "On my way, Akio. I'll land in the field on the other side of the alleyway by you."

The guide gestured for Gater to proceed down the alley to their left, trailing closely behind, all the while clutching his StunGun under his coat. Gater's head was spinning. He walked unsteadily, occasionally reaching for the wall to regain his balance. The alley walls seemed to be closing in on him, and he could hear his breath rasping as it left his throat. As they reached the other side, a TourPod materialized. The pilot, Gracie, stood at the hatch, a glowing blue light from the cabin framing her like an angel. Gater staggered onboard and toward her, following her to the first aid cabinet.

Akio called from the alley, "Best message HQ once you've fixed him up and tethered him. We'll want to know who he is and where he's from."

Gracie gave a thumbs-up as she closed the ramp and turned her attention back to Gater.

Gater, slumped on a chair, watched her intensely as she scanned his shoulder with her FirstAid rod. She applied a nanotape over his broken collar bone and then offered him a sip from a bottle filled with a green solution. Gater felt a little stronger already.

"Thank you," he softly muttered. "Water please."

"Sure." She smiled.

As Gracie turned to the beverages closet and pulled out a bottle of water, Gater pulled out his karambit blade and pounced, cutting her swiftly across her throat. She collapsed in his arms. She was dead within seconds.

Gater hurried over to the tethering cubicle and immediately afterward, jumped into the pilot's seat and set course for 2130.

RACHEL--1893

Rachel cast a desperate glance over her shoulder, her heart pounding as Lars closed in on her. His eyes locked onto hers with a terrifying intensity, arms thrashing grotesquely as if his shoulders weren't properly attached. He was gaining on her, moving with a speed that defied her expectations. A bubbly froth of bubbles streamed from his gaping mouth. Rachel propelled herself forward, darting left and right. There was no losing him. She could not shake Lars, and he gained on her with every stroke. Her lungs were bursting. She twisted towards the surface, broke water, sucked in as much air as she could, and immediately dived again, narrowly missing Lars, who also needed to breathe. Rachel headed farther out, away from the safety of the promenade.

The farther out and the deeper she swam, the icier it got. As she progressed, she searched for a reef or rock formation to hide behind. Anything to shake him. She propelled herself toward a row of moored boats, surfacing behind an anchored cargo vessel. Lars remained submerged, a horror below the waves. She slipped alongside the hull, hoping to shake him off. Her heart sank as Lars emerged from the water with a guttural grunt. His fatigue was evident, but his determination was terrifying.

She dived again and swam beneath a schooner moored alongside the cargo ship. Lars saw her and followed. The cold was suffocating. Rachel surfaced and paddled alongside the schooner, but Lars was still close behind. She simply could not lose him in the water. He had a bloodlust and would not be satisfied until he had destroyed her.

As she ducked behind one ship after another, Rachel felt herself gradually disappearing. Her left arm was already ghostlike as was most of her head, face and her right leg. No matter how quickly she swam, Lars was always right behind her and closing in. He would catch her soon. She needed to do something different. Her thoughts were scrambled. Every part of her that was still flesh and blood was freezing. She was almost out of ideas. Only one dreadful option left. Rachel swam straight down toward the seabed. Lars immediately followed.

As Rachel propelled herself deeper, she started to take short, desperate breaths. She imagined her body disappearing, fading, ghosting. She focused on her torso. The more rapidly she inhaled and exhaled, the more quickly her lungs filled with water. It was agonizing, like she was being enveloped by a relentless, suffocating darkness, where every desperate gasp for air was swallowed by an all-consuming, crushing panic. She was drowning. Gradually, her torso started to dematerialize. She reached the seabed and clung to the rocks, pushing herself off to keep away from Lars. Lars was a few feet away. She could tell that he was running out of air too.

Rachel kept on panting, willing herself into a ghostlike status. She was losing consciousness. Lars was closing in on her quickly. Rachel gave one final push, thrusting herself away from him. Her lungs felt like they were about to explode. She kicked away furiously. As his furious eyes burrowed through her, she gradually noticed that she couldn't feel the burning any longer. She glanced downward and saw that her entire chest was transparent. She no longer needed to breathe to stay underwater. Lars was glaring at her as he thrashed his arms. He was out of oxygen and making his last desperate attempts to grab her. Rachel pushed away from him easily, keeping herself close to the bottom. He began to drift upward, away from her, his hands still grabbing outward toward her as he floated toward the surface. His raging eyes and black mouth with its pointy white teeth grew smaller as he drifted away.

Rachel floated where she was as she watched Lars disappear above her. When she felt he would not return, she swam back toward the promenade and headed farther along the shore. She had no idea if he had drowned or not, but she wanted to be sure to avoid meeting Lars ever again. However, she was more worried about herself. She was already half a ghost and had no strength left to make herself whole again.

TIME TRAVEL COMPLIANCE AND OVERSIGHT COMMITTEE--2130

The fifteen members of the Time Travel Compliance and Oversight Committee were an hour into their monthly session. They were seated in the Lucy Findlay Conference Room on the 250th floor of the TTA headquarters in Rochester, New York. The room was regal and impressive. Its walls were coated with a dark mahogany inlaid with shining titanium and silver. The carpets were a plush royal purple surrounding a polished oak boardroom table with inbuilt holographic screens for each meeting participant. The committee, led by Chairwoman Shinjo, was made up of representatives from each of the united continents as well as two members from industry, two from academia, two from technology, and two senior ethics and philosophy professionals.

Chairwoman Shinjo announced the next item on the agenda. "Please scroll to the compliance reports for the new tour operator applications."

The members all swiped at their screens until Barrett's reports displayed them. Edward Pearson, the North American representative, seated between the African representative, Andile Mabuso, and the Australian representative, Dean Waugh, was quietly stewing. He had looked through the Dark History report prior to the meeting convening. Horrified and apoplectic, he had immediately called Barrett, who wisely didn't pick up. Pearson had made a few more quick calls to gather support for the application and was now ready to refute the report in the committee, though he did not feel as confident. He was convinced that Barrett had purposefully sabotaged him to jeopardize the business.

Chairwoman Shinjo introduced the first of the applications. "The first new tour operator submission is from Dark History Tours. It's North American. Would Senator Pearson kindly provide an introduction and address the issues that have been raised as well as the recommendation from the TTA Compliance Division."

Pearson activated the holographic projector and tackled each of the major categories, starting with the fleet. As visuals of the approved Dark

History fleet flashed around the board room table, he assured the committee that while some of the TourPods were new and as yet uninspected, they all fitted the TTA specifications. This would be verified during a subsequent inspection, which had already been arranged for the following week.

The projector then presented a clip of the uniformed, professional team posing, working, and training. He addressed the Dark History personnel, noting that all curriculum vitaes sat on Superintendent Barrett's desk.

He pointed out that the Time Obscura Institute from which Dark History had sourced most of its tour guides was established and run by an illustrious veteran of the industry who had also been a past committee member of the Compliance and Oversight Committee. Finally, he noted the regrettable incident mentioned in the report.

On cue, the room became gloomier as the projectors projected unflattering visuals of Milo Morton, his old, rusty TourPods, and scenes of him appearing under fire, being cross-examined as the defendant at various hearings.

"The assault on deputized agent Milo Morton was most unfortunate. The employment of tour guide Wanda Evans, who was responsible for the supervised inspection, has been terminated. The security officer on the tour did not return with the ship." A hologram of Dmitri and his young bride displayed. Several members of the committee murmured sympathetically.

"We are investigating Mr. Morton's role in his disappearance. I can assure you that it was an isolated occurrence. No such attack has ever happened previously. I would also like to draw to this esteemed committee's attention the track record of the supervising agent, Mr. Milo Morton."

A clip of Milo looking particularly aggressive as he slammed his fists on a committee table, sound amplified, dominated the center of the room, jarring the committee.

"Those of us who have been involved in time tourism for several years will no doubt remember the volume of complaints, misdemeanors, fines, and irregularities that came from his outfit, Morton Tours. He was a man who was suspended by this committee, so we should surely treat this recently reported assault within the context of his record. I would furthermore suggest that it was highly irregular of Superintendent Barrett to deputize and send Mr. Morton on the inspection in the first place."

The holographic projector turned off, and Pearson paused dramatically, making sure that he had the full attention of the committee.

"Who authorized him to appoint an ex-convict!"

Pause again. Silence. An image on the projector of Barrett, donut filling his mouth as he suspiciously glared sideways, dominated the room.

" I recommend that Superintendent Barrett be censured and suspended. He should appear before this committee to explain why he sent Mr. Morton on this fact-finding report and whether he is also responsible for the ensuing attack and the death of Security Officer Dmitri Kiryenko. Finally, I recommend that the Dark History application be approved without delay."

Senator Pearson, brow furrowed and chest out, silently observed the expressions of the committee members around the table. Several were nodding approvingly. According to his calculation, he had come into the meeting with five members in his pocket and would win over another three votes.

Chairwoman Shinjo requested that he remain behind after the meeting and then requested that the committee members submit their votes by the end of the day. They moved on to the next agenda item.

JOE--1889

Vera put down the PodCom and turned to Ash. The group was hunched over by the Drink Master commiserating Joe's quarantine.

"Well...I guess you were right. That was headquarters. They want us to give Joe an opportunity to find his daughter. They say that they got a formal request directly from the TTA."

Ash sighed, relieved. He'd been expecting the call from head office. Milo had told him that the TTA was making progress.

Vera continued, "I really wasn't planning this. I think it's dangerous. I was expecting a pleasant stopover in Germany to see Carl Geist. Why tempt fate? And how will we find this daughter, anyway?"

"Leave that to me," Ash said, and he went over to Joe's cabin.

Joe was pacing back and forward, staring at the door.

Ash grinned. "We're going to Oslo. Pass me that stolen receiver." He said, while taking a seat across from Joe.

They sat on Joe's bed – Ash swiping at the screen of the device. He activated it and flipped to the lists of numbers, each of them containing twenty-eight integers. The syntax of the listing was complex but to a pilot with Ash's experience, the longitudinal and latitudinal coordinates hidden within the strings were unmistakable. Ash had also noticed date arrangements and had it worked out.

"This is the receiver for a bunch of transmitters that your friend has been planting throughout his trips back in time. I am willing to bet that he plants transmitters at significant events and locations that he feels he might want to revisit. If we can work out the coordinates, which I think I did, and we can get our ship to somehow lock on to them, we will be able to navigate to the exact time in Oslo where he attacked your daughter."

Joe was nervously hopeful. He felt a rush of energy and a determination to get back on the ground. "Let me help with that," he said, distracted as he emptied the remaining vials from his pockets and studied his Universal Key.

Ash continued, "You see the many long strings of twenty-eight numbers. Each line represents a specific time transmitter and will direct us to a time destination. The first set of seven numbers is latitude. The second set of seven numbers is longitude. The next set of eight numbers is a date. The final set of six numbers is a time. Now, this is the latitude and longitude for Oslo. So, if we can find a record in here where the first fourteen digits are close to this, we'll find the coordinates for the transmitter that your friend planted there."

They scrolled through, saving several close matches. Most of them were irrelevant. By comparing the dates, they realized that all but one of the entries was too early in history to be the right coordinates for the Impressionist tour.

"This must be it. I am willing to bet that he planted it after he ran into Rachel. Now let's see if we can set the TourPod's navigation system to take us directly to this signal."

Ash and Joe hurried to the cockpit to prepare for the next jump, while Vera looked on disapprovingly.

CHAPTER 23

BARRETT--2130

Barrett removed his InstaLoss thousand-calorie patch from his neck and turned it, checking the display on the back. Nine hundred calories. He tossed it in the trash before pacing to his window. Far below, workers were milling about parks filled with children. The window zoom activated, tracking his eyes and magnifying the scenes in the park that he chose to watch. The Friday afternoon lunch crowd was slowly trickling back to work. Things slowed down around this time, and Barrett generally looked forward to his Friday afternoon ritual.

Normally Yulia would knock on his door with a tall cup of Himalayan yak butter tea and a small plate of Japanese wasabi cheese doughnuts. He would tie up some of the loose ends from the week, plan his coming work week, and catch up with a few of his agents over a beer, before heading home. This Friday was different. He was sure to hear back from the Compliance and Oversight Committee in a few minutes. He was also expecting a hostile call from Senator Pearson after the Dark History hearing.

The Impressionist tour with Joe Hasselback was also due back today, and he would probably learn the fate of Rachel, the missing daughter. He paced back to his desk and prodded at his calendar. On… off… on. Damn calendar. He couldn't focus on anything, let alone plan his upcoming week. Yulia knocked on his door, and he invited her in with his yak tea and doughnuts.

Yulia sensed that he was anxious and offered him a reassuring smile.

"Things will work out," she offered, leaving the door ajar as she returned to her desk.

Not even a minute later, the phone rang. Answering, she turned to Barrett and put the phone on speaker. Barrett heard the angry voice on the call from his desk.

"Put him through," Barrett muttered.

"Well, you tried to screw me over, didn't you, Barrett?"

"Senator Pearson. Are you referring to my recommendations on the Dark History Tours application?"

"They are a well-funded, highly professional, well-run operator, and you tried to sabotage their application!"

"That is not correct, sir. During our inspection and review, we found several irregularities and undisclosed facts of a material nature. I reported them and recommended that the application be revisited after they have provided us with all our answers That's my job," Barrett returned.

"You had plenty of time before the committee to complete your report, and you didn't. And you sent Milo Morton to do the dirty work for you!"

"Milo Morton is a highly experienced veteran of our industry. He was more than qualified to help us finalize the report. I sent him in an attempt--"

Pearson jumped from accusation-to-accusation, aggressively interrupting Barrett. "He attacked the tour guide, the pilot, and who even knows what he did to the security officer!"

"We have footage, which is on file, of the Dark History personnel attacking him. He was--"

"Well, it doesn't matter. I am confident that their application will get the votes needed, despite your efforts to block it. Oh. And one more thing.

You will be notified later today of your suspension. A disciplinary meeting will be arranged next week. I imagine you will be fired."

Pearson disconnected the call, leaving Barrett bewildered. A few moments passed before Yulia started gesturing to him again. The phone had rung, and this time it was Simon Levinson, the chief operating officer of the TTA and Barrett's boss. He oversaw the day-to-day running of the TTA and reported to the chief executive officer and the Executive Committee. He liked Barrett. They got along well and had worked together for several years. Barrett always found him very fair and direct. Yulia still knew this wasn't the call that Barrett wanted to take on his Friday afternoon.

John Levinson greeted him. "Hi, Dan. How are you?"

"Thanks. It's been a bit stressful, but I am getting to the bottom of everything."

"Look, the report that you submitted for the Dark History application ruffled some very big feathers for some reason unknown to all of us mortals. Senator Pearson went wild, and he is calling for your head."

"I really held back with that report. Something is going on. They are up to no good. I need more time. But I felt we had enough evidence to delay the decision. I wanted the committee to give us a chance to do the job properly."

"The committee didn't. The votes aren't in yet, but Senator Pearson has put in a lot of overtime with the members to get them to vote his way. I don't know why he is so interested in this license. He is also working very hard now to have you disciplined and dismissed."

"Well, let him try. I've done nothing wrong," Barrett responded.

"I believe you. Unfortunately, the committee decided to suspend you, pending an investigation. You'll be called to appear before them next week."

Barrett slumped back in his chair. He felt like he'd been punched in the gut. "Can you stop them?"

"I'll try to find out what is going on. But for the time being, you need to make bloody sure that you can defend every decision you made and every word that you wrote."

"I will Simon. Thanks for letting me know."

His boss wished him a good weekend and they disconnected. Barrett took a sip of his yak tea, forcing it down. It was already cold.

JOE--1889

Joe watched as Ash integrated Gater's receiving device with the Crichton's navigation system. The speed with which Ash scrolled through the complex menus and configured the assemblies and connections was breathtaking.

Feeling useless, Joe asked asinine questions and pointed at holographic endpoints as they flashed across his periphery. Ash smiled patiently as he got on with it. Vera glanced over at their work and huffed as she activated the digital itinerary and replaced the next destination, Grünberg 1906, with Oslo 1893.

Joe turned as Nellie opened her compartment door, a warm smile spreading across his face. "Welcome back," she called out, her voice filled with cheer. She sprinted over and enveloped him in a tight hug. Even Carl, usually reserved, hurried over, giving Joe hearty pats on the back and shoulder. Leaving Ash to his work, Nellie chattered with Joe about an insane woman who shared her room in the French asylum. She related how she had to sit completely still for an hour, too scared to move, while the lady brushed Nellie's hair with a dead mouse. Eventually, Carl interrupted to ask Joe how he got them to safety.

"You know, it's amazing. You anticipated those horses that nearly ran Vera over. And then in the asylum, you knew how to find Nellie. And you knew where the guards would be. How do you do it?"

"It's just since I got here. It never happened to me before."

Vera came to the table. She cocked her head to the side and tapped her foot impatiently.

Joe continued. "I have a sense that bad things are going to happen before they do. I feel it, like a distant memory forcing its way back into my subconscious. Like I have lived it before. I can't explain it. I know it's impossible, but I could feel where Nellie was." Joe shrugged.

"Very strange. And amazing," Carl declared.

Leonard had joined them at the table, and Nellie turned to him incredulously. "What were you thinking with the dogs at the train station?"

Leonard blushed. "I just wanted to make the children laugh. I forgot the dogs weren't synthetic like mine are."

Vera interrupted the conversation.

"Friends, we have had a change of plans. We will soon be travelling to Oslo 1893 to visit Edvard Munch, the famous Norwegian Impressionist who painted *The Scream*. We're going to try to catch him on Ekeberg Hill, followed by a visit to the town square. Go and change. We're touching down in thirty minutes."

There was a murmur of approval. Leonard commented that this was among his favorite paintings. Just then Ash walked over to the mess table and updated them.

"Well, I managed to synchronize that receiver with our navigation systems. We are picking up a transmission, but I can't be certain. It's a bit of a hack. We should get to Oslo 1893, but I'm not sure if we will arrive exactly on the day and time that I set."

Everybody hastily made their way to their respective cabins and put on their new changes of clothing, freshly prepared by the Fabricators. Joe in a neat gray suit, bowtie, and top hat was the first back in the common area, ready to track Rachel down. Once the group was seated and strapped in, Ash readied them for the jump. A small smile tugged at Joe's lips. His eyes were shining. Vera, fearing a loss of order, left the group with one final instruction.

"I would like to make something clear. We are still touring. I am aware that Joe's daughter may be in Oslo. While we will keep a look out for her, we are sticking to our itinerary. I expect all of you to follow my instructions at all times. To the letter."

RACHEL--1893

Rachel propelled herself through the freezing water. While alarmed at her ability to remain underwater, to never have to surface to breathe, her new ability certainly had its appeal. She stopped paddling and lowered her legs down until she was standing on the seabed.

The final rays of the dusk sun broke through the water's surface, providing enough light for her to take in her strange settings. As extraordinary as the underwater life was to her, Rachel was more of a curiosity to the marine life around her. A particularly large spotted wolf-fish inquisitively glided up to her. She reached out to stroke it, and it darted away.

Starry rays and schools of halibut and monkfish bobbed past her as she stepped carefully between the seaweed and rocks, approaching the harbor's edge. Crustaceans scuttled along the sandy seabed. Rachel got to the shore a half mile down the promenade from where she had dived in. She cautiously emerged and scanned the area to make sure that Lars was not lurking.

Two old fishermen watched her as she waded out. They shrieked and abandoned their fishing rods, sprinting away as fast as their legs would carry them. Rachel was disheartened. She could have done with a warm blanket to towel off the icy droplets from her legs. She looked down, studying her body as she stood, dripping, in the shallow water. She was only half there. The fishermen had run from a ghost.

Rachel climbed back up onto the promenade and quickly regained her bearings. The tour groups would generally stop at Ekeberg Hill and the center of town near the National Museum and town square. She was an hour's walk from each. Her first instinct was to set out for the hill, but she paused and thought about the attack that got her into this ordeal in the first place.

If the tour company worked out what had happened and were also looking for her, they might look for her where the attack happened. Pacing as she considered her options, she noticed that she was no longer leaving any wet footprints. Both of her feet had ghosted. She opted for the National Museum and hurried northward, running as quickly as she could. She knew that Munch's painting was first shown at the National Museum. Surely all groups passed by there...

SHINER--1889

Shiner kept a steady watch over the Crichton as it hovered over Saint-Rémy, sharpening his knife as he mulled over Jethro's instructions. He would not make a mistake this time. The mark shimmered on his screen and then disappeared with a faint popping sound. Shiner studied his navigation charts as he followed the tracking signal. It reappeared over Oslo 1893. He knew exactly what that meant. Joe was going to try to find his daughter.

Shiner strapped in and set his destination coordinates to follow them. He ignited the nuclear propulsion system and sat back, feeling the familiar hum beneath his seat. The ship jumped with a crackle. As he arrived, seconds later, he scanned for the Crichton and saw them wasting no time. Ash was already descending from the heavy, gray clouds and heading for a small forest on the near side of Ekeberg Hill. Shiner cloaked his ship as he watched them. He glided to the far side of Ekeberg Hill and landed in a deserted clearing behind an outcrop of rocks. Hurrying back to his cabin, he threw on the newly fabricated checked suit with a high-collar white shirt and bowler hat. He rummaged through his overnight bag and selected a plasma gun, sharpened knife, StunGun, graphene garrote, and PodCom.

Then he disembarked quickly, guided the ship back up into the cloudy sky, and cloaked it. He had to be hasty if he was to track Joe effectively, and finding a path to follow, he set off, making sure to keep low and concealed. He rushed, meeting nobody on the way, and only paused briefly when he realized that he was passing the exact deserted spot where Munch had painted his masterpiece.

He rationed that the group must have been there, seen that Munch wasn't painting that evening, and continued to Oslo. Scrambling between trees and rocks, Shiner eventually heard Vera around the corner. They were already close to the outskirts of Oslo's old town. He pulled out his plasma gun, slowed down, and peeked around the corner, cursing softly when he saw Ash had accompanied the group. Ash would be stronger and more armed than Vera. Shiner crouched low, using the side of the hill as cover, while taking aim at Ash. He couldn't get a clear shot. Leonard was blocking his vision. He waited impatiently for Leonard and the others to move aside. It would be any second now. As he took aim, his finger hovering on the trigger, he realized that Joe was not with them. He released his finger for a second, just before a cloud of gas exploded next to him and he lost his bearings, fading into blackness.

Chapter 24

Barrett couldn't bring himself to eat his Japanese wasabi cheese doughnuts. There was no word yet on the search for Rachel Hasselback. He hadn't received a formal request from the Compliance and Oversight Committee to appear before them and still didn't know why Senator Pearson was so invested in the Dark History application. The laboratory hadn't reported back on the transmitting disk that Milo had brought back. What where Dark History's plans? Barrett felt like a circus juggler, with way too many balls up in the air, and he couldn't catch any of them.

He went back to his desk and called Milo, his hands twitching and his chest tight.

After a lengthy period of ringing and vibrating, Milo picked up, his large frame blocking some of the shiniest, most vicious-looking weapons Barrett had ever seen. "Dan, do you need something else?"

Barrett craned his neck over Milo's shoulder to study the ball and chains, jagged swords, and an old shotgun with an absurdly large barrel. Milo was wearing a vest. He was covered with silver polish and grease., Milo grinned sheepishly and switched his background to that of an office environment.

Barrett spoke up, "Look, I think the Dark History investigation is dirtier than I realized."

Milo asked, "How so?"

"Well. Senator Pearson, the North American member of the TTA Compliance and Oversight Committee, just had me suspended."

"Because you had me do the inspection?"

"I think so."

"Makes sense." Milo granted. "Yeah. I told you they are up to something. Hmm. I'm sure they will cover up everything that I discovered."

Barrett sighed. "I need a smoking gun. I need to find out who is behind this all."

Milo asked about the disk. "Your lab will find that these things are going to guide Dark History tour groups to famous events. That is a fact. It's breaking your laws. Your bosses cannot ignore that."

"I know," Barrett replied. "My sense is that Senator Pearson is involved with Dark History. Maybe he is one of the owners. I don't know how I can prove that. And if I can't...well, he is a very powerful man. He will beat any allegations I throw at him. And get me fired."

Milo said, "You guys supervised my operation for five years. The people at the top only look after themselves. Do you know why they can't even rescue one girl and bring her back to her family? Because they don't care about her. They only care about money and control. You'll never uncover anything or save any tourists as long as you work within the system."

"You might be right," Barrett agreed. "Not sure what you are telling me, though."

"I'm not telling you anything," Milo replied.

"I need something more than what you've already given me?"

"Sorry. I've got nothing."

JOE--1893

Joe cautiously descended from the knoll and approached the pathway below. He inched his way towards Shiner, every muscle tensed, his ears straining for any hint of movement. Titanium rod extended, he prodded Shiner in the ribs. No response. He placed the rest of his vials back in his pocket, took the gun out of Shiner's hand, and tucked it in his pants before he hurried back to the group, catching up with them before anybody even noticed he'd broken away.

They seemed enthralled by Vera's explanation of Munch's *The Scream.*

"It's a pity we didn't run into Edvard Munch. He was known to set up his easel on this path. The fiery red sunset you see, inflaming the clouds, reminded him of an endless scream passing through the world. His sister had just been committed to an asylum."

Joe moved to the front of the group as Vera spoke.

"The sky is a deeper red than any typical sunset you may have experienced before. That is due to the recent eruption of Mount Krakatoa, which tinted skies in the western part of the northern hemisphere for several years."

They were at the foot of the pathway now, and Vera stopped the group. She continued with her presentation. "Back to his sister… She is currently housed in the asylum that we are passing to our right. Let's try to stay away from this one." Vera, enjoying her joke, snorted loudly.

Nellie shuddered as she huddled next to Carl.

"The painting has come to represent the universal state of human anxiety. It is one of the most iconic paintings in the world and has been stolen and recovered several times. Nobody currently knows its whereabouts since its last theft in 2075 from the National Museum in Oslo. In fact, the painting will debut there later this year."

Vera continued, and the group followed. Joe shuffled awkwardly beside her, his heart pounding with anticipation. She edged away, her eyes fixed on the ground, avoiding his desperate gaze. He finally blocked her path. She knew what Joe wanted and Vera pulled out her PocketHolo, expanding the view of Oslo.

"We're going to Grüners Gate, north of the center, where Munch lived. I am going to do another draw so that one of you can accompany me up to Munch's apartment."

RACHEL--1893

Rachel hurried toward the National Museum near the university. With each step, she felt a gnawing doubt as she began to second-guess her plan. She was attacked there when she was with her tour group and assumed that future groups would pass by that way as well. As she got closer to the gallery, she recognized her dreadful mistake. It was nighttime. The gallery would be closed already. It only made sense to wait there during daylight hours. Tours wouldn't pass by in the evening. She stopped running, feeling a growing sense of panic. She felt with all her heart that her dad would come to find her before she completely ghosted. He would never let her go. In the same way he dedicated himself to her mom, spending weeks and months understanding her illness, Joe wouldn't quit now. He added years to Liz's life, and Rachel knew he would be just as stubborn with her. But she had to help him find her.

Her dad was not impulsive; he approached every decision methodically and with precision, weighing probabilities and analyzing outcomes. Rachel's thoughts raced as she tried to get into his mind. If he were navigating an unfamiliar city, he would choose the most logical, central meeting point. She envisioned him arriving in Oslo, scanning a map, and searching for the most recognizable landmarks. As she sifted through the possibilities, she kept wandering back to memories of their family holidays in foreign cities. A pattern slowly emerged: their shared love of fountains, each trip marked by visits to these serene, central attractions. That was where her dad would instinctively wait. With a jolt, Rachel realized she needed to return to the fountain in the town square.

She turned around and ran as fast as she could.

SHINER--1893

Shiner, awake but groggy, leaned over and retched. He rubbed his eyes, coughing as he got back onto his feet. The air was thick with the scent of damp earth and decaying leaves. He could hear the rustling of unseen creatures in the underbrush and the occasional mournful howl of the wind as it snaked through the skeletal trees. Joe was long gone. Bastard! Checking his watch, he estimated that he'd only been out for around twenty minutes. Shiner never considered himself a particularly cold-blooded or ruthless mercenary. He was always the cool-headed operator, biding his time, getting things done. But now, he wanted to kill Joe more than any target he'd ever been assigned. Shiner cursed as he examined himself and his equipment. He looked around for his gun, kicking rocks to the side and parting the overgrowth. Had it dropped when he was ambushed? No. His plasma gun was missing. Joe took it! He pulled out his PocketHolo and tried to guess where the group would be heading. He knew they must have come to see Edvard Munch. They'd passed the site where he painted *The Scream*. They might head to the museum, which housed the painting, though he wasn't sure if Munch had completed it yet. They might want to tour the museum to see other works of his, though that prospect didn't seem so thrilling to him. They might try to visit him at his home. Even a home visit wasn't a sure bet.

He pulled out his receiver with the Dark History transmitter maps and searched for the closest signals. The signal from the disk that Gater planted right after he had assaulted Rachel Hasselback was disseminating from Christiania Square. If Joe or the pilot had taken Gater's receiver, they might also head that way. Shiner sprinted. He would not let Joe escape his clutches again.

JOE--1893

Joe studied the holographic map on Vera's PocketHolo. He thought about Rachel, alone in Oslo, expecting him or another tour to rescue her. He realized that he only had one more chance to figure out where she would be. The problem was that Joe lacked an imagination for most things. Liz was the parent with the ideas, leaving him to his routine. On the odd times he had to plan a holiday morning, he'd always headed for the tallest, oldest or most central sites. Rachel was smart and knew this. If she wanted him to find her, he knew that she would wait in the most obvious places. He assumed that she had barely toured Oslo before she was assaulted. She would wait in any of only a handful of places. Old. Central. Town Square.

He turned the map toward Vera and pointed to Christiania Square. He held her gaze and gestured that they needed to pass through this area. Vera stared at him.

"I am the tour guide, and I say where we will go. And we are going to Munch's apartment."

Vera grabbed the PocketHolo back from Joe. As she did, she noticed the plasma gun sticking out of Joe's belt. She slowly raised her head to confront him, her eyes burning. "Where did you get that gun from?!" Vera seethed.

Joe stood unmoving. How would he explain to Vera how he came to possess a plasma gun? Rooted to the spot, he held his hands in front of him, surrendering to Vera, soundlessly pleading with her to relax. Vera reached for her StunGun and pulled it out. Ash was eavesdropping and jumped in to defuse the situation. He placed himself between Vera and Joe as the rest of the group froze.

Vera demanded that Ash move aside. "Joe has a gun in his belt."

Ash glanced at it. "Where did you get that? The Dark History guys?"

Joe lowered his eyes. He carefully pulled it out with the barrel down and offered it to Ash.

"Did they try to attack us again? When?" Ash asked.

Joe nodded as he indicated that it was a few minutes ago.

"How did you get it?"

Joe pulled out his last remaining vials and showed them to Ash. Ash shook his head.

"Well, thank you, I guess. He could have killed us all with this." He glanced at Vera.

Joe nodded and then pointed to the PocketHolo. He indicated to Ash that he knew where they needed to go. Vera reluctantly handed it to Ash, and Joe showed Ash that they should head toward Christiania Square. Ash nodded and turned to Vera.

"Let's go there. He seems to think it's the most likely place his daughter would be."

Vera glowered, her distaste very apparent. "No way he is getting that gun back though."

Joe had no clue how to use it anyway. Ash handed it to her, and she placed it into her jacket pocket as she disdainfully turned her back on him

"We are taking a quick detour to the town square and will continue with the planned itinerary shortly afterward." Then she set off, sulking. Joe tried to increase the pace a little but knew not to push his luck.

RACHEL--1893

Rachel arrived in Christiania Square. The air was heavy with the mingled aromas of freshly baked bread from a nearby bakery and the lingering scent of coal smoke from chimneys. The cobblestones underfoot felt worn and uneven. She found a quiet corner between an old yellow building constructed from timber and an ancient brick common house. She leaned against the wall as she watched the locals walking through the square. The rhythmic clatter of horse-drawn carriages and the distant murmur of conversations heightened her tension, like a muffled, beating drum. She focused on her breathing, picturing herself slowly becoming whole, starting from the top of her head and working downward through to her forehead, eyes, nose, and the rest of her face.

Slowly, she noticed a sensation return to her face. She had not realized how cold the air was. As she stood, she felt a new uneasiness, as if the beating clatter had suddenly become malevolent. Across the square, she spotted a shadowy figure arrive, stalking as he passed the outer buildings. He reminded her of the attacker who had grabbed her and knocked her unconscious. She watched him as he prowled deliberately, mapping out the square.

It was Shiner. He moved slowly but deliberately, passing the restaurant that Agnes haunted. She slunk back, out of his sight.

GATER--2130

Gater landed the TourPod in the Dark History hangar. The ground crew were visibly stunned when they noticed the dead pilot in a pool of blood, haphazardly covered by a handful of shower towels. Ignoring their protests, he stormed through arrivals and into the admin center. As he approached Jethro's office, he slowed. The ordinary white door pulsed with a hidden menace. Gater took a deep breath, reminded himself that Shiner had left him to die, and knocked politely but firmly.

"Come in, Gater." Jethro's thin, quiet voice answered.

Gater entered and immediately launched into a host of accusations.

"Shiner is a lunatic! He had no place...."

Jethro interrupted firmly and pointed to the seat across his desk. "Sit."

Gater quickly sat as Jethro rose from his seat and made his way around the desk. Gater's gangly, massive frame spilled over the seat, though he felt small.

"You left the girl and her father alive?"

"Sir. I had him, but he got away. I'd have killed him, but Shiner betrayed me. He left me to ghost. He needs to--"

"You stole another ship and killed the pilot?" Jethro now stood in front of Gater. He leaned back on his desk and met Gater squarely in the eye.

"I had no choice. Sir, I need your permission to return to the mission and to make Shiner pay for..." Gater's voice faded as he found himself struggling to form the words he needed to say. His throat began to close. Coughing, his mind fixated on an icy point deep at the back of his mind. It grew into an ancient fear that steadily pushed all other thoughts from his mind. He saw Jethro watching him soundlessly, with laser-like focus, as he grew increasingly terrified and helpless. Jethro's face grew more distant as it faded into a pitch-black tunnel. Struggling to breathe, he caught a flash of flaming, raging redness behind Jethro's cold, dark eyes.

"You failed me completely Gater," Jethro calmly said.

Gater opened his mouth, but no words came out.

"It's too late for you."

Gater clawed at his throat, trying to pry away the invisible grip. His eyes began to roll back uncontrollably. He clawed at them as blood began to drip from his tear ducts. He begged Jethro, pleading as fear and horror filled his mind. Jethro reached out to him and gently held Gater's face. He patted Gater's hair and wiped blood from his cheeks. Then he steadily tightened his grip as he dug his fingernails into Gater's hairline and began to burrow his fingers underneath the skin. Gater uttered a low guttural scream as he pushed against Jethro's arms. They felt like rods of steel. As Jethro began to pull, peeling back the skin from his face, Gater's mind spun into blackness, his last thoughts of searing agony.

JOE--1893

Vera led the group to Christiania Square with an unwavering impatience. At the entrance, she turned to make her point once again about this stop being nothing more than a quick detour.

"This is Christiania Square. It was the first section of Oslo to be developed following the great fire of 1624. The fountain in the center was the spot that King Christian IV declared to be the official site from which the new town would be built. Follow me as we take a quick stroll around. We will leave shortly afterward to resume our actual program." Vera marched off swiftly, commencing her lap, and the group dutifully followed.

Joe scrutinized the passersby, scanning the crowds until he noticed the fountain in the center. Rachel loved fountains. Hope. He imagined her presence already and decided to position himself by the center. If she were here, she would notice him by the fountain. He stood on the ledge, feeling the freezing spray on his back as he looked intently into every building and corner. He couldn't see Rachel…

But she saw him.

And so did Shiner.

CHAPTER 25

It hadn't been five minutes since Barrett and Milo's call when Yulia ran into his office again.

"Superintendent Barrett. Mr. Levinson is here to see you."

"Thanks, Yulia. Leave my door open. Let him through when he gets here."

A visit late in the afternoon on a Friday was unusual. Barrett's boss was usually on the virtual reality golf course or at his beach house in Hawaii by now. Levinson knocked and greeted Barrett before entering.

"Well, Dan, it's probably not the Friday afternoon you were hoping for," Levinson offered.

"What have you heard, John? Is there already news on Dark History?"

"Yes," Levinson responded, "it was approved by ten votes to five. They'll be running their first tours next week."

"Next week already?!" Barrett was shocked, "They already have tours booked? You can't make all the necessary arrangements so quickly. There are hundreds of things to do once a license is approved. They must have known that they would be approved months ago."

"Looks that way," Levinson responded. "Seems there are some

influential people involved over there."

"Well, they have to divulge those details. Operators need to disclose all their owners. The way Senator Pearson pushed for the application to be approved, I was sure that he had some relationship. Who owns Dark History?" Barrett asked.

Levinson's mood changed quickly. His shoulders stiffened, and his gaze hardened.

"You need to get those thoughts out of your head. It's prohibited for anybody at the TTA to own a stake in a tour operator. You know that. He knows that. Suggesting Senator Pearson behaved improperly will get you fired very quickly."

Barrett did not apologize. He lowered his eyes to the clutter on his desk and considered the exchange. The silence became uncomfortable until Levinson finally broke it.

Levinson walked over to Barrett.

"Look, you might not like how it went. The committee made its decision. You just need to accept it and to manage your department. I suspect it will take a bit of effort to keep Dark History honest. I have no doubt that you are up to the task."

He slapped Barrett gently on the back.

Barrett stood and shook his head. "No. They have me appearing before a disciplinary committee next week."

"Don't worry about that. I have some back channels there. The hearing will go fine. The worst you can expect is a minor reprimand."

Barrett wasn't satisfied. "The problem is bigger than that. Dark History was involved in the disappearance of a tourist recently. And nobody in the TTA committees cares about it."

"How do you mean?" Levinson rolled his eyes. "How did a tourist disappear on one of their tours? They haven't started operating. But look…there are always going to be missing tourists. It's just a part of our business."

"A young girl went missing a few weeks ago. In nineteenth-century

Europe. Did you hear about it?"

"I didn't," Levinson responded. "But somewhere in the world, a tourist goes missing almost every month. Nothing we can really do about that, except minimize the losses by making sure that the operators follow all the rules. And you are bloody good at supervising them and enforcing the rules."

Barrett closed a file on his desk and put his hands in his pockets. He had nothing left to say except to tell Levinson that he was planning to resign at his hearing the following week.

"Go home, Dan. You are supposed to be at home now anyway. I came up to tell you that you are suspended. Take a few days of vacation. Go to your hearing next week. Be polite. Suck it up. Accept their rebuke and get back to work. We have lots to do." Levinson gave him a cheeky wink and strolled out of the office.

RACHEL--1893

Joe climbed up onto the stone ledge surrounding the fountain so that he could get a better look at the pedestrians. Most of the young women seemed to resemble Rachel until he examined them a second time. His mood was fluctuating from optimism to frustration with almost every passing moment. He slowed his thoughts down and turned steadily, squinting desperately into the crowds and side streets. At one point, he tripped himself up and almost fell into the bubbling water. Vera, who had been marching the tour group swiftly around the perimeter of Christiania Square, swiveled around and immediately noticed that Joe wasn't following her.

"Where is John…Joe?" she demanded.

Nellie and Carl shrugged. Ash looked around worriedly. Leonard, not paying attention, was admiring the old buildings surrounding them. Vera turned to the center, annoyed, and spotted Joe. She called out loudly as she headed for him.

"Joe! Get down from there. Come join us immediately!"

A passing policeman had also noticed him and gave his whistle a short blast, waving Joe down as he approached him. Rachel had spotted him too. She was feverishly switching between watching Joe and Shiner. It took every ounce of her strength not to charge and jump into his arms. She was bursting with a new hope.

Joe had begun to sense that Rachel was in the square. He ignored Vera and the whistling policeman, continuing to stand on the ledge of the fountain while peering into all the cracks, crowds, and causeways. His gaze lingered on the entrance to the alley where Rachel hid, though she was too well concealed.

Rachel wanted to be found, but Shiner was too close to her now. If she made a move, Shiner would see her too. She had no doubt that he had come to finish her off. She couldn't take chances just yet and decided to wait until he moved on. Whatever happened, she wouldn't let her dad go back home without her. When he left the square with his group, she would carefully follow them. She'd reveal herself when it was safe, even if it meant that she became more ghostly.

Vera called out again loudly, "Joe! I must insist that you that you come here immediately!" She had almost reached him.

Shiner heard her too. He had been watching Joe and now turned catlike to assess Vera. She was fast approaching Joe. A policeman was also heading to him. Shiner, noticing a gun handle sticking awkwardly out of Vera's pocket, zoomed his EyeCam to focus on it. She had his plasma gun. *Bitch,* he thought. Shiner pulled out his blade and crouching low, rushed toward her. Rachel saw him go and instinctively hurried to protect Joe.

Vera and the policeman arrived at the foot of the fountain simultaneously. Vera was shouting furiously now.

"Get down from there. Get down immediately!!"

Joe stopped searching. He felt a strangeness, and the sense was overtaking his whole body. His neck was burning. His hair was bristling. He turned to face Vera and the policeman. Suddenly Joe launched himself off the ledge, diving toward Vera. The policeman quickly jumped in front of Vera, blocking Joe off. Vera froze. Her face transformed from anger, to surprise, and then to shock.

Joe slammed into the policeman, knocking him over. Vera staggered sideways as Joe and the policeman tumbled at her feet. Joe landed heavily. He turned his attention to Vera again, leaving the policeman on the ground. Vera stared back at him, her eyes wide with fright and confusion.

Joe met her stare. Something was wrong. Vera had dropped her bag. She futilely reached behind her back, clawing at it as she staggered, and dropped to her knees, tears streaming from her eyes. Joe moved toward her. She collapsed, still flapping her arms behind her. He caught her and looked over her shoulder. She had a shining black knife handle sticking out between her shoulder blades.

It had pinned her puffy jacket severely against her back. A small stain of blood began to spread around the wound. Joe was helpless to save her. Her arms flailed, weakly now, as her life began to fade. He lay her down swiftly but gently as he scanned the onlookers feverishly. The crowd, dispersed around the square, were frozen in silence. Gradually, a woman's scream filled the silence, followed by others.

Joe spotted Shiner striding toward him, cutting through the cries and sobs with an emotionless determination. Ash, Nellie, Carl, and Leonard nervously approached the scene. Nobody had seen the knife yet. Shiner had thrown it at lightning speed, eliminating his main threat, the gun-bearing tour guide. Now it was time to take care of Joe. Grasping his garroting wire, he descended on Joe. Joe reached into his pocket for his last vial. He felt around frantically but couldn't find it.

Out of time, he raised his arms to defend himself as Shiner reached him. Shiner looked amused as he drew up to Joe. Joe was shaking. Shiner paused for a second and then punched straight through Joe's defense, knocking him backward. Shiner followed him again, fists circling, and lashed out again, catching Joe on his nose and sending him backward a second time.

"We've never met, you and me. But I have a feeling you've seen me before. Seen me following you. You probably don't know why. You've guessed that it's connected to your daughter. It was. But it's more than that now."

He struck out again, connecting squarely with Joe's jaw, this time knocking him down against the base of the fountain. Shiner knelt next to Vera's lifeless body and reached under her, feeling for his plasma gun. He found it quickly and stood again, holding it by his side. He dropped his garrote and pulled the knife from Vera's body, wiping the blood off against his trouser pants.

Ash, alongside the tourists who were just a few feet away, froze in horror, realizing that Vera was dead. Leonard turned to him, his eyes bulging and his face betraying an intense pain. He doubled over, grasping at his right arm. He reached out for Ash, clawing at his sleeve as he struggled to catch his breath. Ash was perplexed. Vera was dead. Too late for her. Joe was under attack. And Leonard had collapsed. He was likely dying. He had to help.

Shiner stood over Joe, ready to shoot him. The sprawled policeman was attempting to get back on his feet; he fumbled for his whistle and baton. Shiner, standing almost motionless, lifted his left leg and stomped his heel down hard against the policeman's neck, driving him back into the stone slabs with a sickening crunch. He turned his attention again to Joe, who was again fumbling for his last remaining vial.

Shiner calmly spoke, "You've been very elusive. Caused us more problems than we ever imagined you would." He lifted his plasma gun, pointing it at Joe's head. Then, to Joe's surprise, he froze. His face began to twist and contort. Shiner gasped and started to choke as he dropped his gun and his knife onto the floor. Rachel stood behind him.

Rachel had crept up to Shiner as he crushed the policeman's neck. She had tried to pick up his garrote, but her ghostly hands had passed through it. Changing her plan, she closed her eyes and focused on making her right hand whole again. As she did, she realized that Shiner would easily smash her aside. She was no match for him, even with a weapon in her hand. So, she stood up again and positioned herself right behind him, sticking her hand through him at the level of his heart. Then she willed her hand to become whole again, using every ounce of her remaining energy. As her hand became corporeal, Rachel grabbed for Shiner's heart and squeezed it, crushing it in her fist.

Shiner fell forward, an expression of tortured confusion forever etched into his face. He took Rachel with him, her hand stuck inside his chest. She caught herself and landed next to Shiner, balancing on her free arm and knees. She looked up at Joe and mouthed, "Hello."

Joe jumped up, ignoring his battered face and bruised body. He raced over to Rachel to hug her as tightly as he could. Rachel was only partly there, and her arm was stuck inside Shiner. Their hug was awkward, fruitless, and worrying. He stroked her face as they sat quietly, heads touching.

It only took moments before they realized how much screaming and chaos still surrounded them. Shiner's and Vera's corpses lay next to a dying policeman, who was twitching intermittently. Slightly farther away, Leonard was lying on the ground, his head in Ash's lap. Ash was remotely and frantically steering the Crichton to a quieter courtyard behind Christiania Square. Nellie and Carl were huddled together switching their attentions between Joe, Vera and Leonard.

Women sobbed and screamed while crowds gathered around the carnage. Ash summoned Carl, and the two of them helped Leonard to his feet. Police whistles shrieked in the distance so they hurriedly staggered off toward the edge of the square.

Joe glanced at Rachel nervously, hurrying her to extract her arm from Shiner's chest. She shrugged helplessly, jerking her arm up. Shiner's lifeless corpse flopped backwards and forwards until Joe begged her to stop. He hurried over to fetch Shiner's knife and pocketed the plasma gun. Rachel started to breathe rapidly to try and dematerialize her fist again. She closed her eyes, mostly to avoid seeing Joe's spontaneous surgical procedure. Joe held one hand in front of his face to obstruct the view as he began to cut. Rachel kept her eyes shut tight and concentrated on her breathing.

Rachel's arm was starting to loosen when Ash appeared, panting heavily. He was bothered and frantic as he spoke.

"Leonard had a heart attack. I need to get him back right now. Ready to go?"

Joe pointed at Rachel. She was still stuck, mostly a ghost, and currently attempting to dematerialize even further. Rachel would not be able to go back with the Crichton in her current state. And not while attached to a dead body.

"We need to leave. I can't wait for you," Ash exclaimed.

Joe held up his hands, pleading with Ash to wait. Rachel began to cry. Ash stepped backward slowly.

"What can I do? Leonard is dying. I will tell Time International to send another tour. I'll insist that the TTA arrange a rescue party. I'll make a plan for you. We can't wait for Rachel now. I'll get you back. I promise. Just get her whole again." Ash turned and ran.

Joe knew that he had no choice but figured there was no chance the TTA would send back an effective rescue mission. They never ever did. He turned his attention to Rachel. Her eyes were watering still, but she wore a small grin on her dirty face. She waved her right arm, wiggling her fingers. She was at least free.

CHAPTER 26

RACHEL--1893

Joe and Rachel staggered up, and he attempted to put his hand around her shoulders. They were no longer physical. His hands passed through them. She had almost completely ghosted. Only her face, neck, and part of her arm were still human. The rest of her had dematerialized, appearing translucent. They looked around as the sound of police whistles grew louder. The Oslo locals were shocked, intimidated, or confused.

Nobody dared approach them as they stood between the corpses of Vera and Shiner. The policeman, barely moving, groaned lightly. Joe gestured to Rachel that they best get out of there. Rachel nodded in agreement. Joe glanced again at Vera. He wished that he had been able to save her. Rachel met Joe's gaze reassuringly, and he was struck by how strong she seemed.

The policeman groaned again, grabbing their attention. Shiner's boot had most likely broken his back. They crouched down to see if he was conscious. His eyes were open, but he seemed critically wounded. Joe patted his shoulder and offered him a compassionate smile. He glanced again at Rachel and noticed, surprisingly, that she did not appear sympathetic. Her look was quizzical and scheming. Almost hungry.

Rachel pulled out her notebook and quickly scribbled.

TRUST ME!

She moved over until she was in front of the policeman's head. Joe edged backward, watching curiously. He tapped on his wrist. They needed to get out of there.

Rachel met the dying policeman's gaze and suddenly gnashed her teeth as she rolled her eyes back. She held her ghostly hands up in front of her and curled her fingers in claws. She passed them through her face and then slowly lowered her face toward the policeman. She opened her mouth as if to bite him as she stuck her fingers through his widened eyes.

Joe stared in disbelief. He began to chuckle, but Rachel quickly shot him an angry stare before returning to her haunting. She pushed her ghostly hands back and forward, passing them through the policeman's face as she silently hissed and wailed. He began to choke as a thin trickle of blood ran from his mouth. He pitifully tried to push himself away but couldn't move. Eventually, he looked upward at Rachel, offering her his last pleading stare as he muttered his last words.

"Please, miss… Let me die in peace."

Rachel, feeling silly, put her hands back to her sides, suspending her display of terror. The policeman closed his eyes and died. Now to follow Harry's advice. She nervously touched his back. Harry had been specific in his instructions that ghosts who scared the living to death could regain their bodies for a short period of time. She doubted that she had scared this policeman to death as much as annoyed him while he was dying. She grimly hoped that she had contributed to his early demise by sapping his remaining strength.

She touched his back and felt a slight tingle. She pushed her hand a little farther into his body as Joe looked on. Then she crouched above him and slowly lowered herself until her whole body barring her head and neck were inside his fresh corpse.

The police whistles were growing louder as they got closer. Joe looked around and saw more of them had now entered the square. They had been met by concerned locals who were pointing toward the fountain. Two large policemen reached for their batons and began to move deliberately toward Joe and Rachel.

Joe moved closer to catch Rachel's attention and gave her a desperate look as he tapped on his wrist again. Rachel lay inside the policeman. She felt a tickling surge of energy circle her body. It grew gradually more intense as it surrounded her, flowing up and down her limbs. And then it abruptly stopped. Rachel rose quickly and moved to stand next to Joe. She held her hands up in front of her face and watched as they steadily became whole again. She brushed her hands down the front of her streaked and stained dress, grasping the material. She turned in a circle, enjoying the feel of the cloth as it floated against her legs. Then she dived onto Joe, squeezing him in as tightly as she could. Joe hugged her back as she rested her head against his chest. They held each other for a moment, then holding hands, ran down the path.

The policemen, seeing Joe and Rachel flee, gave chase, filling the square with shrieking whistles and shouts to halt. Running through the crowds, passing the Gamle Rådhus restaurant, Rachel glanced at the basement windows, imagining she would catch a final glimpse of Agnes. They turned down an alley that would take them outside the square. Once back in the side streets, Rachel pointed toward Kontraskjæret Park. They headed there, hurrying as fast as they could, and ducked behind a row of bushes.

The policemen were slower and bumbling. Joe and Rachel watched as they assembled outside Christiania Square, guessing haphazardly which way the culprits might have escaped. Half of them headed to the left, and most of the remaining officers headed to the right. The last pair of cops approached the park. Joe and Rachel backed hurriedly toward an empty bench and sat. Joe took off his blood-stained jacket and turned it inside out. He ineffectively smoothed his hair. Rachel patted her head, trying to neaten her appearance, and wiped grit from her face. They calmed themselves and spread out on the bench. Rachel had a thousand things she wanted to tell her dad. Joe was just relieved, proud, and exhausted. They stared at each other as the policemen approached.

Joe looked up and raised his hat as they drew near. The policemen squinted suspiciously at them and passed, finding nothing particularly unusual or suspicious in seeing a father and his daughter seated on a bench. Once they were safely alone, Rachel pulled out her notebook and began to write.

I knew U would find me dad.

Joe took the pen.

100%. How was your tour?

Rachel shot Joe an indignant glance and pushed him on his arm playfully.

U know. Sightseeing + fighting ghosts & demons.

Demons?

Will explain later. When we get home.

Joe pondered that point for a moment as he took the pen.

Getting home…

He drew a sad face with a big question mark.

What's up with your hair?

Joe tried to push it flat again and shrugged.

Rachel looked at him. She bit her lip and nervously began to fidget with her sleeve. Then she wrote:

That guy said he would come back for us

They've never come back for anybody before. You will be the first.

Rachel took the pen back. She straightened up again.

I believe he will come back

She meant Ash.

They will need to find us. We must help them.

Joe was not as confident as Rachel. He knew that Ash would not be able to come himself. The tour operators would never send a TourPod just to find them. The chances of success were tiny, and the cost of sending a ship was significant. Joe imagined that the TTA might send drones. If a drone located them, the chances would increase slightly. Joe wrote:

We might be here for a while. Is there a place we can go?

Rachel wrote back:

Ghosts hide away until they vanish forever.

They sat on the bench for a while, waiting, feeling hungry and exhausted. Rachel lifted her right hand and turned it over, studying the crusty blood under her fingernails. She had taken a man's life. Violently. She balled her hand into a fist, the same way she had when crushing Shiner's heart. Turning her face away, she dropped it back to her side. Joe, noticing her anxiety, put his arm around her. The voices around them grew more still as the din of the night insects intensified.

As precious time passed, he stood, paced, and then sat again. Rachel repeatedly walked to the river's edge and studied the horizon. They were growing more anxious. Rachel wrote in bold letters:

WE HAVE TO DO SOMETHING.

I know.

He emptied his pockets, handing Rachel all the equipment: A knife stained with Vera's and Shiner's blood. Garrotes. One vial that would emit some gassy surprise. And Shiner's plasma gun. Rachel held the gun and turned it over. It was a sleek, shiny black device with a series of controls positioned intuitively near the trigger. Neither she nor Joe had held, let alone shot, one before. Joe took it and studied the series of buttons and options. Neither could tell how to activate it or what to expect if it did shoot off a blast of plasma. Joe picked up Rachel's notebook and wrote:

Let's see what it does.

Rachel agreed. She seemed intrigued. The park bench was a few hundred feet from the edge of the port. They made their way to the bank and then headed along the shoreline until they were in a remote spot. Joe figured out how to turn off the safety features, and Rachel grabbed it from him.

Holding it up and pointing it upward and out in the direction of the open ocean, she squeezed the trigger, firing off the first shot. The gun let off a strong fizzing sound as a powerful blast of white energy shot out and headed up into the horizon. It resembled an upside-down bolt of lightning and only dissipated miles out to sea, and not before they noticed a distant sailboat catching fire. Joe stared at Rachel, alarmed. She shrugged sheepishly and handed him the gun. Rachel wrote:

If anybody is looking for us, they'll see THAT!!

Joe agreed. He aimed the gun directly overhead and shot it again. The blast of plasma shot up into the sky. They heard locals in the distance shouting and alarmed at seeing bolts of lightning appear out of nowhere. He waited another minute and shot again and then again.

They could hear more and more voices. People were gathering close by, wanting to find the source of the upside-down lightning. And then, from behind the trees, they heard:

"Are you trying to shoot me out of the sky?" It was Milo, beaming.

Joe raised his arms in joy, forgetting that he was holding a deadly weapon. He ran over and hugged Milo. Rachel rushed over to greet him, and he squeezed her shoulder warmly.

"You must be Rachel. Some people have been very worried about you. Are you a ghost?"

She patted herself up and down as she shook her head vigorously.

"Let's get you both home. Follow me."

Milo's ship was only a few yards away. It was not the sleek, new TourPod that had brought Joe and Rachel to the past. Milo's ship was older and more beaten up. It was a faded blue color with a crooked rim. The peeling and cracked Morton Tours sign on the side informed Joe that the rescue was not official TTA business.

Milo slammed his fist against the side, and an entrance hatch slid open. He kicked the underneath of the ship, and a set of stairs unfolded and descended. Rachel stepped slowly and lightly as she climbed into the ship. She remembered Harry telling her how he climbed aboard a ship, only for it to take off right through him, leaving him stranded. She ran her hands along every surface to reassure herself that she was still whole.

"Who wants to talk?" Milo asked as he held up a device.

Rachel jumped, pushing Joe aside. Milo scanned the device on both of their voice boxes, removing the magnetic field. Rachel sang with joy, followed by launching into a series of curses and exclamations that were too fast for anybody to hear. She wanted to tell her dad everything, but she wanted to get home and safely first.

"Let's go home."

Milo said, "You also must be starving."

He gestured for them to sit around the table in the common room and threw an assortment of prepacked laboratory-grown meat sandwiches and sodas on the table. The interior of his tour ship was as rustic as the exterior. The cockpit had handheld manual steering and navigation capabilities. And a dusty green carpet pulled the common area together.

Joe urged Milo, "We're not sure how much time Rachel has before she starts to disappear again."

"Right. We'll jump back now. We can talk once we're there."

He got up and went to the cockpit, booted up the navigation and nuclear propulsion systems while Rachel and Joe chose sandwiches. Rachel opened hers immediately, picked out the giraffe meat, and stuffed the slices of bread into her mouth. The ship started to come alive while she ate, and Milo filled them in.

"Ash got back two days ago. Leonard was taken to the Anchorage Medical Center. He had a massive heart attack. He'll live. Strange guy. Doesn't recognize anyone. His family is still very worried about him."

"Glad to hear. How can anybody tell that he is acting strange?" Joe commented between bites.

"Ash came to see me right away. He told me that Time International wasn't going to send a search party. They have another Impressionist tour running again next month but refuse to come to Oslo again. We called Barrett. Ash told him how they found you and Rachel, as well as how Vera was killed. He asked why he had to leave you behind. He is still beating himself up over it."

"He came through for us in the end," Joe responded, crumpling the wrapping.

The engine was humming now, and Milo set the coordinates to home.

"Ready?" he shouted, and he stabbed his finger at the start button. Joe put his sandwich down and sat back in his seat. A crackle reverberated around the ship, and the interior of the craft started to shake. The sodas vibrated and bounced around the table. Seconds later, the ship engine expelled a long *whooosh*, and the mess table stopped shaking as the TourPod came to a standstill above present-day Oslo. Rachel had not even missed a single chew. She touched her clothes and her hair as she took another bite.

Milo came back to the mess table to sit with her and Joe, who put his bread to the side and picked at his and Rachel's meat while Milo continued. "Barrett's back was really up against a wall. We uncovered that a time touring company called Dark History was behind Rachel's attack. Rachel can tell us what happened when she's finished eating."

Rachel was so hungry and thirsty that she was somehow managing to eat and drink at the same time.

Milo continued, "Barrett sent me on a Dark History inspection, and he was suspended for it. He wasn't even able to get a ship to come back for you until late next week at best. Probably never, if you ask me. So, I came back for you."

"Is this your ship?" Joe asked.

"Technically, this ship doesn't exist. The TTA ordered me to decommission it after I lost my time tour operator license five years ago."

"Is this what you keep hidden in the vault under your house?"

"I don't know what you are talking about", Milo answered with the faintest of grins. "Nobody can know how you got back. So, don't go writing thank-you letters to anybody. And don't write complaints to Time International or the TTA. You're still supposed to be trapped in the past."

"Yay, no school," Rachel commented.

Joe raised his eyebrows at Rachel as he stood. "I will make a plan." He threw the empty cans and wrappers in the bin and turned to Milo. "You could have waited a week to see if the TTA authorized a rescue. It wouldn't have made a difference to us. You would have still arrived by us exactly when you did."

"The wait would have made no difference to you, I guess, but I figured that it would make a difference to your Daniel if I could get you back a week earlier."

Rachel put her sandwich down. She had tears welling in her eyes.

"Thank you," she said, trying to control herself. "It makes all the difference in the world to us that he doesn't need to worry or miss me and Dad for another day. He's already growing up without a mom. He might have grown up without a big sister as well, if it hadn't been for all of the people you mentioned. Especially you, Mr. Morton." She held her hands out.

Milo winked. He was moved and took her hands.

"Do you want to tell us what happened to you? Why we had to cross space and time to find you?"

Rachel related to Joe and Milo everything that had happened to her. She told them about Gater's attack, her slow transformation into a ghost, her control of the process through breathing and focus, Agnes, Lars the demon, her underwater ordeal, and why ghosts scare people.

Finally, she told them about Harry and how she had promised that she would come back for him. Joe could not take his eyes off her. Rachel was stronger than he ever imagined.

"Wow," Milo exclaimed.

Joe hugged her again. "You are so brave and extraordinary," he said softly into her ear.

Milo checked the clock. "Everybody fed? Then we'd better be off. Back to Vermont."

He went back to the cockpit as Joe and Rachel strapped in.

"Rachel, that is a truly amazing story. Learning how to control your body will serve you well if you are ever interested in a career in time travel. But, from what Ash tells me, you've got nothing on your dad."

Rachel cocked her head, surprised. "What do you mean?" she asked.

"Somehow, he seems to know what's going to happen before it happens."

CHAPTER 27

The ride back in Milo's TourPod was the bumpiest Joe had experienced since he'd shared a horse-drawn wagon with Vincent van Gogh on the way to the asylum. He squeezed the armrests tightly. Milo was right back in his element. He whooped as he accelerated to Mach 2 over the Atlantic Ocean.

They arrived at Milo's illegally built cottage in Leddy Park minutes later. A green patch of lawn opened behind his home, and he gently lowered the ship down into the well-concealed basement. It was Friday, late afternoon. Joe had set out only two days earlier, while Rachel had been gone for around a month in present-day time.

"Welcome back," Milo proclaimed. "I expect you'll want to get back to your son."

Joe and Rachel stepped out of the ship and thanked Milo again. He took them up through the cottage and showed them to the edge of the forest.

Rachel stopped suddenly on the path and patted her dress. She had a shocked expression. Joe froze. His heart stopped beating for a moment. Was she losing feeling?

"What's wrong?" he said anxiously.

Rachel laughed. "Look at your clothes."

She and Joe were still dressed in their nineteenth-century outfits, which also were caked with blood, mud, dirt, and grime.

"Milo, do you have a change for us before we head out?"

"Hmm. Not much that will fit you. I might have some tracksuits from the twentieth century," he answered, and they went back inside. "I'll also call you a Bubble. And I am lending you a SmartGlove with a hundred credits on it."

Milo gave them both sweatsuits, and they went back outside to wait for the Bubble. It came moments later, and they climbed in.

Before gliding off, Milo stopped them. "Listen, you two. I spoke to Superintendent Barrett. He would like to meet you both on Monday afternoon. Back here at my cottage. He has something to discuss with you. Is that all right?"

"I think so," Joe replied. "I think I'll take a few days off next week to recover, and I guess we can wait a bit before Rachel goes back to school."

"Great. See you then," Milo answered. He winked and patted the roof of the Bubble.

As the Bubble slowly started to pull away, Rachel shot out a last question through the open window: "Milo, how are you allowed to live in a cottage in a forest?"

Milo waved them off.

SHINER--1893

Shiner floated above the chaos in Christiania Square, watching the scenes of confusion and panic. He felt the energy around him intensify as he studied the carnage. The air around him was rejecting him. He tried to focus. He saw his own lifeless body sprawled on the cold stone ground in a puddle of his blood.

Lying next to him was Vera, that stupid tour guide that he'd killed with his knife. The throw he'd made was perfect. He'd have killed Joe too, if the missing daughter hadn't stabbed him in the back.

Shiner was filled with an unquenchable rage. How had they gotten the better of him? He'd been careful. He hovered above the corpses observing the crowds. He ached. It felt as if the air was nibbling at him, taking tiny bites at the remaining parts of his very being. He shifted as he waited to see what would happen to his dead body.

Joe and his daughter escaped earlier, and the police were reassembling. He waited as they tried to cordon off the area, feeling more pained with every passing minute. One of the officers, a lanky man with the largest hat and a thick moustache, stepped into the crime scene and took charge.

"Keep those people away from here," Chief Lovland barked at some junior officers.

Shiner hovered, watching the officers bustling around, pushing the crowd away. Lovland moved over to Shiner's corpse and pulled out a notepad. Shiner descended farther, wanting to make sure that nobody touched him disrespectfully. His being started to itch more and more as the atmosphere clawed at him.

A hunger began to build inside. It intensified, the closer he drew to Lovland. He knew that if he didn't do something, the itching, biting sensation pulling at him would tear him apart completely. He would be lost forever. Shiner's craving was all-encompassing. He sank right down until he was inches away from Lovland. He stared into the officer's face, leaning in closer and closer, until all he could see was Lovland's mouth.

The officer was directing his subordinates while simultaneously dictating what he observed. His moustache moved around his mouth, rising and falling, wiggling animatedly. Shiner drifted right under his moustache, so close that he could see the stains on Lovland's teeth. The nibbling sensation around him now felt like a tearing. He felt an irresistible draw to be sucked down the policeman's throat. He plunged into Lovland's mouth and spread himself out. His essence reached out to every part of the officer's body. The tearing and biting ceased as he explored his new host's mind.

Lovland, who was crouching next to Vera's corpse, suddenly lurched backward. He stood motionless, his mouth hanging open, and a choking sound growled upward from his gut.

The junior officer beside him asked: "Sir, is everything all right?"

Shiner had burrowed deep into Lovland's consciousness and seized control, crushing any thoughts or impulses that he could muster to fight for control of his own body. Shiner directed Lovland to stare straight ahead.

Slowly, he blinked and closed his mouth but opened it again when he realized he couldn't breathe through his nose. Turning his head from side to side, his gaze settled indifferently on the junior officer, who was looking slightly concerned. He turned back to the corpses and lifted his hands, turned them around, studying his palms.

Old and stiff, Shiner thought as he started to get used to his new body. He ignored the junior officer and crouched back down to examine Vera's body. He touched the drying blood on her back and began to feel gently around her body. Sticking his hands into her pocket, he quickly located her equipment. He pulled out her PodCom, concealed it under his sleeve, and dropped it in his pocket. With his other hand, he found her StunGun and quickly pocketed it as well. Then he searched his own body, pulling Gater's chain from his neck and pocketing it.

"Sir… Chief Lovland?" the junior officer nervously called.

So, I am Chief Lovland, Shiner thought. *This could be interesting.*

"Go find me some witnesses. Where are those suspects?" Shiner barked. "And I sense something over there. Tell me about this square. I want to know about all these offices, shops, and restaurants."

"Restaurants, sir?"

JETHRO--2130

Vinod raced down the passage to Jethro's office. He knocked on the door and waited until Jethro called him in.

"Thank you, Senator Pearson," Jethro was saying. "I am sure things will move quickly now." Jethro disconnected and turned his attention to Vinod.

"Sir. I was just informed by Mike Brown from the TTA operations department that our tour schedules were approved." Vinod stood stiffly, hands in his pockets.

"Yes," Jethro confirmed. "Our shareholders are very grateful. Thank you, Vinod."

Vinod nodded. "Our tours are due to start running next week. We have a Victorian murder tour scheduled to launch this Monday. As well as a Viking tour."

Jethro studied Vinod intently. "Very good. I want everything to be perfect. Tell me all the arrangements for the launch."

"The press conference is set to commence at 10:00 a.m. tomorrow. Kendra from marketing will be running the event. She will call you up to cut the ribbon at around 10:20. Following cocktails and snacks, we will announce the winners of the auction. The gates will then open at 11:30, and the tours are due to depart at 12:30 and 1:00 p.m."

"Who are the winners? Who are our guests for the first tours?" Jethro asked. He stood up and walked over to Vinod.

"Lord Beaumont; Lady Beaumont; Lenny Price, the founder of Dream Systems; and Minister Arusha were the highest bidders on the Viking tour."

"Five million credits each?"

"Correct, sir."

"The tour is going to the Battle of York, correct?" Jethro confirmed.

"Yes. Our guests will be given traditional weapons and customized, period-appropriate, nano-coated armor and will participate in the beginning stages of the battle."

Jethro now stood directly in front of Vinod. "Great. And the other tour?" Jethro probed.

"For the Victorian murders tour, we have Victoria Ming, founder of Android Sciences; the Thomason twins, Giles Almidovar, the football player; and Edward Pearson."

"Twenty million credits. Correct?"

"Yes, sir," Vinod confirmed.

"This is the Jack the Ripper tour?"

"Yes, sir."

"Everybody gets to kill one prostitute?"

"Yes, sir."

Jethro lifted his hand and placed it on Vinod's shoulder.

"And you have taken all necessary precautions? All of the equipment has been manufactured?"

Vinod shifted nervously, too afraid to speak in case he said the wrong thing. He nodded.

Jethro patted him gently on the shoulder. "Excellent. Just make sure that nothing goes wrong. These murders have never been solved. They must always remain unsolved."

Vinod nodded.

"I want our unsolved crime database completed. Every serial killer who never got caught. Every murder, disappearance, burglary. Everything."

"We are working on it, sir."

DANIEL--2130

Joe and Rachel arrived back home moments before sunset. They took the elevator to the 415th floor and hurried to their apartment. Joe's mom, Pam, answered the door and embraced them both at the door. Daniel heard and sprinted to the door.

"Rachy," he yelled as he ran to smother Rachel with a hug.

"Let dad in, love," Pam said as Daniel hugged Joe. She turned to them as they stepped inside. The synthetic wolf strolled out of Daniel's room slowly. "Did you not bring back your bags? Did they lose your bags?"

"It's a very long story," Rachel said.

"Wow. Nice wolf!" she exclaimed to Daniel as she bent over to stroke its thick gray fur.

"Whose clothes are those?" Pam asked.

Joe and Rachel both grinned at her sheepishly, brushing the question off. Joe had not yet decided how much they should tell Daniel. Rachel had agreed to gloss over those parts of her story that were too horrifying and gory. She would not mention the ghosts and demons that she had met, except maybe Harry. Nor would they discuss the various deaths.

"It was pretty crazy, Mom. Definitely no vacation," Joe responded.

Pam sat them down and poured them drinks. Daniel prompted them to start explaining what happened.

"Rachy. What happened to you? Why were you gone for so long? What was the world like then? Is it easy to get lost?"

Daniel jumped on Joe's lap.

"Well, Danny boy. For you, I have been away for a month. But I was only on the tour for a few days. I was thoroughly loving it. We went to Paris, London, and the South of France. On our last stop in Oslo, a man crept up behind our tour and mugged me. He clubbed me over the head and knocked me out."

Rachel lifted her hand and slammed it into her fist.

"Then he dragged me away to steal my stuff. I was separated from my school group, and they left me behind."

"And did dad find you?" Daniel pressed.

Joe puffed out his chest. "I sure did. The tour that I went on mostly retraced Rachel's steps. It took a little convincing, but I got them to travel to Oslo. Once we were there, it wasn't too hard to track her down."

He took a sip of his coffee, pausing for dramatic effect.

"She always lands up in a fountain. I just needed to find the biggest one."

"But how did your TourPod arrive at the same time Rachy was there? And did you find out who attacked her? Was it just a criminal? Were you turning into a ghost already, Rachy?"

Joe and Rachel looked at each other. They realized that it was not going to be so easy to answer all of Daniel's questions. Rachel answered first.

"I was. I reckon Dad got to me just in time."

Daniel jumped off Joe's lap. He strutted up and down as he fired off more questions: "What was it like? How did you reverse it? Did you just go back to being a person after you got back on Dad's TourPod?"

"It's terrible. You can't feel anything after a while. Not your clothes on your body. Not the wind on your face. Nothing at all. I fought to slow it down. I must have done enough that I became whole again before Dad came to bring me home."

"You could just reverse it with your mind? That seems too easy. And Dad. why do you have a huge bruise on your face?" Daniel reached up to touch Joe's face.

"Well. The man who mugged Rachel also attacked me when he saw me with her. You should see what he looks like now." Joe smiled.

"What? But why was he following Rachel?" Daniel wanted to know everything.

Pam interrupted. "One question at a time, love."

Joe hugged Daniel again. "Rachel and I need to get cleaned up. I should also go take care of my bruise. And we're starving. We've hardly eaten for 240 years. We'll tell you everything over dinner?"

Rachel followed Daniel to his bedroom while Joe turned to Pam. They heard Rachel shriek with delight as she saw the snake.

Pam asked, "What really happened?"

"It was crazy. Rachel…I don't know how she survived. I would have crumbled under the crazy pressure she went through." Joe took off the sweater and SmartGlove that Milo had loaned him. "Except, I didn't crumble. I really found something in me while I was in Europe. It was like I'd been there before. Often, I could sense things were going to happen before they did."

"How do you mean?" Pam asked.

Joe told her about the prickle he felt in his neck and his crazy static hair and fingers whenever he was in danger.

Pam started to clear away the dishes as she listened.

"Maybe you should look into it, love. These gene scans can tell you a lot about your body that you don't know."

He thought of Liz.

"Sometimes it's best not to know what's going on."

"Don't be silly. It sounds important," Pam said as she walked over to hug him again. "Maybe you will learn something about your biological parents as well."

The following Monday, Joe and Rachel returned to Milo's cottage in the forest. Milo welcomed them at the door, and Rachel blurted, "Milo, did the government just let you build a house in their forest?"

"Come in." Milo sidestepped her question. "You already know Ash. I want you to meet Superintendent Barrett."

Barrett was waiting for them by the glowing fireplace in Milo's cozy wooden lounge. He jumped up to greet Joe and Rachel, telling them how happy he had been to hear of their safe return. Joe and Rachel thanked him for his part in their rescue.

Milo served black, instant coffee, lamenting that he had not invested in a DrinkMaster yet. Once they were seated, Barrett thanked everybody for meeting.

"I run Regulations and Compliance at the TTA. I am supposed to make sure that all the time tour operators follow the rules. It may not sound exciting, but it's sometimes nerve-racking. Every time something goes wrong on a tour, it's up to my department to find out what happened and try to prevent it from happening again."

"I do a similar job but with synthetic animals," Joe interjected.

Rachel nudged him with her foot, willing him to shut up, while Barrett paused. Joe apologized for interrupting, and Barrett continued.

"So, every time a tourist goes missing, we try to figure out and document what went wrong. We pass our file over to the operations department, who are supposed to try get them back. To this day, they have never recovered a single person. It's heartbreaking. More than four hundred people are missing. They are all ghosts, floating around in time. Haunting old buildings, basements, and battlefields. Yearning to come home to their loved ones. Rachel, you are the only one who ever came back."

"All thanks to Dad, Milo, Ash, and you," she replied.

"Yes. And no thanks to the TTA. I was just censured for trying to do my job. I have no faith that things will change."

He paused and sipped his coffee.

"This brings me to my point. Tomorrow, I'm being disciplined. I've been told that they value me too much and will go light. I plan to tell them that I will only continue to work for the TTA if they allow me to hire outside companies to help me investigate and recover lost tourists. My boss has already agreed to support me. For a trial run."

Milo interrupted this time. "There are no companies that can help recover lost tourists."

Barrett smiled at Milo. "Come on, Milo. You know what I am asking you to do."

Milo frowned. "They will agree to hire me?" Milo asked.

Barrett answered him, "They will agree to hire all of you. And they will pay you well. I am told that you all have unique gifts. Milo, there is nobody in the world with more on-the-ground time travel experience and grit than you."

Milo agreed.

"Rachel, you figured out how to rematerialize yourself. You literally came back from the dead. And I bet you could do it again. And help others."

Rachel was flattered, and her cheeks blushed. "I really wouldn't want to try," she said. "To do it again myself," she clarified.

"Joe. Ash tells me that, somehow, you can preempt danger. You know when bad things are going to happen before they happen. "

"It was only when I was on the time tour. I really don't know how."

"Well, I'd like to investigate how that worked. And Ash, there is no finer, more capable and trustworthy pilot than you."

Ash gave a playful salute.

"I want you all to form a company that will find lost tourists and bring them back."

"You know that Rachel is still in school?" Joe reminded Barrett.

"I will make sure that she continues. She can enroll in our TTA programs and study whatever she wants."

Joe looked from side to side. Rachel was tapping her feet quickly. Ash sat back in his chair, holding his hot beverage.

"Who will we be dealing with at the TTA?" Milo asked.

"Only with me," Barrett answered. "I will initiate and supervise every mission. You will report only to me."

Ash answered, "I'm in."

Joe turned to Rachel. "What about the synthetic animals?"

Rachel shouted, "Let's do it!"

"This will be dangerous," Milo said. "The TTA will need to pay us well."

Barrett looked relieved and pleased. "So, it sounds like we have an agreement."

Joe pursed his lips. He was still thinking.

"For me, there is one condition," Rachel concluded. "I choose the first assignment. I left a friend behind in Oslo."

"You'll need to tell me more. But in principle, I'll agree to that."

Rachel clapped and turned to Joe. "I can join, right, Dad?"

"I don't know. It was pretty dangerous the last time we time traveled."

Barrett answered, "You won't have maniacs following you again. It's just straightforward rescue operations and information gathering."

"Just try it for a few months. You can pay me back for saving your ass," Milo suggested. He held Joe's gaze, and Joe realized there might be more to the comment than the others realized.

Barrett persisted. "We'll throw in a holiday. Have you ever seen the Hanging Gardens of Babylon? I heard they had pretty impressive fountains."

Rachel grabbed Joe's arm and shook it.

Joe nodded.

The Ghost Investigation and Rescue Agency would be launched.

RACHEL--2130

A few days of rest passed without incident. Rachel was happy with the quiet. She'd picked up her paintbrushes again and even painted her own version of *The Scream*. The screamer looked like Agnes, so she added a thick mop of blond hair and makeup. Joe went back to work and handed in his resignation. He'd notified Rachel's school that she was back but needed time to recover. The principal was compassionate, helpful, and relieved that Joe wasn't planning to sue the school for losing his daughter in the first place. Sara called and offered to structure a timetable to suit Rachel, giving Rachel the opportunity to go with Joe for a three-month tour guide's course at the Time Obscura Institute. Barrett had booked it for them, citing their newness and the fact that most of the Dark History guides had been trained up by them. He wanted to know if the two organizations were connected. Rachel was excited to kick off the adventure. It was due to start this winter.

Daniel proved to be a willing art student, mostly taking to painting ghosts. And he and Rachel renewed their virtual-reality racket-sports rivalry. It had been stormy and windy the last week, giving Daniel the opportunity to prove his indoor athleticism once again. He'd just retaken the lead with a bounding overhead smash, when the door glowed green, announcing a visitor.

"I'll get it," Daniel bellowed as he removed his VR glasses.

He bounded to the door and swiped it open while Rachel scratched the sleeping wolf's furry side.

"Hello, young man," Leonard, the historian, wheezed. His nose completely blocked; he gaped air into his mouth between words as he extended his hand to shake Daniel's.

Rachel instinctively stood up, nudging the wolf with her foot.

"Is your father home?" he continued. "I am a friend from his European art tour."

"He's not here," Daniel replied. "He's at work."

"May I come inside?"

Daniel stepped backward, allowing him to enter. The wolf stood up and stared quizzically at Leonard. Rachel advanced toward him as well. Something seemed off.

Leonard reached down, gently cupping Daniel's chin in his bony hand. Daniel jerked backward. Leonard's hands were freezing cold.

"You must be the precious daughter," he said, looking over at Rachel. "I didn't get a chance to say goodbye to him. The tour ended so abruptly. You know, he forced me to take the group to Oslo for you. I didn't want to go there."

Rachel squinted at him as he slowly walked toward a bar stool at the kitchen counter. Catching his eye, she saw a flashing glint of redness behind his iris. A lurking dread surrounded her. The same sense she had felt when Lars, the demon, stopped her in Oslo.

"Come over to me, Daniel," she said forcefully.

The wolf, staring at Leonard, cautiously walked over and placed its body between him and the children. He growled, a low, grumbling snarl.

"Settle down, boy," Daniel urged, patting the wolf's head.

Leonard was unfazed. "I'll just wait here for your dad to come home, if that's OK. We have some catching up to do."

"That's fine," Rachel replied, holding Daniel's shoulders firmly.

"You know, I am starving. OK if I eat here? It feels like I haven't had a bite in years." Leonard burst into a cackle of laughter.